Seeker of Time

A Novel by J.M. Buckler

Seeker of Time

Copyright © 2017 by J.M. Buckler

Cover Art Illustrated by: Adam Rabalais

This is a fictional novel written by J.M. Buckler

Visit my website at www.jmbuckler.com

Printed in the United States of America

First Printing: September 2017

Published by: Sojourn Publishing, LLC

Published for: Gratus Publishing, LLC

Hardcopy ISBN: 978-1-62747-119-0
Paperback ISBN: 978-1-62747-122-0
E-Book ISBN: 978-1-62747-117-6

Table of Contents

Dedicated to:

The greater good.

Prologue

Starring down from the giant precipice, he reflected on his choice as the cold gray waves crashed against the white, jagged rocks below. Anyone else would have felt uneasy at this height, but other concerns occupied his mind. He knew what he must do, for he had spent the last nine years waiting for this day.

The past nine years had been anything but easy. Running, hiding and surviving had been his way of life; the life of a criminal; the life of an outcast: a life filled with uncertainty.

The winter's icy breeze cut through his dark hair like a freshly sharpened blade. Fine bits of ice crushed loudly under the weight of his boots as he took a cautious step forward. Exhaling deeply, he closed his piercing blue eyes, mentally preparing himself for the task at hand. Doubt clouded his mind as his eyes shot open, filled with concern.

Why was he hesitating? He had gone over this day a hundred times; spent countless nights working through every detail. This was unlike him; hesitation was not in his nature.

Maybe it was the thought of the unknown. How would she react when she learned of the truth or heard about the life he had lived? Would she believe any of it?

The young man threw his head back, sighing loudly. He watched the warm breath leave his mouth like smoke from a chimney. The sun had begun to set and the time was rapidly approaching. Looking out over the gray water, he observed the last bit of daylight fade away like a candle's dying wick. He took one final breath of the crisp, cool, night air, closed his eyes and jumped.

CHAPTER 1

It was hot and I was sweating. I had always despised the heat but this was beyond hot and I suddenly felt claustrophobic. I peeled my legs from the gray, leather seat of our family's eco-friendly sedan, attempting to resettle myself. Collecting my long hair into one hand, I slid a small hair tie off my wrist, securing it tightly into a high pony tail. I tried craning my neck between the driver and passenger seats only to feel my seatbelt lock me into place just inches from the cool air. I had officially reached my breaking point.

"Mom, can you *please* turn up the A.C.? I'm dying back here!"

"Honey, it's on as high as it can go. We told you it would be much warmer down here than back home. I don't know why you insist on being such a drama queen! Your father and I think it feels nice for a change," she replied, eyeing my father.

"Feels nice? It feels nice if you like being glued by sweat to a leather seat," I murmured, just loud enough for my mother to hear.

"Come on Elara, it's only a few more hours 'til we get there," urged my father in his pleading, "your mother is about to lose her temper" tone.

Riding for twenty-nine hours in a car with your childhood idol would probably become irritating at some point, but twenty-nine hours in a car with your parents? The once-spacious sedan now felt like the cockpit of a fighter jet: small, cramped and nauseating at times. My father's driving ability consists of blowing through red lights that apparently don't apply to him and high speed, illegal lane changes. I braced myself, grabbing the handle above the window as he maneuvered in and out of traffic.

"I just don't understand why we had to leave so suddenly," I managed through clenched teeth as my father crossed four lanes at once to avoid missing the exit.

I watched in the rear-view mirror as his eyebrows scrunched together, preparing for my mother's reaction.

"ELARA DUNLIN! We've been over this a hundred times!" yelled my mother from the passenger seat. "Your father has accepted a wonderful job offer. I'm tired of listening to you complain! We're going and that's final."

I sighed, catching my father's reflection in the small mirror once again, only this time to see "I told you so" written on his face. I returned his gaze with an apologetic smirk while silently mouthing "I'm sorry." He winked, flashing me his famous quirky side smile, reassuring me that he was not actually upset by my behavior.

I giggled quietly to myself thinking how different my parents are from one another. Not only are they complete opposites physically, but their personalities could not be more dissimilar. My father Roger – or Rog, as my mother likes to call him – is average height for a male, with sandy brown hair and matching eyes. He is shy, quiet and thoughtful. Emily, my mother, is the most petite woman I've ever known. By the age of thirteen, I could casually rest my elbow on her shoulder. Four years later, I towered over her. Her short, blonde hair and abrasive personality make her a force to be reckoned with. Sometimes I wonder how they ever ended up together. Being the hopeless romantic that he is, my father told me it was love at first sight. When asked, my mother says it just works.

Letting out a sigh, I wondered how it was humanly possible for my breath to feel cooler than the air temperature inside of the car. I pressed my head against the back-passenger window hoping for some relief, but was disappointed when it stuck to the glass. Watching the other cars zip in and out of traffic, I reflected on why I found myself sitting in this hot, uncomfortable car for twenty-nine hours.

The job offer came out of thin air. My father wasn't even searching for work when the thickly packaged envelope arrived in our rusty old mailbox. It must have sat on our kitchen table in the junk-mail pile for days, because no one seemed to notice. One evening during dinner, my mother sifted through the pile and asked us how the large envelope managed to get stuck between Wal-Mart and Shaw's Supermarket coupon flyers. When she finally opened it, she discovered that the package contained an offer letter to my father for a Senior IT Manager position with an oil-and-gas company located near Houston.

"Texas?" I managed, nearly choking on a spoonful of Hamburger Helper.

I was quickly cut off by my mother as she continued to read the details of the letter, louder than before. I watched her pupils grow to the size of bottle caps when she reached the part about the proposed salary. Her hand shot to her mouth while my father's fork dropped loudly against his plate. At that exact moment, I knew what she was thinking. That sort of pay increase would allow her to finally quit her job, something she had wanted to do for ages. I only had to glance at my mother to know that the inner dictator had spoken: we would be leaving Maine and moving to Texas.

I peeled my forehead from the hot window, wiping the mark I had left behind with the sleeve of my shirt. The sun sat low in the sky, mocking me by shining its blistering rays into my face. I reached for the cheap travel pillow, tossing it on the empty seat next to me. I twisted uncomfortably underneath my seat belt. Surrendering any hope of comfort, I let myself collapse like a fallen tree onto my left side. I listened to my father snicker at my unsuccessful attempt, then closed my eyes, imagining what my new school would be like.

Forcing me to move across the country at the start of my senior year in high school was a crime in my opinion, but then again, no one ever asked for my opinion. The school I attended back home was small and the students were decent enough. I had never been the bubbly, popular cheerleader type or the wild, "get into mischief" type either. I was just … me. Making good grades had always come naturally to me, and so was staying under the radar. My high school career thus far had trained me to be a master at blending in and observing. My fair skin and long, bone-straight ebony hair wasn't a feature that high school boys found attractive. I had always been lean and lanky and unfortunately lacked the curves of the popular girls. The only compliment I ever receive is about my uniquely colored blue eyes. They are not just an everyday blue, but a piercing, bright, sapphire blue.

I was interrupted from my thoughts by the sudden jolt of my seat belt holding me in place. My father yelled profanities at a fellow commuter, all while reassuring my mother that the other guy almost ran *him* off the road. I rolled my eyes, doubting my father's claim before resettling myself onto the warm seat. I sighed, draping my arm over my face in hopes of blocking out the bright afternoon sun.

"Maybe a fresh start wasn't such a bad idea," I thought.

It had always felt as though I were on the outside looking in, living someone else's life. I glided through the motions but never felt like I was on *my* own path. Waiting, always waiting for something great to happen, only nothing ever did.

"Maybe a new state, a new house and a new school was just what I needed to propel me on the right path," I wondered.

I jammed my fist into the small travel pillow, attempting to fluff up the synthetic cotton, only to be discouraged when I laid my head back down, feeling my bony wrist digging into my temple once more. I exhaled deeply, thankfully allowing myself to drift off to sleep.

I wasn't aware of how long I had been sleeping, but I didn't have to open my eyes to know that the sun had set. The temperature inside the car had dropped drastically and I was wide awake. It was the same way I felt every day when the sun finally decided to sleep. It was night and I felt refreshed. I could think more clearly and my senses were awakened, alert.

I lifted my head from the sad travel pillow, wiped the drool from my chin, and stretched.

"Welcome back," my father said cheerfully. "We should be getting close soon."

I leaned forward, wedging myself between the driver and passenger seats, attempting to get a closer look. In the distance, I could make out the words of a bright green road sign.

"I think we're already here," I corrected, rubbing my eyes.

My father craned his neck forward. I watched a smile slowly cross his unshaven face as he proudly read the sign aloud.

"Welcome to Houston."

CHAPTER 2

The drive to our new neighborhood was pleasant, once we veered off the bustling highway. Woodward, as it was so appropriately named, appeared like a hidden oasis in a desert of industrial mayhem. Tall pine trees and man-made lakes filled the night skyline. Wide sidewalks interwove hike and bike trails like a thick labyrinth.

"I think it's the next left up ahead," my mother said, squinting to read the sign.

"Mom, where are your glasses?"

"I can see just fine, thank you very much!" she snapped.

It was no surprise when we turned down the wrong road. I laughed at our misfortune as my father finally convinced my mother to put on her glasses. Two more wrong turns, followed by a sharp right, led us to our new home. We pulled into the freshly paved driveway, leaving the U-Haul trailer sticking out into the street as if we owned the neighborhood.

"Great," I thought. "We're already one of "those" neighbors."

I unfolded out of the car, resembling a contortionist, then stretched and popped my neck loudly.

"Elara! Don't do that! You know I hate it when you pop your joints like that," demanded my mother, loud enough for the entire neighborhood to hear.

"Shhh, mom it's late," I hissed.

"Don't tell me to shhh!" she countered.

I rolled my eyes, opening my mouth to defend my argument when …

"Girls!" my father interjected. "Come on, we're all tired. Let's go inside and check out the new digs," he pleaded.

My father always had a way of being the buffer between my mother and me at the most opportune time.

Snapping out of our sister-like behavior, we quickly headed toward the front door. Our home in Maine was nothing to be desired. A small, one-story with only two bedrooms and one very small bathroom was all I had ever known. Built in the late 1970s, it had plenty of "character," as my father would say. What he really meant was lack of functionality. Old appliances that you had to either shake, hit or beg to turn on made the simplest task a chore. A dishwasher that had a mind of its own, popcorn ceilings that resembled stalactites, retro brass fixtures and wood paneling that made me cringe every time I walked down the old hallway.

I was distracted from my thoughts by the smell of fresh paint and the feel of cool air, as my father opened the newly installed front door.

"Why is it so dark in here?" complained my mother, searching for a light switch.

I joined in the search, listening to my shoes thump loudly against the hard surface below.

"Voila!" sang my mother in her best French accent.

Light flooded the spacious room. Dark walnut wooden floors flowed through the open concept design. White crown molding trimmed the rich mocha-colored walls while brushed nickel covered every door knob and chandelier in sight.

My mother glanced at me and our earlier bickering was forgotten as we ran hand-in-hand like best friends to the kitchen.

"Holy…" my mother's voice trailed off, admiring the new kitchen.

"This … is … awesome," I stuttered, trying to take in the new surroundings.

Sparkling, white granite glowed under the beautiful recessed lighting, covering every counter top in sight. A plethora of gray colored cabinets lined the kitchen walls. Brand new, stainless steel appliances seemed to smile as I walked by. While passing the dishwasher, I could have sworn I heard it whisper, "I am at your beck and call, my lady."

I let my hand brush against the cool counter tops, marveling at the automatic ice maker.

"No more annoying ice trays," I yelled toward my father, where he stood, still admiring the entry way.

"That's great kiddo," he laughed.

Placing her petite hand on my shoulder, my mother whispered, "Why don't you go pick out your room upstairs?"

"All right," I nodded, feeling more awake than I had all day.

I ran from the kitchen, taking off up the wooden stair case, skipping every other step. As I reached the top of the stairs, I was hit with total darkness. Quickly, I put on the brakes, stopping dead in my tracks. I had never been fond of the dark. Something about it always left me feeling uneasy, like someone was watching me. Again, I began searching for a light switch, only this time with more determination. My heart thumped, until my hand finally rested on the white, plastic switch. Once illuminated, the upstairs appeared less like something out of a creepy movie. I laughed at my child-like behavior, reminding myself that at seventeen years of age one should not be afraid of the dark.

I walked through the vast, empty bonus room and then down a hallway which led to three different bedrooms. The first room I entered was a perfect square with one small window that overlooked the driveway. I peered through the blinds, gazing down at the quiet street. The newly planted oak trees wobbled unsteadily in the slightest breeze. The closet was a decent size, not that I needed a lot of space, considering my

9

pathetic excuse for a wardrobe. I found another door that opened to a Jack-and-Jill style bathroom. It was small with a double sink that would have been convenient if I had a sibling, but two sinks were unnecessary for an only child.

I made my way through the narrow bathroom into the next bedroom. This room, more rectangular then the first, had a window directly facing the neighbor's brick home. I glanced down, noticing our two A.C. units churning away. The view was far less impressive then the first room, so I mentally cut it from the list.

Eager to see what the last room offered, I hurried down the short hallway. I smiled, walking into the spacious room. It was better than I could have ever imagined. Moonlight poured in from two large windows that occupied the entirety of the back wall. Even with the lights off, I felt at ease with the amount of light that shone forth. I marveled at the built-in desk located next to the wall of windows. The attached bathroom was large with finishes equal to that of the rest of the house.

"This move is looking better by the minute," I thought, walking over to the wall of windows to inspect the view.

My eyes scanned the freshly landscaped back yard. A wooden fence bordered two sides of the house, allowing privacy only between neighbors. The un-fenced portion of the back yard connected seamlessly with the heavily wooded area.

Satisfied with my decision, I bolted down the hallway, eager to tell my parents the good news.

"Mom...Dad...," I yelled, bounding down the stairs.

No answer. This house was much larger than our previous home and shouting was something we would all have to grow accustomed to. I located the master bedroom hiding just around the corner of the living room and to my surprise, found both of my parents sprawled out on our old air mattress.

"Uh...you guys awake?"

"Barely," they whispered in unison.

Without opening her eyes, or changing position my mother pointed to a small roll up camping mattress.

"I guess I'll see you guys in the morning?" I asked, quietly picking up the faded red mattress.

Waved away by my mother's hand, I hurried out to the car to retrieve my back pack before proceeding upstairs. I unrolled the old mattress, placing the travel pillow just right so that it looked somewhat inviting. I frowned, shaking my head at the pitiful attempt before heading to the bathroom. I didn't have any towels, so as good as a shower sounded it would have to wait until the next day. I washed my face, brushed my teeth, changed into an oversized shirt with cotton shorts and combed out my long, straight hair.

Checking the time on my cell phone, I was surprised to find that it was already after midnight. As usual, as with every night, I didn't feel the least bit tired. I walked over to one of the large, freshly cleaned windows, allowing my eyes to take in my new surroundings. I smiled at the full moon resting high in the night sky. My eyes scanned the back yard, admiring the vast wooded area behind our house when suddenly I gasped, feeling my entire body go rigid with fear.

A man stood at the edge of the woods, only feet from the entrance to our yard. My breathing stopped, as his eyes found mine. The room was silent, except for the rhythmic sound of my heart pounding on overdrive. Time stood still while the man and I stared at one another. I was immobilized with panic, but for some reason had no urge to run or call for help. There was a strange familiarity about his presence. It was the same feeling as when one experiences déjà vu.

He took a small step forward, allowing the moonlight to expose his perfect features. He was younger than he first appeared; looking only slightly older than myself. He was tall,

11

with a muscular yet slender frame; I watched his chest rise with every breath that entered his lungs. A subtle breeze pushed his jet-black hair into his face, disturbing his statue-like appearance. A flood of emotions surged through every vein of my body: fear, excitement and caution clouded my mind.

"What is he doing? Why is he just standing there, watching me like some sort of creepy statue?" I wondered anxiously.

Every scary movie I had ever seen and every Dateline my mother forced me to watch, told me this situation would end badly. I dropped to the floor, taking cover below the windowsill.

"Great, now what?" I asked myself. "Do I yell for help, or remain silent?"

I closed my eyes, wishing to be back in Augusta. I longed to be in our small, two-bedroom home where my parents were just a wall away and there wasn't a strange man watching me from outside the window.

"Come on Elara!" I scolded. "You're not a child, stop being ridiculous. The doors are locked and there is no way he can scale the side of the house up to your bedroom windows."

I breathed slowly, commanding my body to raise its head just enough to see out the window. Only pine trees filled my vision. I lifted my head higher, frantically searching the area for the young man. Regaining my confidence now that the mysterious visitor had vanished I stood, my mouth gaped looking out the window.

"Where did he go?" I thought, my eyes straining to see through the dense brush.

I ran to the first bedroom with the view of the street and searched as far as my eyes could see, then walked back to my room, scanning the yard once more. Doubt took over as I started to question my mental state.

"Maybe I'm seeing things," I thought. "It is late and my mind does have the capacity to play tricks when alone in the dark."

My heart continued to thump in my chest as I slowly inhaled, attempting to calm myself.

"Relax," I reassured myself, closing my eyes. "Your parents are downstairs and you are safe."

Giving up the search, I laid down on the thin camping mattress, finding it challenging to get comfortable. I flipped over onto my left side, facing the door. The vivid image of the man still lingered in my mind while I played out our brief meeting once more. He seemed focused with a look of determination, a look of wanting. I shuddered at the idea of him having a hidden agenda. Shaking my head, I tried clearing my mind of the foolish games it was playing. I exhaled a long, deep breath, deciding to play the, "I imagined it" card.

"Yes, it was probably my fear of the dark that initiated this entire event. It was dark when I first walked upstairs and it is dark outside. It's late and I'm probably just exhausted from the drive and not thinking or seeing clearly. That's it! The dark scared me, simple as that."

I lay quietly, forcing my eyes shut in hopes that I had imagined his visit, but something deep inside told me otherwise. I continued to toss and turn, wondering about the young man, until I finally drifted off to sleep, convinced I made the whole thing up.

CHAPTER 3

It was late afternoon as I lay watching the chain of the fan sway in a steady rhythm, resembling the pendulum of a clock. The past few weeks had flown by in a blur. My father and I had been assigned various tasks, which included breaking down boxes, numerous visits to The Home Depot and endless re-arranging of furniture. As busy as my mother kept me, only one thought constantly occupied my mind: who was the mysterious man outside my window? I went back and forth daily trying to convince myself that he was real, only to change my mind when fearful thoughts took over.

I let out a sigh, rolling over. Even far away in my secluded room, I could still hear my mother complaining about the pictures not hung to her perfection.

"Rog! Where is the level you bought the other day? The picture in the dining room is still crooked," she barked.

I laid the cool pillow over my face, trying to drown out the sound of my mother's voice.

"Now is the time," I thought.

I had felt like a trapped prisoner for days and my grand escape needed to be put into action, immediately. I quickly changed out of the gray cotton pants I had been wearing on and off for a week, changing into an old pair of jean shorts with a light blue tank top. I slipped on my barely worn flip flops, whipped my hair into a messy bun, grabbed my poor excuse for a cell phone and darted down the stairs.

"Mom? I'm going to get some fresh air and check out the neighborhood. I'll be back before it gets dark," I yelled.

"Don't forget your cell!" she shouted back from the dining room.

"Got it," I called, closing the door quickly behind me.

The sun sat low in the sky, without a cloud to hide behind. The summer breeze whipped across my face as I closed my eyes, taking in its warmth. I had never cared for heat, but it did feel nice for a change.

I ventured down the sidewalk toward the main two-lane road. I had noticed a trail head somewhere close by during one of our many runs to the local hardware store and figured it shouldn't be too hard to find on foot. While walking along the wide paved sidewalk, I watched as children bobbed and weaved in and out of a sprinkler on a corner lot. I laughed as one young boy tormented an even younger girl with a classic game of kiss chase. They ran after each other in circles, the small girl giggling loudly.

Up ahead, I noticed the entrance to a park and figured that was probably as good a place as any to look for the trail. My prediction was correct and before I knew it, I was standing in front of an old wooden sign just feet from the main road. The sign read:

Nature Preserve Trail Head
No Motorized Vehicles Permitted
Pets Must Be Leashed at All Times
Stay on Trail
Watch for Snakes

My eyes darted directly to the ground where my feet lay, barely protected by the thin rubber thongs. I began contemplating whether I should go back home and change into hiking boots when suddenly, two young boys zipped past me, almost knocking me over while running down the trail in nothing but swim shorts and bare feet.

"Sorry!" yelled one of the boys in my direction, not taking the time to look back.

I laughed at my paranoia, slipped my cell into my back pocket and started on the mulch-lined path.

As I walked down the trail, I kept a watchful eye out for snakes and found myself jumping at the slightest scuffle or shake of a branch.

"Try to be practical, a snake is not going to fly out of a bush and attack you," I scolded myself.

I giggled at my own thoughts, imagining how ridiculous I would look running wildly back toward home with my arms flailing like a mad woman.

The comedic imagery melted away my fears, permitting me to absorb the natural setting. Birds chirped, squirrels chased one another up and down the tall pine trees while something small scuttled around the dense brush below. It was peaceful on this path and for the first time since we left home I felt at ease, relaxed.

The path wound in and out of the preserve. The only part maintained was the trail itself. Overgrown shrubs and tall weeds made it difficult to see through the heavily wooded area. The deeper the path led into the preserve, the darker and cooler the air temperature felt. Tall evergreens and live oak trees blocked out most of the sunlight, allowing the tiny sweat droplets that had formed on the back of my neck to evaporate within minutes. Farther down the trail, I noticed a small wooden sign carved into an arrow which read Woodward High School.

Not sure how much farther down the path I needed to walk to find the school, I decided to take my chances, following the brightly painted arrow. The trail continued, twisting and turning, becoming less maintained and more rugged. My eyes carefully followed my feet, in hopes that I didn't trip over any exposed branches or roots.

"I guess kids don't really walk to school around here," I said aloud, as if someone were listening.

At that exact moment a strange, loud popping noise sounded to my immediate left. My head snapped toward the peculiar noise as my eyes frantically searched the thick brush.

"Hello?" I whispered.

Silence; I could no longer hear the chirping of birds or scurrying of squirrels. Chills crept slowly up my spine as my mind rushed back to the night I saw the man outside my window. The eerie feeling that someone was watching me made blood pump through my veins at an incredible rate. I was alone on the trail and the closest public place to my knowledge was the high school. The casual pace I had been maintaining quickly turned into an Olympic speed walk as I maneuvered over fallen branches and pinecones. My head rotated quickly, scanning the woods all the while attempting to guide my feet through the gauntlet of debris. Minutes passed, though it felt like hours before I finally reached a clearing. A massive, red brick building surrounded by parking lots and tennis courts filled my vision. I sighed with relief, slowing my pace as I left the trail.

Feeling more relaxed, I eased my way down the grassy hill to observe the school from a closer distance.

"Geez!" I thought. "My old high school could fit in half of the parking lot alone."

Behind the vast parking lot towered a massive stadium. Large bleachers bordered the dark red track; in the center as if on display, sat a well-manicured, elaborate football field. I had heard rumors that Texans took pride in their high-school football programs, but this stadium was equal to that of a college field back east. Permanent banners placed precisely at the entrance to the field read Home of the Titans: 5A State Champions. The perfection with which the field and stands were designed and built overflowed to the school building itself. Perfectly laid brick and limestone decorated every wall with red and black mosaic tiles spelling: Woodward High School. Tall pine trees and well-maintained shrubs outlined the school, making it the perfect set to film a popular teen film. My back pocket vibrated, causing me to flinch.

"What, mom?" I answered.

"Elara, where are you?" she asked, a sudden urgency in her voice.

"I'm exploring the trails and found the high school. You should see this …."

"I don't want you wondering around on those trails by yourself!" she began. "Come home! Your father is hungry and it will be getting dark soon."

I rolled my eyes at her paranoia, but agreed to her request. I slipped the dated phone into my pocket before heading back up the hill toward the trail. The sun was beginning to set and anxiety took hold; I knew the trail would be darker than when I had first begun the journey. I tried reassuring myself with the simple fact that it was a beautiful trail and the only thing I needed to worry about was a rabid squirrel or a snake. I summoned every ounce of courage I could find, stood up straight and began the long walk home.

The birds chirped as critters scurried up and around the tall trees. It was quite a bit darker than before, but I kept my mind focused on the impressive school, allowing myself to daydream about what my new high-school life would entail.

My thoughts were interrupted by the same loud popping noise I had heard earlier. I froze, holding my breath. My heart pounded, but my senses moved in slow motion. I could feel someone's presence right behind me. The hairs on my neck prickled as I listened to the sound of steady, rhythmic breathing.

A quick breeze brushed against my back as the strange presence moved to my right side. Overwhelmed with fear, I found myself physically unable to move. I had always wondered what it would be like to find myself in a situation where my instincts would kick in and take me into survival mode. Unfortunately in that moment, my instincts were out of commission. My feet, feeling as though they were made of iron, remained glued to the mulched trail.

"How could I run if there was no oxygen entering my body?" I thought. "Motivation! I need some motivation."

I turned my head ever so slowly to the right. Standing within five feet from my location, was a young man. Not just any young man, but the same young man who stood outside my window only weeks ago. He looked exactly as I had remembered: dark hair, sharp features, fair skin, but this time I noticed his eyes. They were a piercing blue, appearing to blink only when necessary. I met his gaze and felt utterly helpless. His stare was intense and he broke eye contact only by scanning my body, reminding me of a predator summing up its prey before an attack. This break in eye contact was all I needed to snap me into action.

I assessed the situation; I was alone in the woods with the same man who I caught watching me only weeks ago and had no means to defend myself. The heavy, iron feeling in my feet suddenly melted away as blood surged through my veins. I inhaled, allowing oxygen to rush into my lungs as I sprinted down the trail, never looking back. I leapt over broken tree limbs and hurtled roots that had refused to stay underground. My throat burned from the heavy breathing as my side cramped in pain.

"Why didn't I ever take track, or any sport for that matter?" I asked myself, racing down the trail.

My legs burned as if on fire. I was not sure how much longer I could keep up the fast pace. The intensity of his presence lessened as I continued the mad dash toward home. The adrenaline pumping through my body was wearing off; the quick breaths entering my nose and mouth were not sufficient to fill my lungs.

I skidded to a stop, slipping on the loose mulch, falling hard. I was too out of breath to inspect the large gash covering my knee, but could feel the warm blood trickling down my leg. Everything started spinning faster than my eyes could focus. It took every last ounce of energy to keep my body from collapsing. Hyperventilation set in as I tried holding my breath to slow the heavy breathing while my heart pounded in my ears.

"Don't pass out, don't pass out! You can't pass out, Elara!" I pleaded with myself.

This is what a lonely, injured gazelle must feel like after trying to outrun a big cat; exhausted and helpless. I looked up ahead, noticing the entrance to the trail head no more than a few yards away. Knowing I must stay focused, I commanded my body to stand. I winced at the pain radiating from my knee, then froze once more, hearing the familiar popping noise. Feeling like a trained circus animal following a command, I turned toward the direction of the noise. This time, the young man stood several yards away, maintaining his steady breathing.

"Who is this guy, a tri-athlete or something?" I wondered. "We just sprinted a half mile and he's barely winded."

Our eyes locked. The intensity of his focus lessened as he took notice of my bloodied knee. His dark eyebrows furrowed, as he slowly shook his head. Cautiously, he took a small step forward.

Once again, that was all the motivation I needed. I hobbled into a steady run, ignoring the searing pain coming from my knee. Moments later, I darted through the entrance of the trail head, resembling a first-place finisher in the New York City marathon. My senses were overwhelmed with the sounds of cars rushing by, children laughing and the feeling of safety. I was no longer alone. If mystery man was going to attack, he would have to do it in front of the entire neighborhood. I whipped my head back toward the trail entrance and to my surprise, there stood the same two young boys I had seen earlier. Together, they rushed out of the trail, laughing as one tried tackling the other.

My jaw dropped.

"They were right behind me the whole time and I never saw them?" I asked myself, taking a seat on the warm ground to rest my injured leg.

"Am I imagining things? There's no way! I saw him! Twice! I heard that strange noise."

I racked my brain, going over every detail.

"On my way to see the school, I had heard the noise but didn't see anything. On my way back, I heard the noise and then saw him," I thought, confusion taking hold.

I winced, attempting to steady myself onto two feet. Painfully, I stretched out the wounded leg, inspecting my bloodied knee.

"How am I going to explain this to my mother? If I told her the truth, she would never let me leave the house again and with all the other recent changes in my life, that was the last thing I needed," I thought, touching the tender gash. "I would just have to tell her I tripped over a fallen branch and explain that flip flops are not the best thing to wear while hiking."

I gazed back toward the trail, perplexed by my muddled thoughts. I couldn't have imagined it. This wasn't like me. I wasn't some paranoid girl who imagined creepy men, or who ran from them, for that matter.

I shook my head, limping back toward the sidewalk, continuing to examine every thought that flew into my mind. He had to be real, he stood there clear as day. I could make out every feature. His dark hair, the way it hung in his eyes, his perfect posture and those deep blue eyes. First, I see him outside my window and then again today? These encounters can't be random coincidences. The more I racked my brain, the more obvious it became. If he had wanted to harm me he would have done so when I tripped and fell. He had the perfect opportunity to attack, but instead, just stood there in silence, staring. It was almost like he had something to tell me, but couldn't get it out.

The vibration coming from my back pocket startled me as I quickly reached for the device, placing it to my ear.

"Where are you?" my mother asked, irritated.

"I'm just around the corner. I'll be there soon."

"Your father and I were beginning to worry. It's getting dark out!"

"I'm sorry. I got lost on the trail," I lied.

"That's the exact reason I don't want you to be on the trail alone!" she barked.

"I'll be home in a few minutes," I noted, hanging up the phone, refusing to listen to anymore of her scolding.

I took one last glance at the trail, curious about the young man. While limping home, I took the time to devise a plan in case I were ever to see him again.

"I need to stop acting like a child and start handling the situation like an adult. If I do see him again, I will confront him about his stalker-like behavior and simply ask why he keeps following me," I thought, stepping over a large crack in the side walk.

Just then, a loud crashing noise sounded in the distance. I turned my head in every direction my eyes scanning wildly for the mysterious man. The sound crashed again. A few streets down, I noticed a large dump truck busying itself with the construction of a new home. My nerves calmed, but immediately began rethinking my strategy.

"Maybe, confronting a total stranger isn't the best idea. Maybe the best thing to do is to avoid him at all cost," I confirmed, nodding my head, pleased with the newly devised plan.

I rounded the corner, only to find my mother pacing back and forth in our driveway like a solider on watch. Even from this distance, I could see she was irritated, anxious to give me a lecture on the dangers of the world. Slowing my pace, I started exaggerating my limp in hopes of distracting her from the unavoidable speech. She stopped pacing once she noticed my injured knee, then crossed her arms tightly while tapping her foot anxiously. I walked cautiously onto the driveway, preparing myself for the wrath of my mother.

CHAPTER 4

I could feel his warm breath on my neck as I tried to outrun my predator. Running farther than I ever had, my feet carried me effortlessly down the rugged path, knowing exactly where to step without conscious effort. My breathing was slow and rhythmic, but my heart pounded rapidly with every step I took. He was right behind me. I had to get away. My vision was sharp and clear. I could make out the delicate patterns on the bark of the pine trees even in the moonless night. I burst out of the trail and onto the street, only to be met by an oncoming car. I raised my hands, shielding my face from the inevitable impact. Halting with a screech, the car's wheels locked, sliding against the black pavement. The horn sounded in a consistent pattern. Beep ... beep ... beep ... beep. Time stood still, as everything faded to black.

My eyes shot open as I lay still, motionless, taking in my surroundings. The loud beeping persisted. Turning my head, I squinted, noticing 6:37 a.m. flashing brightly on the alarm that rested on my bedside table. My heart began to slow. I was covered in a sticky layer of sweat; my sheets were soaking wet. I hit the off button violently with my hand, took a deep breath and sat up while pulling my knees into my chest. I played the dream over again in my mind. It was crystal clear, like I was just there. I could still smell the cool night air and feel his strong presence around me. I shuddered at that thought, snapped back to reality by the sound of my mother's voice on the stairwell.

"Elara! Are you up? You don't want to be late for your first day of school."

"I'm up," I yelled back.

I sighed, rolling out of bed, avoiding the cool, moist spot of sweat. Looking out the window, I noticed the sun's poor attempt to break through the dense layer of fog that consumed our yard. The ominous sight reflected the vivid dream I was unable shake.

After a quick shower, dressing took ages because I hadn't a clue what to wear. I changed four times, before deciding on a pair of old faded jeans with a navy blue tank top. My other selections were strewn across the floor like fallen comrades. I brushed my long ebony hair, then tied it into a messy bun, staring at my reflection in the mirror. I let out a deep breath. It was a poor attempt, if I planned on impressing anyone during my first day of school. My mother would have words with me about my lack of enthusiasm, but I didn't care. This was me, take it or leave it.

I grabbed the nearly empty back pack before darting down the stairs, skipping every other one. I could smell cooked bacon as I approached the kitchen. My mother was humming loudly while she set the dining room table with eggs, bacon, pancakes, and freshly squeezed orange juice. Her hair and makeup were meticulous and to top it all off she wore a flowered apron that I had never seen before.

"Mom. What's going on?" I asked, confused by her dolled-up appearance accompanied by the elaborate breakfast.

"I just thought since we are starting out fresh, it would be nice if I tried to fit into my new role as a stay-at-home mom!" she sang, twirling around while making exaggerated hand gestures toward the food.

"Um ... okay," I replied, trying to make sense of this "new" mother.

"Elara, you could at least say thank you for the elaborate breakfast, or that I look nice."

Nope, I was mistaken. Her new appearance could not mask her true self. This may have looked like a new mother, but she was still my "take everything personal" mother.

"I'm sorry," I managed, plastering a fake smile onto my face. "You look really nice, mom. Thanks for the fancy breakfast."

She smiled, pleased with my response but then frowned as she noticed my appearance.

"Elara! What are you wearing?"

"I couldn't decide on anything," I stated, pouring myself a glass juice.

"Well, you could have at least tried to make somewhat of an effort. Don't you want to give a good impression on your first day?"

"Not really," I mumbled under my breath, sipping the thickly pulped orange juice.

"I'm disappointed in you," she scolded, reaching for a pancake.

It was too early in the day to start an argument with my mother. Instead, I chose to eat in silence, listening as she shared her detailed plans for the day.

After breakfast, she insisted on driving me to school even though I argued I was fully capable of walking there alone. This new, stay-at-home-mother act she was trying to pull was already getting on my nerves. I was hopeful this midlife crisis she was going through would soon end, allowing her to resume her less involved approach to parenting.

I climbed into the car flustered, throwing the worn back pack onto the floor board. We slowly pulled out of the driveway, then made our way through the newly built community. As we passed the entrance to the trail, my mind instantly recalled the vivid dream. The frustration I had with my mother instantly vanished, as I now found myself grateful she had insisted on driving drive me to school.

Due to our community's proximity, we arrived at Woodward High within minutes. My jaw dropped observing the spectacle before my eyes. It looked like something out of a popular teen movie. Expensive luxury cars lined the circle drive at the entrance to the school, waiting to unload students while upperclassmen zipped into the parking lot, music blaring. I gawked at the numerous customized SUVs and suped-up sports cars that zipped into the lot. A pack of cheerleaders piled out of a shiny new BMW, laughing while straightening each other's uniforms.

"Can you just pull over here?" I asked, anxiously.

"Elara, the main entrance is still some ways up," she spoke, confused by my request.

"Exactly," I answered.

The last thing I needed was for my future classmates to see my mother dropping me off at the front door. I had always tried to avoid extra attention at school and seeing that I was apparently the only senior without a car, getting dropped off as far from the main entrance as possible looked like the smartest option.

The car rolled to a stop. I had successfully managed to exit the vehicle unnoticed by my peers. Thankfully, my first day was going far smoother than I had imagined. This thought quickly dissolved once I heard my mother's voice sound loudly out of the passenger window.

"Have a great first day, sweetie!"

I cringed; her timing was impeccable. She somehow managed the farewell at the exact moment the perfectly manicured cheerleaders I had observed earlier strolled past where I stood. A tiny blonde snickered as she tossed her tousled locks off her shoulder, resembling a shampoo commercial.

"Perfect," I thought, nodding farewell to my mother.

Quickly, I walked toward the entrance of the school wishing I could blend in with the gray sidewalk. Not far past the main entrance was a large open rotunda, bustling with noisy chatter, accompanied by the squeaking sound of new sneakers on the freshly polished floor.

I unfolded the wrinkled class schedule I had received only days earlier from the guidance counselor. Glancing over what would occupy my time for the next few months, I sighed with frustration remembering that Spanish 1 would take up the first half of my morning. At my previous school it was mandatory for students to take French as a foreign language, considering the Canadian border was only a stone's throw away. In Texas, you were "encouraged" to take Spanish. Just days ago when reviewing my transcript with the guidance counselor, I begged her to allow me take French. Disapproving my request, she smiled and handed me the unrevised schedule.

I reviewed the details for first period. Spanish 8:05 a.m. to 9:35 a.m. with Melinda Lopez in portable B Room 4. I looked around the large rotunda, my eyes scanning for some sort of direction as to where the portables were located.

Giving up, I pulled the campus map from the front zipper pocket of my back pack. I squinted, trying to decipher the convoluted maze of hallways and wings that created the vast campus.

WHACK! My head snapped forward like a rocket. I stumbled, catching myself on a wall of bright red lockers. The sound of the slow bounce of a basketball rebounded loudly through the hallway. Holding my sore neck, I turned in hopes of finding an apologetic peer, but instead found a sea of laughing faces. I smiled, nodding at the fellow onlookers, hoping the phrase "if you can't beat them, join them" might work this time.

A deep voice bellowed close by.

"Dude! A pass like that won't get us to state this year."

I flinched at the harsh tone, surprised to find the owner of the deep voice standing beside me. He was tall, easily towering over me; covering his lean frame was a well-fitted, red and black t-shirt that boldly read 2014 & 2015 5A BASKETBALL STATE CHAMPIONS.

"She walked right in front of you!" argued his counterpart from across the hall, gesturing in my direction.

The deep-voiced player effortlessly picked up the ball with one hand, spun it on the tip of his index finger and began dribbling it toward his teammate, continuing to further ridicule him along the way. The matching pair, continuing their banter, walked side by side, oblivious to the fact that I was the casualty of their failed pass attempt.

I exhaled slowly, attempting to redirect my focus to the task at hand: finding the portable buildings. I looked down to review the complex campus map, only to see my empty pale hands.

"I must have dropped it when attempting to brace myself from the blow," I thought, feeling myself getting flustered.

I scanned the floor, my eyes desperately searching for my only lifeline. A sea of shoes in every style imaginable made it a challenge to see the floor, much less the missing map. I paused the frantic search, noticing a sudden warming sensation move throughout my entire body. The gentle pressure of rhythmic tapping on my shoulder caused me to flinch. I quickly turned, my eyes locking onto the young man standing before me.

I might as well have been face to face with a modern-day gladiator. His dark eyes; amber in color, exuded confidence and displayed a strong since of fearlessness. Though only a few inches taller than myself, he easily outweighed me by 100 pounds. His tan, muscular body appeared to flex, without any effort. The short, white blond hair covering his head mirrored his pearly white teeth that sat neatly in his handsome smile.

"Are you looking for this?" he asked, casually waving the folded map only inches from my face.

"Uh …..," I was at a loss for words.

"What has staring at this Greek god done to me?" I wondered, my mouth gaped.

"It's a simple yes or no question," he continued, playfully.

"YEAH!" I blurted out.

He stepped back, surprised by my severe tone.

"I mean yes, thank you," I managed in my normal speaking voice.

"You're new here," he stated, observing my nervous posture.

"Yes," I replied.

He cocked his head to one side, as though analyzing my response. Pointing at me, he continued.

"You sure do say yes a lot," he noted, his tone playful once more.

"Y..e… No! You almost got me on that one," I pointed, wagging my finger.

Flashing me his Colgate worthy grin, he unfolded the small, blue map.

"What class are you trying to find?" he asked, handing me the creased paper.

I sighed, "Spanish I, Room 4, Portable B."

A confused expression crossed his tan face.

"Are you a freshman?"

Noticing my agitation, he quickly recovered.

"I mean you don't look like a freshman."

J.M. Buckler

The strong, tingling, warming sensation intensified as blood rushed through my veins up to my cheeks. Embarrassed, I looked down at the wrinkled map.

"The portable buildings are behind the school. Just go out the large door by the library. That will lead you to the parking lot. Trust me, you can't miss them."

Slowly I raised my head, making eye contact with his amber eyes.

"Thank you."

"Anytime," he said, still smiling.

We both stood silently starring at one another. My skin prickled with heat while my hands buzzed excitedly. There was something playful about his presence. I wondered if he had this effect on every girl he met.

"I'm going to go ... find the portables," I stuttered.

"Good idea," he replied, his voice solid and steady.

A tiny smirk slowly broke at the corner of his mouth as I spun around.

"The portables are the other way," he shouted, loud enough for me to hear over the bustling hallway.

I turned around to see a large grin cross his face as he pointed toward the opposite direction I was heading.

"Right," I sighed.

I walked quickly past where he stood; the warming sensation intensifying. Without thinking, I whipped back around, finding his handsome face in the sea of other students.

"It's Elara!" I yelled, loud enough for him to hear.

"What?" he asked.

I was unsure if the quizzical look that crossed his brow was because he could not hear me over the background noise or if he didn't understand what I had said.

"My name. It's Elara!" I shouted, even louder this time.

32

"That's an unusual name," he remarked, his voice raised over the noisy hallway chatter.

I threw my arms up in a "what am I supposed to do about it" gesture. He laughed, pointing to himself.

"Cyrus."

"Like that's a common name?" I asked sarcastically, my voice still carrying over the busy hallway.

He threw up his arms, mocking my previous gesture.

I laughed, shaking my head. He waved before heading off in the opposite direction.

The walk to my first period class was simple thanks to Cyrus's accurate directions. He was right, the portables were impossible to miss. Clustered together, the small buildings were painted in red, black and white, covered with murals of alumni sport stars. Was it obnoxious? Yes, but more entertaining than the usual, boring, khaki-colored building.

Being early to first period had its advantage. The classroom was empty, so I had first pick of the numerous available seats. I headed straight to the back row, hoping to go unnoticed by the teacher who sat quietly reading the paper at her desk. I chose the last seat on the aisle that sat directly under the window air-conditioning unit. I loathed being hot, so its location was perfect. I would be under the radar and cool, exactly how I preferred to attend class.

Sitting down on the hard-plastic seat, I bent over and unzipped my back pack. I fished out a new spiral-bound notebook and mechanical pencil. I never received a list of school supplies from the guidance counselor, so these two items would have to suffice for the day. Resituating myself in the uncomfortable chair, I observed that the teacher was no longer reading her paper but staring directly at me.

"Are you comfortable?" she asked, getting up from her desk.

"Yes, I think so," I replied nervously.

"It is Si, Señora Lopez," she corrected.

"Why couldn't I have taken French," I thought. "I don't know a lick of Spanish."

"Si, Señora Lopez," I stammered.

"You will have to work on rolling your R's if you want to succeed in my class. Who told you that you had the privilege of choosing your own seat? Señorita…?"

"It's Elara and I'm sorry, I thought I could sit wherever," I squeaked.

"Well, you thought wrong. Every freshman has an assigned seat, so therefore you will sit where you are told."

"But I'm not a freshman," I stuttered.

She inhaled slowly, closing her eyes briefly.

"That may be, but you are in a freshman class so therefore you shall be treated as one."

Her voice, irritatingly calm, was quiet and soft. I would have preferred her to yell then continue speaking to me in such a patronizing tone.

"Yes…" I stopped myself. "Si, Señora Lopez," I corrected.

A small smile broke at the corners of her mouth. I felt like a dog trying to join a pack of wild wolves. She was the Alpha and after successfully winning the challenge left me feeling like a defeated, submissive pup.

"Where would you like me to sit?" I asked, through gritted teeth.

"A senior with so much maturity should only be front and center," she answered, her voice lingering on every word.

She snapped her fingers, pointing to the front and center desk and then motioned for me to quickly collect my things. For some reason, the new seat felt more uncomfortable than the last. The fluorescent lighting that hung over my new desk, flickered and flashed annoyingly, mimicking that of a strobe light. I could hear the window unit hard at work, but sadly felt none of its efforts.

I closed my eyes, rubbing my temples. I had a headache. I wasn't sure if it was from the earlier collision with the basketball, or the encounter with my new teacher. At least I would only have to deal with her for a few months. Woodward High's curriculum followed block scheduling, which meant I had four classes in the fall and thankfully, four new classes in the spring.

My head popped up at the sound of the bell. Students flooded into the classroom, their cheeks rosy from the outside heat. Each one lined up like obeying soldiers, against the front wall. Some whispered, pointing toward me with looks of confusion crossing their face.

Señora Lopez smiled at the freshman, greeting them with a warm and friendly tone.

"Bienvenido clase!"

"Hola!" They replied in perfect unison.

My mouth gaped.

"How was I supposed to know that was first-day protocol!" I thought, bewildered.

"Welcome to Spanish 1. My name is Señora Lopez and we are all going to have a great semester together. Let's begin with finding your seats. I will first call your name, then kindly take a seat where instructed."

She smiled once more at the zealous freshman.

I watched the enthusiastic students effortlessly take their seats one by one. When Señora Lopez got to my desk, she made sure to introduce me to everyone by letting them know I was a senior taking a freshman class. Some giggled while other's gasped, if I had committed a crime.

The morning dragged on painfully. I sat quietly, trying to avoid any further interaction with my new teacher. She smiled as the obedient freshman opened their glossy new textbooks, then frowned in my direction when noticing my empty desk top. Eager student's hands shot up, excited to answer her questions while I struggled to follow along in my neighbor's text.

"Why were these kids taking Spanish 1?" I thought. "Half of them already seemed fluent."

I was completely lost and felt more and more anxious with every passing minute. Señora Lopez, sensing my uneasiness, found great joy in continuing to ask me questions she knew I was unable to answer. A small sense of satisfaction crossed her face with every unanswered question. I closed my eyes, pushing down the intense frustration that was slowly building. My teacher had it out for me, plain and simple. I placed my forehead down on the cool wooden desk, surrendering. This was going to be a very long day.

CHAPTER 5

To my surprise, the remainder of the morning went by swiftly and uneventfully. After a disastrous first period, I was grateful to have Calculus, an all senior class, where I was permitted to choose my own seat and easily answered any of the teacher's questions. I felt confident back in my comfort zone. Math, my favorite subject, had always come naturally to me. Mr. Randal was an easy-going teacher and cared less that I showed up to class unprepared. He kindly let me borrow his teacher's copy of the textbook and informed me to purchase a scientific calculator at my earliest convenience.

English Literature followed directly after Calculus. My stomach loudly protested the lack of sustenance and I was eager for the upcoming lunch hour. Fortunately, I lucked out with another all senior class, effortlessly finding a cozy seat located in the back of the room. Mrs. Jenson, a tiny woman who smelled strongly of coffee and cigarettes, paraded around the class, full of life. I found her enthusiasm about the new school year endearing. I had never seen anyone talk so passionately about the Scarlet Letter or Wuthering Heights. By the end of class, I found myself so engaged with her lesson that I had forgotten all about the burning hunger pains churning loudly from inside.

Lunch hour followed English and instead of joining the noisy crowd of students in the cafeteria, I opted to eat alone on the vast patio located just outside. It was hot, but the tables were shaded and the warm breeze felt slightly refreshing against my cool skin. I selected a small table that faced the enormous glass windows that looked directly into the cafeteria. There I sat, picking the crust off the sandwich my mother had made while watching fellow classmates file into the cafeteria.

Woodward High was no different from any other typical high school. Freshman flocked together like wading ducks, unsure where to sit in their new environment. Upperclassmen effortlessly found their friends, casually filling up tables located at the back of the large open lunchroom. The popular group of cheerleaders I had encountered earlier that morning bounced excitedly to their table, which sat directly in front of my current view; the only thing separating us was a thick layer of glass. Apparently, one must enjoy rabbit food to sit at their table because each girl's lunch tray held nothing more than a simple salad and a bottle of water. All six of them were tan and thin with similar hair styles. Beach wave curls draped over their toned shoulders while their flawless skin glowed under the bright fluorescent lights. The center of attention and clearly most popular one of the bunch was the platinum blonde who just so happened to be the exact same girl that had snickered at my mother's salutation. She tossed her hair out of her face every few minutes, using exaggerated hand gestures while she spoke.

Taking the last bite of the dry sandwich, I tossed the empty Ziploc back into the brown paper bag. My eyes glanced to the large window, noticing Cyrus enter the cafeteria. My heart leapt seeing his smiling face once more. My skin, thankfully, felt cool to the touch.

He was greeted by friends who slapped him on the back or offered fist-bumps while walking past. The entire mood of the room appeared to change. There was something about his presence that was contagious. Peers wanted to be around him. Even teachers stopped briefly to chat, smiling and laughing, while patting his shoulder. Regardless of social status, Cyrus seemed to acknowledge anyone who approached him. Even wide-eyed freshmen were given a warm smile when he stopped to talk with some of the junior varsity football players. His posture was relaxed, confident, reminding me of a politician working the crowd on a campaign trail. I thought back to our meeting earlier that morning, instantly feeling deflated.

"I guess he's that friendly with everyone," I thought, frowning.

Lingering on that thought, I watched a large grin cross his face. He waved a tan arm casually in my direction, heading straight toward the back doors of the cafeteria. I almost choked on the remaining piece of sandwich while I stood entirely too quickly, knocking my head against the canopy umbrella that shaded the table. I smiled, waving back energetically.

Cyrus moved through the cafeteria with a purpose. I watched as he neared the exit door that lead to the patio, my heart thumping in my chest. The large smile across my face quickly dissolved as he took a sharp turn, heading away from the patio and straight to the table of cheerleaders. Cyrus was met with open arms by none other than the popular platinum blonde. The hug, lingering longer than I would have liked was followed by a passionate kiss as his lips locked with hers. The other girls at the table giggled with delight as though watching a romantic film.

They slowly broke away from one another. Cyrus's arm slid gently down her back and then settled comfortably around her tiny waist. The thin brunette at the table pointed in my direction. Cyrus's apparent girlfriend flipped her blonde locks behind her back, turning curiously to see where her friend was so eagerly pointing. To their amusement, they found my arm frozen, stuck in the mid-wave position. They laughed aloud, amused by my reaction. I could have sworn I saw one say, "What is she doing?"

My arm fell to my side like a dropped dumbbell as my face burned with embarrassment. Cocking her head sharply to one side, the popular blonde proceeded to make an exaggerated pouty face while waving her hand cutely as if acknowledging a young child. I rolled my eyes, shaking my head and letting out a deep breath.

Quickly, I stood and grabbed the empty lunch bag before tossing my back pack over one shoulder, then headed straight for the side gate of the fenced-in patio. Unfortunately, I had to walk directly in front of their view to reach the exit. I kept my head down, but could feel their eyes following my every move. I glanced up in time to see Cyrus remove his hand from her waist, noticing a look of disapproval in his eyes.

A giant oak tree that had taken claim of the sidewalk with its vast root system looked like the perfect spot to find solace. I strolled down the grassy hill away from the patio and away from any further humiliation. Laying my back pack against the rough trunk, I sat leaning against the mature tree, reflecting on my less-than-perfect first day. All I wanted to do was blend in, but had somehow managed to do the complete opposite. My Spanish teacher's goal was to make my life miserable; the extremely attractive guy and only peer who had spoken to me all day was claimed by my new arch rival. At lunch, I had tried to avoid any social awkwardness by sitting outside away from everyone, only to be humiliated. Now, I found myself sitting under a lonely tree like some outcast in a B movie. I shook my head, trying to mentally erase the day.

"How did I get here?" I wondered.

Only months ago, I was back home in a familiar environment, flying under the radar, effortlessly gliding through the motions. Now I found myself stuck in an unfamiliar place, flying above the radar while stumbling through every motion. My eyes began to sting with warm tears. I forced them shut, trying to stop the inevitable waterworks.

"Not now, Elara. All you need is for someone to see you crying and your current situation will go from bad to worse," I lectured myself.

Taking a deep breath, I popped my neck, encouraging myself to brush the day off. My thoughts were distracted by the sound of the bell signaling the end of lunch. I rubbed my eyes and grabbed my bag before making my way back toward the main building. One more class and I would be free of any further humiliation.

I was the first one to enter the bright and open classroom. An entire wall of windows covered one side of the room, allowing ample afternoon sunlight to flood the large space. Displayed across the teacher's desk was a large pile of used textbooks. Without saying a word, the heavy-set, gray-haired instructor motioned for me to take one. I chose a worn copy of The Physical Universe: An Introduction to Astronomy and headed to the last seat of the last row, closest to the wall of windows. I eyed the black board which read "Mr. Lawson's Senior Astronomy," scribbled faintly in large letters. Underneath it was written, Homework- Read Chapters 1-2 & complete chapter summaries before next class. Having nothing better to do, I decided to get a jump start on the assignment. Opening my book to page one, I quickly began skimming the first paragraph, but stopped at the sound of the bell. Students began filing into the classroom in groups, taking seats next to their friends. The room filled up quickly and only a few available seats remained.

I began to relax as the number of students entering the classroom slowed. I enjoyed the idea of having empty desks around me. Just as I settled comfortably into my new surroundings, two girls ran into the classroom right as the final bell sounded. My mouth gaped as the thin brunette cheerleader who had so kindly pointed me out at lunch walked closely with her blonde friend, Cyrus's girlfriend. Casually, they walked up to the teacher's desk, carelessly grabbing copies of the text. I felt my heart begin to race. Only three empty seats remained. All of which surrounded my desk.

"You made it right under the wire, girls," murmured Mr. Lawson.

"We are so sorry," they replied in unison, smiling sweetly at him.

"Please take your seats, Ms. Russel and Ms. Clark," he instructed, motioning toward the vacancies in my direction.

Not only were these girls popular with their peers, but apparently with the teachers as well. He didn't have to glance at the roster to know their names. The two girls quickly walked to the two empty seats on my immediate right.

The hair flipping was getting out of control. It was like they could not speak or move without tossing their tousled locks every which way. I let out an exaggerated sigh, louder than anticipated. It appeared they had not noticed my presence until that very moment. Simultaneously, both of their heads snapped in my direction, displaying looks of disapproval. I rotated my head back to the blackboard, pretending to be invisible once more.

Mr. Lawson stood slowly from his desk, adjusting his overly large pants by the worn belt loops, then hobbled over to the lectern. The walk from his desk to the lecture stand could not have been more than ten feet, but he panted uncomfortably with every step he took. Though the room was ice cold, beads of sweat dotted his creased forehead before he finally settled into position in front of the classroom. Grabbing a pen from behind his large ear, he began calling off names from the roster. Mr. Lawson had only finished the B's, when the classroom door suddenly swung open. My heart skipped a beat. It was Cyrus.

"Please, let him be an office aid delivering a note or something," I silently pleaded with the universe.

"I'm sorry I'm late Mr. Lawson. Coach Burnell needed to speak with me after lunch. It won't happen again," he apologized, his voice calm, unwavering.

Mr. Lawson exhaled, irritated by the intrusion, "Make sure it doesn't happen again, Mr. Lofton. I do not like my class being interrupted. Now hurry and take a seat."

Cyrus reached for one of the two remaining Astronomy books before heading toward the last available desk, which was located directly in front of my own. As he approached the last row, my skin began to prickle as the familiar heat wave surged through my body once more. The closer he got, the warmer I felt; my cheeks flushed and my heart raced. Everyone, including his girlfriend and her sidekick, watched as he walked to his desk. His foot gently brushed against mine as he settled into his chair, causing my face to flush even more. The tiny brunette pointed her thin finger at me for the second time that day, teasing loud enough for everyone to hear.

"Awe... Hillary I think the new girl has a crush on your boyfriend!"

The entire class laughed aloud. I closed my eyes, forcing down the lump of anxiety that had formed in my throat.

"Please, like she would even have a chance," Hillary murmured to her friend.

A quiet "ooohhh," fell over the class.

Cyrus shifted in his seat, his head continuing to face forward.

"That's enough!" Mr. Lawson barked.

Everyone diverted their attention back toward the front of the class, quickly losing interest in what they had just witnessed. I, on the other hand, sat there stunned and once again humiliated.

"Was this whole day some sort of cruel joke? Had I enrolled in the School of Social Injustice? Did I have a sign on my back, saying 'Make her life miserable at all cost?' I wondered, glaring at my enemies' perfect profiles.

I couldn't believe this was happening to me. I hadn't even done anything to these two girls. I couldn't help it if physiologically my blood pressure rose when Hillary's very attractive boyfriend was near. Frustrated, I slammed shut the large textbook, gazing out the giant window. Mr. Lawson continued roll call, allowing me to learn the names of the tiny brunette and Cyrus's girlfriend. Kayle Clark and Hillary Russel were two names I would not forget.

The rest of the period dragged on dully. Astronomy appeared like an interesting subject, but somehow Mr. Lawson managed to make it dreadfully boring. His voice, monotone, displayed zero inflection while he read directly from the book, word for word, line by line, page by page. I found myself suddenly feeling tired. Everyone else in the class seemed equally as bored, but were occupied by rubbing their arms and hands together trying to stay warm. Unlike my peers, I felt warmer than when sitting outside at lunch.

"Why am I like this around Cyrus?" I wondered, running my fingers through my long hair. "I don't feel nervous or anxious anymore, but my skin feels like I have a mild sunburn. Maybe it's because I'm so close to the window? No, that can't be it," I thought, watching the other students.

Everyone in my row, looked as though it were mid-winter. Even the back of Cyrus's neck was covered with tiny goose bumps.

RING, RING, RING!

I jumped in my seat at the sound of the last bell. Books slammed shut and desks scraped against the newly polished floors as Mr. Lawson attempted to talk over the commotion of students gathering their belongings.

"Don't forget your chapter summaries for next class!" he bellowed.

Cyrus stood from his chair, slowly stretching his long arms overhead; then he popped his neck loudly.

I leaned over the bar connecting my chair with the wooden desk, snatching my back pack off the floor. I sat back up in my seat, rotating my body to exit the small desk, then paused when I noticed Cyrus standing only inches away from me. My face flushed.

"Well you survived your first day," he proclaimed cheerfully.

"What is he doing? Why is he speaking to me? Wasn't he aware that his girlfriend had it out for me?" I asked myself.

"Barely," I quietly answered, storing the heavy book in my bag.

Out of the corner of my eye, I could see Hillary and Kayle waiting for Cyrus at the door. Hillary's eyes never left Cyrus as Kayle whispered quietly in her ear. Quickly, I zipped up my bag, and tossed it over my shoulder, refusing to look at Cyrus.

"You okay?" he asked, sincerely. "You seem much quieter than you were this morning."

Was he completely brain dead? Had playing too much football finally caught up with him, or was he too self-absorbed to even notice the events that had surrounded me that day, all while he was present. In that moment, any initial attraction I had toward Cyrus Lofton disappeared. He was just the typical, popular, high school jock, that every girl wanted to date and every guy wanted to hang out with. I was over it. His girlfriend was downright mean and if he couldn't see that, then I wasn't going to spell it out for him. Hillary Russel and I would never be friends, so it seemed pointless to waste my time trying to become his.

"Why don't you ask your girlfriend?" I asked, staring him right in the eyes.

His expression was that of utter confusion. I squeezed past him, knocking my shoulder against his muscular arm; the intensity of heat in my body growing to an all-time high. He turned, watching me leave, saying nothing.

Impatiently waiting by the door, Hillary and Kayle parted like the Red Sea when I approached. One of them snickered loudly as I walked by. I froze in my tracks; enough was enough. I was never one for drama, or for stirring up trouble, but something about these two girls brought out the rebel inside of me. Turning around, I tossed my hair over my shoulder in a dramatic mocking motion as I smiled a wide sarcastic grin at the pair of them. I finished off my performance by returning Hillary's earlier condescending wave. The look of shock on their faces was priceless. Both mouths gaped as if their jaws had become unattached. For the first time that day they were speechless. I turned back around, feeling satisfied. Happily, I marched down the hallway toward the rotunda. Though my heart was racing with adrenaline, my skin was cool to the touch.

Opening the main doors that led to the parking lot gave me a sense of freedom. I had made it through my first day in one piece, even though at times it felt as though I had been torn apart. The warmth of the late summer air was refreshing on my now-cool skin. I stood, looking at the long line of vehicles waiting to pick up passengers.

In the distance, I noticed my mother waving anxiously from the carpool line. Hours ago, I would have been mortified by her behavior but now, found the situation humorous. Something inside of me had changed. I decided in that moment, I would not let Hillary or her friends get the best of me. The only reason they behaved cruelly toward me was because they somehow felt threatened by my presence. Afraid to show anyone their insecurities, they felt the need to lash out at others. Yes, it felt good to mock them, but the only person I was truly hurting was myself. I didn't need to stoop to their level to make myself feel better. I could look at the big picture, realizing that I didn't have to like them, or even hang out with them but I could show compassion toward these girls, even if they showed me none in return. I could also try to see Cyrus differently. Maybe he was a jock and oblivious to his girlfriend's behavior toward me, but who was I to judge? He had been nothing but kind to me thus far, so I would do the same.

I took a moment to laugh out loud at my new posture on high school life before bounding down the stone stairs, skipping every other step. Smiling, I waved to my mother, acknowledging her presence while walking over to the passenger door. I climbed into the cool car, gently tossing my bag onto the floorboard, then leaned over to give her a hug. Stunned by my behavior, she paused, hugging me harder than she had in a long time.

"So, how was your first day?" she asked, pulling out of the carpool lane.

I hesitated, taking a moment to reflect on the long day and the positive shift in my newly found attitude.

"It wasn't exactly easy, but it wasn't all bad," I said smiling, watching the school disappear from view as she drove away.

CHAPTER 6

The month of August passed by quickly and painlessly, thanks to my new attitude. I found a smooth rhythm, which allowed me to glide effortlessly through the motions of my senior year. The plan I fashioned on the first day of school had worked brilliantly. I apologized to Cyrus and he was equally apologetic for Hillary's rude behavior. I was right not to judge Cyrus Lofton. Yes, he was Mr. Popular and at times could act like a stereotypical jock, but underneath that façade was a kind, gentle person who truly cared for others.

Cyrus's mood was as steady as the consistent beat of a drum. He was funny, light-hearted, and always looked at a person's entirety, before casting judgement. He did not dissect their every flaw, as I tended to do. We could not have been more opposite. My emotions ebbed and flowed like the tides of the ocean, but Cyrus was emotionally steady, driven and thoughtful. The one thing we did have in common was our ability to always find the subtle humor in a situation.

One day during Astronomy class, in the midst of a mind-numbing lecture, a bird slammed into one of the large windows that bordered the room. The entire class jumped in unison at the loud thud against the glass. Mr. Lawson slowly turned his head toward the direction of the sound while letting out an irritated sigh, then quietly mumbled, "Damn bird, interrupting my class."

The rest of the student's eyes glazed over, while he continued the lecture on celestial orbits, but Cyrus and I hysterically laughed aloud at his added commentary. Our "obnoxious behavior" as Mr. Lawson so gracefully proclaimed, sent us to the hallway for the remainder of class. We didn't mind the break from his lesson on orbiting patterns. It allowed us to chat about our day and gave Cyrus a chance to warm up from the freezing classroom. A friendship was blossoming and even though I didn't allow myself to look at him romantically, I enjoyed having him in my life. He was the only person at school I could be myself around. Even if it were a silly smirk in the hall, or casual eye roll only I was meant to see, we somehow understood each other. Yes, my skin still prickled with a fiery heat every time I was near him, but whatever the strange phenomena was, I could live with it.

On the flip side, I wasn't making much progress with Hillary or Kayle, but their rude remarks lessened and their constant pointing diminished; finally they began to ignore me altogether. Life was beginning to feel normal. I was excelling in all my classes, except for the dreaded Spanish 1, which kept me up late most nights but I refused to let Señora Lopez win by my failing her class. The mid-term exam was rapidly approaching and if I could scrape by with a C, I would feel victorious.

I yawned, rubbing my eyes, slamming shut the Spanish text book. Glancing over at the dated digital clock resting on my bed side table, I gasped when the dull blue numbers read a quarter past three.

"I have got to start going to bed earlier," I thought to myself, shoving the heavy Spanish book off the bed.

Every morning I felt exhausted, but as the day went on I felt more and more awake. By dinner I felt refreshed and by midnight it was as though I had consumed two shots of espresso. This behavior irritated my mother. It was not "normal" as she so gently reminded me every night at exactly eleven o'clock by popping her head into my room, demanding that I get some rest.

My eyes felt heavy as I dozed off, dreaming of Señora Lopez storming into my bedroom, yelling about strict bed times in Spanish.

A dull, repetitive beeping sound grew louder and louder until I could hear the faint yell of my mother's voice somewhere in the distance.

"Elara! YOU ARE GOING TO BE LATE!"

My eyelids felt like lead weights as I squinted to read the clock. The time of 7:33 a.m. flashed back at me like a bad omen. There was no way, I could be dressed and in class before 8:05 a.m. I felt like a zombie and the thought of turning the light on made me want to …

"ELARA!"

My mother's voice pierced through my ears as she flung open the bedroom door, switching the fan off and the light on in one clean swoop.

"MOM! Why do you have to do that?" I yelled, shielding my eyes with a pillow. "I'm up," I mumbled, rolling over.

"Apparently, you are not up! You're still in bed half asleep. What's wrong? Are you sick?" she questioned quickly, like a mad interrogator.

"What? No mom, I am just tired. I went to bed…"

"You went to bed late again! This is what I am talking about Elara! You can't keep doing this. You must go to bed at a reasonable time, or you will just exhaust yourself. I have been up since seven, waiting to drive you to school, but what are you doing…sleeping!"

"Well, you don't have to drive me to school!" I reminded her, throwing the pillow off my face. "I can take the trail and that way you can sleep in and not have to worry about what time I go to bed or what time I wake up," I scoffed, tossing the covers off the bed, while making my way toward the bathroom; my mother following closely behind.

"Do *not* use that sarcastic tone with me, young lady!" she demanded.

I turned to face her.

"Mom, no offense but I'm not twelve years old anymore. I'm frustrated, because I am tired and now very late for class and instead of backing off, you're doing your usual, overbearing mother routine. I'm going to be 18 soon, on Thursday for that matter. When are you going to stop treating me like a child? Why do you care if I go to bed late? Why do you care if I miss my alarm? For once in your life just BACK OFF!"

Her mouth opened slowly. Tears began to form in her eyes, as her bottom lip quivered.

"Fine," she managed, in a cracked voice. "Find you own way to school."

Turning around quickly, she marched out of the bathroom, slamming the door shut behind her. I groaned, throwing my hands up in frustration.

"Great," I thought. "Not only did I oversleep and would be late for Spanish, but now my mother is furious."

I prepared for the day, quickly changing before heading downstairs. I found the house eerily quiet, my mother nowhere in sight. Unfortunately, there was no extra time for me to find her and apologize. It would have to wait until after school. The positive side was that my mother had the rebound rate of a toddler, so more than likely by the time I got home she would be back to her usual self, acting as though nothing had happened.

I gave up running to the trail after the first block; my lungs were burning and my side was cramping in pain. I was already late and could not find any reason to continue torturing myself. I slowed the quick pace to a brisk walk, catching my breath. The morning air was sticky, and beads of sweat began to form on my brow.

"Why is it so hot in September?" I complained, longing for Maine's cool weather.

By the time I reached the trail head, sweat had already begun dripping down the sides of my face and my shoe had rubbed a large blister onto my heel.

"I should have kept my mouth shut this morning," I thought, regretting the earlier confrontation with my mother.

The trail looked much different in the morning than the afternoon. Besides the loud crunching sound of mulch coming from beneath my shoes, the brush around me was silent. The trees above, on the other hand, were full of life. Birds sang and chirped loudly as squirrels leaped from branch to branch. I had been so preoccupied with school over the past few weeks, I had barely spent any time thinking about the strange encounters with the young man. Maybe it was because of the amount of time that had passed since I had first seen him, or the simple fact that I was so late to class I didn't have time to let my mind play tricks. I stayed focused on the task at hand; get to class before second period and don't let your mind scare you into thinking you will run into him again. Before I knew it, I was staring at the vast high-school campus.

"Well, that was easy enough," I thought proudly. "I could probably handle that every day."

A small sense of accomplishment washed over me as I exited the trail. I was sweating and decided to take a quick moment to adjust the large wet spot on my shirt where my back pack had been resting. The goal was in sight. I could see the portable building from the hill which I was standing on. I checked the time on my cell phone one last time before jogging down the grassy hill toward Spanish. I reached the portable door at 8:37 a.m., exactly thirty-two minutes late to first period.

Taking a deep breath, I opened the door as quiet as humanly possible. About twenty or so heads turned in unison, observing who was entering the classroom unannounced. One of the heads belonged to Señora Lopez. I froze, watching a look of loathing cross her face. Only then did I realize I should have skipped first period all together.

"What are you doing?" she asked.

"I … am walking into class," I answered, without thinking.

I watched the vein on her neck pulsate, quickly regretting my response.

"Sarcasm is not a trait I admire Señorita Elara. Can you kindly explain to myself and your fellow classmates why you are…,"

Slowly she turned to the classroom clock hanging on the back wall.

"… exactly thirty-three minutes late to my class?"

I quickly thought how Cyrus would answer her question. He would get straight to the point, no fluff, just facts.

"I didn't have a ride to school this morning, so I had to walk," I answered firmly.

"I am unsure as to how that is our problem," she said, gesturing to my fellow classmates. "Detention. Thursday, after school. You can help Coach Burnell deep-clean the bleachers before the big game on Friday night."

I nodded, taking my seat, feeling more defeated with every passing minute.

Thankfully, the rest of the day flew by in a hurry. By the time I arrived at Astronomy, I felt more awake and less frustrated by the morning's events. I was early to class as usual and the first one to take my seat in the large empty room. I stared out the windows overlooking the campus, watching large, ominous, gray storm clouds gather in in the distance.

"Great," I thought. "Knowing my luck today, I'll have to walk home in the pouring rain."

My skin prickled with heat as a smile crossed my face. I didn't have to look at the door to know that Cyrus had entered.

Walking confidently as always, he headed toward our row, sliding quietly into his seat before turning around to face me.

"You're early to class today," I said.

"Hillary is out sick, so I had some extra time," he responded, refusing to look me in the eye.

I nodded, snickering. Everyone knew that he and Hillary had "alone" time every day after lunch behind the portables. I had the misfortune of taking a detour one day, only to be met with the two of them lip-locked with no signs of coming up for air.

He shivered. "Why is it always so cold in here?" he asked, quickly changing the subject.

"Cold? I think it is always burning up. My other classes are freezing, but not this one," I said, leaving out the reason as to why I found Astronomy so uncomfortably hot.

"You're crazy," he laughed. "It's FREEZING!"

Students began filing noisily into the classroom, taking their seats while chatting to one another. I noticed Kayle walk quietly to her seat, absent of her usual counterpart.

"Hey, are you coming to the big game on Friday?" he asked, stretching his muscular arms over head.

"Doubt it," I replied. "Sports aren't really my thing."

"You should go! It's our first district game. We're playing our big rivals; the more the merrier," he winked, teasing me.

"I can't make any promises, but at least the bleachers will be in pristine order! I get to spend Thursday afternoon in detention with Coach Burnell, courtesy of Señora Lopez."

"You, a trouble maker?" he asked, gently nudging me.

I flinched as my shoulder tingled with heat.

"Hardly, I was just late to class because I had to walk today. Her only goal is to make my life miserable."

"Why were you walking?"

"My mom and I got into some stupid fight this morning, so I didn't have a ride."

"I can give you a ride home today if you want," he added.

"Oh, I'm sure Hillary would love that," I noted, fishing my Astronomy text out of my bag.

"Well, Hillary isn't here today, is she?" he pressed.

I laughed, amused by his response.

"Yeah, but I don't think…"

Our conversation was cut short as Mr. Lawson entered the classroom, slamming the door behind him only moments before the last bell rang.

Pulling his pants up by the empty belt loops, he walked over to the lectern and grabbed a large stack of papers. He then motioned for a student at the front of class to stand up and assist him with handing out the illustrated flyers. The bright blue flyer read, Solar and Lunar Eclipses: A Key to Our Future and Past.

Cyrus glanced over his shoulder, rolling his eyes. I giggled quietly, attempting to avoid eye contact with Mr. Lawson.

"In December, we will be taking a field trip to NASA," Mr. Lawson explained. "Attendance is mandatory, so you can forget about skipping class."

A unanimous groan filled the classroom.

"QUIET!" He barked. "You will be paired into groups of two and will be completing an assignment during our visit. I am expecting everyone to act like adults during this trip and will not tolerate any horseplay or obnoxious behavior," he said, glaring between Taylor and Cliff, the known class clowns.

"See the flyer for more details. We will be taking the school buses…"

A larger groan echoed around the room.

"…so, don't be late, or you will miss the bus and receive a zero for your assignment."

Mr. Lawson turned his back to the class of irritated students and began writing the day's lesson on the board. I rotated my head toward the large window, watching the inevitable storm take shape. The dark clouds moved slowly over the vast campus. Moments later, lightning flashed, with thunder shortly following, causing the large windows of the room to vibrate. Rain began tapping against the glass, slowly at first, drop after drop, then in sheets carried by the strong winds. I exhaled, wondering how long the storm would last.

My skin prickled with heat, feeling Cyrus's fingers touch my hand. Discreetly, he passed me a neatly folded piece of paper. Slowly, I opened the note, keeping my eyes on Mr. Lawson at all times. I gazed down at the barely legible writing, quickly placing a hand over my mouth to keep from laughing.

In all capital letters read: PLEASE CHECK A BOX and beneath it were two drawings. The first picture was of a frowning stick figure, standing in the rain with an arrow above its head that read "YOU." The second picture was of two stick figures sitting inside of a car, out of the rain. One of the figures smiled with an arrow above its head reading, "YOU."

Even though I sat behind him, I could tell he was grinning, overly proud of himself. I rolled my eyes, checked the box with the two stick figures, then nudged the back of Cyrus with the refolded piece of paper. My hand tingled as he grabbed the note from me. Unopened, he tucked it inside his jean pocket, focusing once more on Mr. Lawson's lesson.

The bell rang, putting life back into the students as they jumped from their seats while gathering their belongings. Cyrus stood and stretched, just as he did after each class, then turned to meet my gaze.

"I parked in the back lot, close to the field house, so you may get a little wet out there," he warned, reaching for his bag.

"How do you know I've accepted your offer?" I asked, picking my bag up off the floor. "You didn't even see what box I checked," I teased.

"I didn't have to," he smirked.

My forehead creased, perplexed with his response.

"You're different Elara, that's for sure, but you aren't crazy. Only a mental person would volunteer to walk home in this," he affirmed, nodding toward the large windows.

Another loud rumble of thunder echoed nearby, sealing my fate.

"Lead the way!" I exclaimed, pointing toward the door.

The hallway was bustling with students eager to leave the building for the day. Lockers slammed shut as shoes squeaked loudly on the wet floors. The main doors leading out to the rotunda blew open and shut, allowing rain to pour inside. I laughed while watching two of Hillary's friends debate how they were going to get out of the building without getting wet. One dramatically gestured to her shoes while the other one pointed to her neatly curled hair.

Cyrus began opening the door only to have the wind rip the handle from his hand. The strong gust slapped at my face as I squinted, trying to see through the downpour. It was raining so hard I could barely make out the parking lot. I tried covering my head with my back pack while following Cyrus down the steep concrete stairs, but eventually gave up, tossing the drenched bag back over my shoulder once more. Cyrus ran effortlessly through the crowded parking lot, hopping over puddles while dodging reversing cars. I panted several strides behind him, managing to somehow run through every puddle and was almost struck by an oncoming vehicle.

The headlights of a shiny, black Camaro flashed with the chirp of an alarm. Relieved, I exhaled once approaching our destination. Cyrus, being the gentleman that he was, hurried to open the passenger door.

The smell of new leather accompanied by men's cologne, overwhelmed my senses as I slid onto the warm seat. My eyes darted around the fully loaded coupe: a low-profile radar detector attached to the rear-view mirror, a pair of Ray Ban sunglasses sat in a wide cup holder, a football play book, stacked with papers taking up most of the driver's seat, with a pair of girl's cheerleading shoes resting on the floor board. Quickly, I moved my soaking wet shoes as far away from the stark white Nike's as possible.

"What would Hillary say if she knew I was sitting in her boyfriend's car?" I asked myself nervously.

The driver's door swung open and instinctively, I reached for the playbook and papers just before Cyrus sat on top of them.

"Thanks," he smiled, taking his belongings from my hands, then carefully rested them on the back seat.

Letting out a long sigh, he turned, looking over at me.

"We made it," he said, shaking water from his blond hair.

"Hey!" I complained, shielding my face from the flying water droplets.

"Like a little more water is going to hurt?" he laughed, gesturing at my appearance.

I looked down, frowning. It was as though I had jumped into a pool fully clothed. I gathered my long black hair over one shoulder, twisting it hard with both hands. I watched as water poured from the ends.

Cyrus let out a loud laugh, shaking his head.

"It's all fun and games until Hillary finds out you gave me a ride home," I declared, continuing to ring out my hair.

"Don't worry about Hillary. She won't mind."

59

"Yeah, right!" I exclaimed. "She seems a little bit like the jealous type," I said, glancing at Cyrus out of the corner of my eye.

Continuing to laugh, he rested his blond head against the leather head rest.

"Yeah, you're probably right. We're going to be in big trouble," he chuckled.

"Cyrus, that is not funny!" I snapped.

"Well, I couldn't let you walk home in this weather. She wouldn't want me to leave a woman stranded," he protested.

I rolled my eyes, turning to face him.

"Of course she wouldn't," I teased.

A large smile crossed his tan face.

"Let's live on the edge for once, huh?"

"No! Let's not!" I pleaded.

Cyrus twisted in his seat, reaching for something on the back floor board. I grimaced as his arm pressed against my shoulder. The burning sensation intensified the longer we made contact.

"I knew I had one in here," he exclaimed, facing forward.

I did a double take as Cyrus began pulling the drenched shirt off his tan, muscular body.

"What's he doing?" I thought, rotating my entire body toward the passenger window.

"I'm just putting on a dry shirt," he announced, sensing my discomfort.

"Yeah, of course you are," I replied, waving him off like it wasn't a big deal.

I blushed. Emotionally, I had let go of any romantic feelings toward Cyrus, but physically, I found it impossible not to find him attractive.

Embarrassed, I turned my body to face the windshield once more. Without saying a word, Cyrus started the car. The engine rumbled loudly and the exhaust sputtered even louder as he shifted into reverse. The wipers worked diligently trying to keep the windshield clear.

We followed the long line of cars out of the parking lot, stopping at a red light farther up the hill. Through the heavy downpour, I noticed a man standing at the corner of the intersection, only feet away from Cyrus's car. A long, black rain jacket covered his torso, its hood draped carelessly over his head. His boots were covered in mud and sat motionless beneath him. Rain fell from the tattered hood in large drops to the ground.

"To think that could've been me," I thought, feeling even more grateful that I was sitting inside the dry car.

The light changed to green, and Cyrus shifted the car into first gear, slowly entering the intersection. As we drove by I focused on the unfortunate man. His head slowly lifted as we passed, acknowledging our presence. I gasped as two, piercing blue eyes locked onto mine.

CHAPTER 7

"Stop the car!" I yelled, gesturing wildly with both hands.

"What?" Cyrus asked, looking over at me. "I'm in the middle of the intersection. I can't stop the car right now!"

My head turned uncomfortably, watching the young man's eyes fixated on Cyrus's passing car.

"Do you see that man?" I stammered, turning to face Cyrus.

Giving a quick glance in his rear-view mirror, Cyrus shrugged, shaking his head.

"I don't see anyone, Elara. Why would someone be standing out in the pouring rain?"

"He's right there," I sputtered, turning my body once more, only this time to find the man nowhere in sight. "Well, he was right there."

"What's going on?" Cyrus asked, his voice concerned. "First you tell me to stop in the middle of the street, then you want me to look at some man standing in the rain?"

I sighed, feeling foolish.

"I'm sorry Cyrus. I just keep seeing this guy; that guy to be exact in the strangest places. It's like he is following me, or something."

"What do you exactly mean by following?" Cyrus asked, slowing to a stop at another red light.

I informed Cyrus of the three times I had seen the mysterious visitor. First, outside my window, then on the trail and now, only moments ago. Cyrus sat quietly, listening to my story, keeping his eyes focused on the wet road.

"What part of Woodward do you live in?" he asked, approaching the busy intersection.

"Uh … I live in the Riverside Community. Do you know where that is?"

"I do. I pass by it every day. My house isn't too far from there."

The car slowed, approaching another red light. Once stopped, Cyrus turned to face me.

"I don't know what to tell you about that guy. It's probably just a coincidence."

"A coincidence? He ran after me on the trail!" I argued.

"You don't even know if he was really chasing you, Elara. Maybe seeing him again, just freaked you out and you only *thought* he was chasing you down the trail. I didn't see him today, but maybe he was … waiting for a ride?"

I rolled my eyes, not buying his explanations.

A horn honked loudly behind us, causing me to flinch. Cyrus quickly shifted the car, sending the tires squealing on the wet pavement as he hurried to make it through the yellow light.

"I doubt he was waiting for a ride at the corner of an intersection in the pouring rain," I argued.

"Fine, then maybe he doesn't exist. Maybe you are the only one who can see him," he teased.

"Not funny!" I cried.

"Of course he was real, wasn't he?" I asked myself, my pulse quickening.

I was never one who believed in ghost or the supernatural, but Cyrus did have a point. I was the only one who saw him staring into my window that night, the only one who saw him on the trail that day and between me and Cyrus, the only one who saw him standing at the intersection. I shivered at the icy chill creeping up my spine.

"I'm sorry," he apologized, noticing my body shiver at the cold chill.

He reached for the heater, turning the knob up to high. I flinched as the warm air blew into my already hot face.

"Thanks, but I'm not cold," I said, turning the vent in the opposite direction.

"My mistake," he said, reaching for the knob once more. "It just looked like you were cold. Girls are *always* cold."

"No. I'm just hot natured," I lied.

What was I going to tell him, that I only got hot flashes when he was near, or that my skin radiated with heat anytime he brushed up against me or got too close? Cyrus was probably already questioning my mental state after our conversation about the mysterious stranger. The last thing I needed was for my only friend to think I was a complete lunatic.

The rain slowed to a gentle drizzle as we approached the entrance to Riverside. Switching on the blinker, Cyrus turned into my community, slowing the car.

"It's the third street on the left," I said, pointing ahead.

The heavy rains had formed large puddles on the dark, green grass. Lightning flashed brightly in the distance as Cyrus turned down my street.

"Do you think I'm crazy?" I asked.

He laughed, down-shifting the car.

"No. I don't think you're crazy, but I do think you might be over-reacting."

Accepting the first half of his statement, I nodded, pointing to the driveway of my residence.

"Well, good, because I'm not."

He chuckled, easing the car into the wet driveway.

"Thanks for the ride," I said, reaching for my bag.

My face dropped when I noticed my mother standing in the open doorway of our home. Her arms were folded tightly across her chest with a look of deep concern on her face.

Noticing my facial expression, Cyrus followed my gaze toward the front door.

"Someone's in trouble," he teased, giving my mother a subtle head nod and wave.

I grimaced, watching her worried expression shift to that of anger.

"Perfect," I groaned, opening the door before climbing out of the car.

"Good luck!" Cyrus yelled.

I nodded, then waved, taking a moment to watch the black car pull away from the driveway. Taking a deep breath, I turned, surprised to see my mother unmoved from her menacing pose. The earlier hope of my mother forgetting our morning altercation was quickly forgotten as the next hour consisted of shouting and yelling at one another.

She immediately began her interrogation, by yelling "Whose car were you in?" and "Who was that boy?" Followed with "Why didn't you tell me you were getting a ride home?" and "How dare you not apologize for speaking to me the way you did this morning!"

The back and forth banter was exhausting. I had a bad habit of being stubborn, never backing down from a verbal fight until my point was clearly heard. My mother had a bad habit of shutting people off by switching the subject. This behavior of ours left these battles always lasting longer than necessary.

Eventually, I gave in, tapping out of the fight gracefully. I suddenly realized that most of her anger was coming from the simple fact that in two days, I would be eighteen and no longer her little girl. My mother feared a lack of control, which caused her to dislike any disruption that occurred in her life. I think her feelings had been building for a while now and this morning, reminded her of that truth: I was turning eighteen and there was nothing she could do to stop it. I would be lying if I said that was the only reason I let her win the argument. I knew my mother well enough to know that if she didn't feel as though she had won this battle, I would be taking the trail to and from school for the rest of the year. Regardless of Cyrus's theory about the mysterious man, I was not stepping foot on that trail unless forced.

CHAPTER 8

Arriving to Astronomy class early as usual, I sat admiring the shiny new phone my parents had given me earlier that morning. I didn't know what surprised me more; the fact that my parents finally upgraded my phone to the current decade, or that they had spent more than forty dollars on a gift. When noticing a look of uncertainty cross my face, they excitedly reminded me "you only turn eighteen once" and expressed how proud they were of the "woman I was becoming." The entire situation made me uncomfortable, not to mention made me feel old, like I was turning forty or something. Regardless of their unique way of telling me Happy Birthday, I was thrilled to accept the new gift.

I had not seen Cyrus all day and found myself eager to show him that I now had the capability of taking photos with my new phone, since he often teased me about joining the current century. Turning to face the wall of windows, I explored the advanced camera feature by zooming in on a small tree in the distance. My thumb moved to press the large red button occupying the lower portion of the screen, but I quickly turned when I felt the familiar warm sensation radiate through my body.

"Aw, man, I was going to sneak up on you," admitted Cyrus, tossing his bag onto the floor, before taking his seat.

I snickered at my little trick, flashing the new phone at him proudly.

"Welcome to this century," he teased.

Our heads turned, noticing Kayle enter the classroom alone.

"Is Hillary still sick?" I asked. "She's been out all week."

"Yeah, the doctor said she has mono, so she won't be back to school until next week," he answered, slightly disappointed.

Kayle turned down the aisle, smiling in our direction.

"Happy Birthday!" she beamed.

I was shocked.

"Firstly, how did she know it was my birthday and secondly, why is she being so nice to me?" I wondered, a small smile crossing my face.

"Thanks!" I replied.

"I was talking to Cyrus," she answered coldly, tossing her long brown hair over her shoulder while taking her seat.

Cyrus quickly turned in his chair, a quizzical look crossing his brow.

"It's your birthday?" we asked one another in unison.

"Why didn't you tell me it was your birthday?" Cyrus questioned.

"Why didn't you tell me it was yours?" I countered.

We laughed, both confused yet excited at the same time.

"So, what big plans do you have for your eighteenth celebration?" he asked curiously.

"Oh, I don't know, spend a glorious afternoon in detention cleaning the bleachers," I replied sarcastically.

He grimaced.

"I forgot you had detention with Coach Burnell. Well, don't worry, he's a cool guy and will go easy on you."

"What about you, Cyrus? Plans with Hillary?"

"No. I have football practice after school and she's really sick so I think just dinner with the family as usual."

"Wow! We really know how to celebrate, don't we?" I asked, chuckling.

My laughter quickly ceased, once I noted Cyrus's expression. His upbeat attitude was suddenly replaced by a look of melancholy.

"Sometimes Elara, I don't think my life can get any more predictable."

I sat motionless, taking in his words, unsure of how to respond to his sudden change in behavior. Cyrus turned, facing the front of the class, hearing Mr. Lawson enter the room. I spent the rest of afternoon watching the back of Cyrus's head, curious as to the deeper meaning behind his comment. I thought back to our conversation, but couldn't quite put my finger on the reason why. It made me feel uneasy to see him the slightest bit uncomfortable. I wanted to pry, ask why he felt that way, but quickly canceled these thoughts, knowing it wasn't my place.

After class, I walked to the football stadium for detention with Coach Burnell. The sunny afternoon was cooler than usual. Not cool by my standards, but it was in the low 80's, which was apparently cool for Texas in late September.

I noticed an older man wearing khaki pants with a red and black collared shirt, standing underneath the silver bleachers. A shiny whistle hung around his neck as he smiled, acknowledging my presence. Casually, he waved me over to where he stood.

"You must be Elara," he said, extending a hand.

I nodded, shaking his strong hand.

"I'm Coach Burnell. It looks like you've got your work cut out for you this afternoon," he exclaimed, pointing to the underside of the bleachers.

"You have got to be kidding me!"

The look on his face said otherwise.

"Yeah, I know it's a lot. Just get off what you can by the end of practice and we'll call it good, okay?"

Before heading back to the football field, Coach Burnell handed me a large metal bucket with a small paint scraper. The amount of gum covering the underside of the football stadium bleachers resembled that of an abstract tile mosaic. Rolling my eyes, I began chipping away the dried chewing gum.

"It would take forever to scrape all of this off," I thought, watching a faded blue wad of gum land into the empty pail below.

My head snapped quickly to the field, hearing a loud whistle blow in the near distance. Practice had commenced, as male students eagerly ran onto the field covered from head to toe in protective padding. It didn't take long to find Cyrus in the crowd. Not only was he more muscular than any of the other players, but his bright blond hair was an easy marker. I watched as he held his shiny black helmet under one arm and joined the other players huddling around their coach, listening intently. The huddle broke quickly with a loud unanimous clap. Team members began breaking into small groups, preparing for what looked like some sort of drill.

Plop. Another wad of dried gum landed into the metal bucket. I had successfully removed all of three pieces from the gum-lined bleachers. I sighed, turning away from the distractions on the field.

"I better get this bucket halfway full before practice is over, or Coach Burnell will think I took advantage of his offer," I thought.

A strong breeze blew, tossing my long hair into my face. Removing the black hair tie from my wrist, I turned to face the field, allowing the oncoming wind to assist in my pony-tail assembly. I gathered my long, black hair into a tight pony-tail, then turned to grab the bucket, but paused when I heard commotion coming from the field.

Two players were in each other's face, throwing offensive hand gestures back and forth. One player, the taller of the two, grabbed the shoulder pads of the other, while the shorter one went for his opponent's face mask.

Sliding the paint scraper into my back pocket, I inched forward, squeezing the upper half of my body between the metal slats of the bleachers, hoping to get a closer look. Noticing the confrontation, other members of the team headed toward the two angry players. Cyrus was the first to approach.

By this time, the two young men had begun shoving each other violently back and forth. Cyrus, being the assertive person that he was, quickly placed a hand on the chest of each player, attempting to create a safe space between the two of them. This appeared to only escalate the situation. The shorter of the two, clearly irritated, used both hands to push Cyrus with all his strength. The next few moments were like nothing I had ever witnessed. My jaw fell open in shock as I watched the events unfold.

Cyrus stood, unscathed and unmoved from his place on the field. His reaction time to the offense was faster than one could blink. Before the angered player had time to remove his hands from Cyrus's chest, Cyrus, in one quick move, pushed his teammate, sending the player flying five yards across the football field. I couldn't believe my eyes. The force behind his smooth movement was effortless, imitating that of a super hero in a movie.

An eerie silence swept over the field. Everyone appeared stunned by the event that unfolded. Even Coach Burnell froze in his tracks. Cyrus, looking down at his shaking hands, was equally as shocked as the teammate standing next to him. A small group of players ran to the aid of the player who lay motionless on the field. Slowly, they helped him to his feet. Looking completely bewildered, he turned to Cyrus and began yelling profanities, accompanied by matching hand gestures. Other players held him back, violently shaking their heads from side to side, urging him not to initiate another challenge. Cyrus, still in disbelief, stood unmoving and alone, as everyone quickly moved to the other side of the field.

Coach Burnell cautiously approached, his hands up as though Cyrus were armed. Confused, Cyrus quickly began gesturing to his body and hands, mouthing inaudible words to his coach. I had never seen Cyrus anything other than calm and collective. Yes, he could be assertive, but he never looked disheveled or frantic. Coach Burnell motioned for Cyrus to calm down, then pointed firmly toward the field house. Looking defeated, Cyrus threw his head toward the sky, then quickly turned and walked to the exit gate.

Without thinking, I grabbed the paint scraper out of my back pocket, tossed it into the metal pail and quickly jogged away from the bleachers to the exit. I felt Coach Burnell's eyes follow my every move. Refusing to acknowledge his gaze, I kept my head down, eager to catch up to Cyrus. I would pay for leaving detention early, but I had to see if he was okay. I wasn't sure why it bothered me so much, but a strong, protective instinct took control of me.

I paced outside the boy's field house, anxiously waiting for Cyrus to appear. I didn't have to wait long. Only a few minutes had passed before he exited the locker room. He had changed out of his football uniform into athletic shorts and matching shirt. He kept his head down as he quickly walked away from the locker room. Had I not side-stepped his fast approach, he would have walked right into me.

"Elara? What are you doing here?" he asked, both confused and startled by my presence.

"I'm sorry, but I had to check and see if you were okay after …"

"You saw that?" he interrupted, a look of worry crossing his face.

"Uh … yeah," I stammered.

Immediately, I began regretting my hasty decision to follow him.

"I had detention with Coach Burnell, remember? I just wanted..."

"I've got to go, Elara," he interrupted once more, stepping around me, heading toward the parking lot.

"Cyrus, wait!" I yelled, jogging after him.

He stopped, turning to face me.

"Now's not a good time. I don't know what the hell happened back there, but I need to get out of here."

His hands clenched into tight fists as he popped his neck loudly. It was obvious Cyrus was agitated. I had never seen him like this and wanted to help but didn't have a clue where to start.

"It's okay, Cyrus. I'm sure there's some logical explanation as to what happened back there," I said, trying to sound casual and upbeat, hoping that a change in tone would lighten the mood. Unfortunately, my efforts were a lost cause.

"No, Elara! A logical explanation is a play not going the way you expected, later to find out you thought Coach called a different one. Logical is getting a problem wrong in calculus, but later realizing you followed the wrong formula. What is not logical, is me waking up one day with super-human strength!" he snapped.

I took a quick, step back, surprised by his sharp tone; Cyrus's eyes were instantly full of regret.

"I'm sorry. I didn't mean to yell at you like that. I just don't know what happened back there," he apologized, shaking his head.

Running a hand over his short blond hair, he looked back at the field, observing his teammates.

"How are you getting home today?" he asked, meeting my gaze.

"Uh..." I stuttered, confused by the quick change of subject.

"Come on, I'll give you a ride," he stated, turning once more toward the parking lot.

"Are you sure?" I asked timidly, watching him walk away from the field house.

Cyrus didn't respond, but I followed, already knowing the answer.

The familiar chirp of the alarm and flash of lights reminded me that the car was now unlocked. I quickly swung open the door, helping myself onto the passenger seat. Cyrus slid onto the driver's seat. His hand dangled the keys inches from the ignition as though contemplating whether to start the vehicle.

The black leather seats were uncomfortably hot, as the afternoon sun poured in the passenger window directly onto my already warm legs. I debated whether I should remind Cyrus, that one must put the keys into the ignition to start the car, but changed my mind when the loud rumble of the engine echoed around me.

We both stared quietly out the windshield, unsure of what to say to one another. The A/C was cranked up as high as it could go but only warm air blew into my face. Awkward silences always made me uncomfortable and this was one for the record books. I inhaled deeply before turning to look at Cyrus.

"Do you want to talk about what *you* think happened back there?" I asked, cautiously.

He paused before answering, continuing to stare out the windshield.

"I haven't a clue. I keep playing it over and over in my mind. Dustin and Omar were arguing about something and it looked like it was getting heated, so I went over to break it up. Dustin, over-reacting as usual, told me to stay out of it, that he and Omar would work it out. I told him to calm down and then placed a hand on each one of them and that is when he tried to shove me."

"Yeah, I saw his lame attempt to do so," I added.

Cyrus, looking more serious, quickly responded.

"Here's the thing though, Dustin may be on the shorter side, but he's a beast on the field. We call him the 'stone' because he's small, but tough as nails. In practice, or during a game, if he tackles someone, they ALWAYS go down. I may have height on him, Elara, but I do not have his strength. As hard as he shoved me back there, I should have at least been thrown off balance. I didn't even feel him touch me!" Cyrus pressed, his voice raising. "You should've seen the look in his eyes. He was frightened!"

My already warm skin began tingling uncomfortably as the heat surged through my body at a rapid rate.

"Well, probably because he was caught so off guard," I suggested, squeezing my hands tightly. "Adrenaline can make people have super human strength!"

"Elara, that was not adrenaline! I get pumped up during games, but never have I come close to showing that sort of strength! It was like this strange feeling came over me. My hands felt..." he finished, his voice trailing off.

I glanced down at my own hands, wondering if I should try explaining to Cyrus the way my body felt when he was near. I shook my head, ignoring these thoughts. The context of our situations was completely different. I only felt flushed when around Cyrus, I did not have the ability to display the strength of ten men.

"Maybe you should talk to Hillary about this?" I asked, unsure of what to say next.

He laughed, "Yeah right! The only thing Hillary ever wants to talk about is the latest gossip, or what our chances will be at becoming homecoming king and queen. She prefers to listen to herself talk rather than listen to anything I ever have to say."

I was shocked to hear Cyrus speak so harshly of Hillary. I had always assumed they had a good relationship.

"Honestly Elara, as of lately, you're the only one I find myself comfortable around."

I felt my cheeks blush, quickly turning my head to the passenger window. Over the past few weeks, I thought our relationship had been one-sided, with me being the only one who appreciated our time together. It was nice to finally know that the feeling was mutual.

"Cyrus, I don't know what happened back there, but crazier things have happened in the world. Maybe it was just some strange anomaly. I'm sure your teammates will eventually come around. There is the possibility they will think the whole thing was just an exaggeration in their own mind."

Cyrus turned his head away from the window, forcing a smile.

"Thanks for the encouraging words, but regardless of how you think they may see it, you didn't see the terrified look on their faces. Did you see them all run away from me like I was going to hurt them or something? Even Coach Burnell looked frightened. I would never hurt anyone intentionally. Those guys are like my brothers."

"Well, then I'm sure they'll let it go and things will go back to normal tomorrow," I said in an extra upbeat tone.

"I won't hold you to it," he sighed.

Cyrus shifted the car into reverse, easing out of the parking space and headed toward the main road. Squinting from the glare of the bright sun, I flipped down the passenger visor to shield my eyes. Simultaneously, Cyrus reached for his black sunglasses, quickly placing them over his eyes. It was a quarter to five and the two-lane road that wrapped around the vast campus was empty. This was a stark contrast from the usual zipping and zooming of cars entering and exiting the school grounds.

As we rounded the sharp curve, Cyrus shifted the car into a lower gear, assisting in the climb of the steep hill. I watched as he reached for the knob of the radio. At first, I was confused as to why it made such a loud popping noise when he turned it on, but that thought quickly dissolved, as the reality of our situation sunk in. My head snapped forward, recognizing the familiar sound. I gasped, as two piercing blue eyes, starred directly at me, only feet away from the hood of the moving car.

CHAPTER 9

There was no time to warn Cyrus. I braced myself for the inevitable impact, shielding my face with one hand, while using the other to grab hold of the handle above the window. Cyrus's reaction time was equal to that on the field. Using both hands, he forcefully turned the steering wheel first to the right then to the left, over-correcting, sending the car spinning into the other lane. My head whipped around, leaving me light-headed as the car spun round and round. Everything moved in slow motion, like a dream I could not wake from. I held my breath as the car slid off the road, down the embankment toward a large oak tree.

Once again, I braced for impact. The tree would surely make contact with the passenger side of the vehicle. Quickly locking me into place, my seat belt burned against my already warm skin. My head jolted to the right as the car abruptly stopped only inches from the enormous tree. The only sound that could be heard was Cyrus inhaling large, deep breaths. Realizing that I was still holding my breath, I gasped for air, resembling a person who had been held under water for entirely too long.

"Are you okay?" he asked, turning to face me.

I looked down at myself, assessing the damage. My chest and waist were both sore from the restricting seat belt, but other than that I appeared uninjured.

"Uh ... yeah I think so," I panted, my voice shaking.

Slowly, I turned my sore neck to look over at Cyrus. My mouth gaped. The once attached steering wheel now lay in his lap.

"Cyrus?" I stammered, motioning to his hands.

He looked down, utterly bewildered, then pointed equally as confused, to my right hand.

"What?" I asked, looking up at my hand still holding onto the handle above the window.

I gasped, realizing that it was no longer attached to the door. Letting out a small scream, I dropped it from my shaking hand.

Breathing hard and feeling as though I were going to pass out I tried opening the passenger door only to be blocked by the large oak tree. I unbuckled my seat belt, and placed my head between my legs taking slow, large breaths. Coming to my aid, Cyrus placed his hand on my back, trying to calm my shaken nerves.

"Hey, everything is going to be okay, *we* are going to be okay," he assured. "How we didn't hit that guy, I'll never know ..."

"You saw him?" I interrupted, picking my head up from between my legs.

"Of course I saw him! I almost ran him over with my car," cried Cyrus.

My mind flashed back to the moment just before Cyrus swerved. The young man stood directly in front of the moving car. It would have been impossible for him to move himself safely away from the vehicle that quickly.

"Are you sure you didn't hit him?" I asked, turning to look out the back window of the car.

"What?" he asked, his facial expression changing from that of concern to that of panic.

Unsure of what to do with the detached steering wheel that rested in his lap, Cyrus quickly opened the driver side door and carried it with him as he exited the vehicle. Awkwardly, I climbed over the center counsel, eager to escape the car. Cyrus and I both began frantically inspecting the vehicle for any signs of impact as we raced back and forth, sliding our hands over the sleek car checking for dents or scratches. Relieved to find the car untouched, we ran up the steep embankment, continuing the search for the mysterious young man. Reaching the top of the hill, my eyes scanned the paved road.

"Do you see anything?" Cyrus asked.

"No. Nothing," I replied, agitated.

"He couldn't have gone far," Cyrus declared, walking toward the middle of the empty road.

I threw my hands up in the air, completely shocked by his disappearance.

"At least now I know I'm not crazy!" I said, looking at Cyrus.

"No, you're not crazy Elara. I *definitely* saw him this time," he affirmed, his eyes now searching the dense brush.

"Why does he keep following me like this? What was he doing in the middle of the road? How did we not run over him … and why are you still holding that steering wheel?"

"What?" Cyrus asked, looking down at his hands, then laughed aloud.

"Cyrus! This is NOT funny! First, you show super human strength. Then we almost run over my stalker and now this?" I said, pointing to the steering wheel.

Still laughing, Cyrus walked back toward the embankment. He tossed the steering wheel onto the grass, then climbed down to the ground beside it. Sighing loudly, he closed his eyes while resting both hands behind his head.

"What are you doing?" I asked, walking over to him.

"It has been quite the afternoon so I think we should take a moment to relax," he said, patting the ground next to him.

"Okay…" I said, awkwardly settling myself next to him on the soft grass.

"Better?" he asked.

"Not really," I mumbled.

A warm breeze blew, causing the trees to rustle in the distance. The sun, only recently shining brightly, now rested lower in the sky. Observing my surroundings, I quietly reflected on the last few minutes of the day.

"No one will believe any of this," I began, staring at the late afternoon sky.

"I wasn't planning on telling anyone," he responded.

"Well it's not like you can drive your car home without a steering wheel."

"True," he noted, smirking.

I rolled over onto my side, facing Cyrus.

"What's the story, then?" I asked.

Eyes still closed, Cyrus spoke in a steady tone.

"Well, let's just say a deer jumped out in front of the car, so I swerved and the steering wheel, obviously being defective, just came right off," he explained, opening his eyes.

"Okay, that sounds plausible, but what about the handle above the window? Was that defective too?" I asked, my eyebrow raising.

"Absolutely," he nodded. "I found it just lying on the seat after the near miss."

Using both hands, I pushed myself into the sitting position, observing Cyrus. His tan skin glowed under the bright sun as his blond hair moved gently in the slightest breeze. He was calm and relaxed as though soaking up the sun at some exotic beach resort. I found myself anxious, worried and fearful about what we had just experienced.

"Don't worry about him," Cyrus said, as if reading my mind. "I'm sure you will figure out why you keep seeing him."

"That's a great thought!" I replied, sarcastically. "So when I don't show up for school one day, you can call the police and give them an accurate description of my abductor," I said, glaring.

He laughed, sitting up next to me.

"I was just trying to make you feel better. This guy really does have you completely freaked out, huh?"

"With good reason, Cyrus! This is the fourth time I've seen him! I'm telling you, he's stalking me or something," I said, shuddering at my own words.

"I don't know what to tell you, Elara. It's not like you can go to the police and file a report on a man you just keep seeing in public places. He hasn't done anything to you, he hasn't threatened you, he hasn't even said anything to you. Maybe he was just crossing the street today? It was really bright driving up that hill. I guess I just didn't see him."

"I know," I groaned. "It's just getting creepy. Every time I see him we make eye contact and he looks so ... serious, like he's on a mission or something."

"Mission to freak you out maybe," he smirked, climbing up to his feet.

Reaching out a hand, Cyrus gently pulled me to the standing position.

"Do you want me to call a tow truck?" I asked, taking note of the idled car.

"No, it's okay. I got it. It will probably take a while for them to get here anyways. Why don't you call your mom and have her pick you up back at the field? That way, she won't worry thinking you were in a car wreck."

"Good point," I said, walking back over to the car.

Climbing into the driver's seat, I reached onto the passenger floor board to collect my bag. I cringed, realizing I had left it under the bleachers back on the field. I hoped practice was over, so I could retrieve it unseen by Coach Burnell.

"Well, thanks for the ride," I said, walking back up the hill toward Cyrus.

"Both times have been slightly eventful, haven't they?" he asked.

I nodded in agreement, standing next to Cyrus once more.

"So, we should probably not…"

"Tell anyone we were together?" Cyrus asked, finishing my sentence.

"Right. I was in detention, but left early to check on you, then my mom picked me up from the field."

"And I left practice early, just like Coach requested and then this happened," he finished, pointing to the car.

"Sounds like a plan," I replied. "But, I feel badly leaving you to clean up this mess by yourself."

"It's not a big deal. People run into deer all the time out here, my parents will believe me."

"You sure?" I pressed, looking back at the car.

"I'm sure," he said, smiling.

"Then I guess I'll see you tomorrow!" I said waving, before heading back toward the football field.

"Elara!" Cyrus called, still standing where I left him.

Quickly I turned, meeting his smiling face once more.

"Happy Birthday!" he beamed.

I chuckled, shaking my head at the irony of it all.

"Happy Birthday, Cyrus."

CHAPTER 10

The following couple of months passed smoothly, without any incidents or visits from the mysterious young man. Cyrus and I kept our promise to one another and for the most part, life went back to normal. Hillary was back at school, fully recovered from her bout with mono; Kayle at her heels. Cyrus had been given a "break" from full-contact practice with the team during the afternoons. Apparently, Coach Burnell thought it best that Cyrus focused on weight training, since he already knew the plays so well. Gossip flew around the school for a week or so, about Cyrus's super-human like strength. Fellow classmates avoided him, keeping a safe distance, but all was forgotten after he threw five successful touchdown passes during the home coming game; sending Woodward High to the playoffs.

I shuddered at the crisp breeze, zipping my hoodie up to my chin. I waited impatiently outside the front of the school with the rest of my frigid Astronomy classmates. It was early December and a sudden cold front had blown in the night before, dropping temperatures into the low forties. A stark contrast to the warm seventy-eight degrees of the previous day.

Clenching my fist in the thin cotton pockets, I sighed, wondering if I would ever acclimate to Texas weather. Shifting my weight back and forth, attempting to stay warm, I watched as Cyrus, Hillary and Kayle huddled together, laughing at whatever story Hillary was telling. Cyrus found my gaze, rolling his eyes quickly, so only I could see. I laughed, swiftly looking away as to not be caught by either Hillary or Kayle.

I missed spending time alone with Cyrus. Now that Hillary was back, our only communication was cautious note passing during Astronomy class, or telepathic facial expressions. I never understood why he stayed with her. At first, they made sense together, but now that I had become friends with Cyrus, I found myself completely dumbfounded as to the reason why.

A large, faded yellow school bus pulled into the circle drive, its breaks squealing as it slowed to a stop. Mr. Lawson ungracefully exited the bus with a clip board in hand. Waddling only a few feet to the huddled group of students, he stopped, catching his breath before speaking.

"As you all know, today is our field trip to NASA. We will be gone most of the school day. Depending on traffic, we should be back before the last period bell rings. I am going to divide you into groups of two, where you will work together to fill in the missing information inside the packet I have provided."

A unanimous groan reverberated through the crowd as Mr. Lawson waved the packets above his head.

"That's enough!" he barked. "This packet will count as a project grade, so if you choose not to complete it you will receive a zero," he continued, turning his attention directly to Taylor and Cliff.

"Now, for your groups," he began once more.

Mr. Lawson began pairing off students by calling names from his brown clip board. I frowned when Cyrus and Kayle's names were called together. My heart sank, when he read Hillary's name followed by my own.

"This is going to be a very *long* day," I thought, watching Hillary complain to Cyrus about Mr. Lawson's decision.

Cyrus, seeing my reaction mouthed a silent "sorry" followed by a smirk. I returned his gaze attempting to glare angrily, but giggled when he shook his head laughing, amused by my little game.

When the pairings had finished Mr. Lawson turned, hobbling to the bus. I was the first to follow, nearly slamming into the back of him when he suddenly stopped. Turning around quickly, his face hardened, exposing wrinkles I had never noticed before. Startled, I jumped back almost knocking over a fellow classmate.

"One more thing," he stated firmly. "There will be NO HORSEPLAY while we are visiting, is that understood?"

A quiet murmur of agreement swept over the crowd of frigid students.

"I will not tolerate ANY misconduct. We will be getting a behind-the-scenes tour of NASA today and you will all be on your best behavior. I do not want to be embarrassed by a lack of maturity on your part. Do I make myself clear?"

The class stood shivering while nodding up and down, eager to gain entry onto the warm bus. Mr. Lawson, satisfied with the response, turned once more, heading up the steep stairs.

The warm air enveloped me as I walked onto the old bus. I unzipped my gray hoodie and selected the first seat on the right. Students filled the empty seats one by one. I watched out of the corner of my eye as Cyrus, Hillary and Kayle headed toward the back of the bus. Noisy chatter filled the warm space as we slowly pulled out of the circle drive. I rested my head against the cool window, observing the puffy, steel gray clouds move gently across the sky. I must have dozed off, because the hour-long bus ride was instantly over as my nodding head jolted me awake.

Mr. Lawson stood at the front of the bus motioning for everyone to quiet down.

"The trams are outside waiting for us. Please be respectful of the tour guide and do not tell me you forgot your packet on the bus," he chided.

I blinked my eyes quickly, trying to shake the post-nap fog.

Classmates slowly walked off the bus talking about everything from the latest gossip to how annoying Taylor and Cliff were on the long ride. I smiled, grateful I had napped the entire way. The cool air outside stung my still-warm eyes. Using both hands, I rubbed them trying to adjust to the stark contrast in temperature. Slowly, I opened my blurry eyes only to find a smug looking Hillary standing only inches away from my face.

"Whoa, there," I noted, taking a step back, surprised by her lack of personal space.

"Okay, so here's the deal," she began, speaking to me as if I were her subordinate. "You do the first five pages, I'll do the last five and then we'll exchange answers at the end of the day. Okay? This way we can complete the assignment and I won't have to spend any time with you. Sound good?" she asked, her voice overly peppy.

Before I could answer, Hillary did an abrupt 180-degree turn, tossing her blonde locks off her shoulders and began walking toward the open-air trams that waited for our class in the parking lot.

Feeling utterly speechless, I shook my head, walking toward the last tram, only to find myself halted once again by Hillary.

"Oh, and stay away from Cyrus," she hissed, meeting my gaze once more.

Before I had time to react, she once again turned and bounded happily toward Kayle and Cyrus, sliding onto the off-white vinyl seat between the two of them.

Frustrated, I climbed into the last empty car and began previewing my "assigned" portion of the packet. The first page of questions was strictly about the tram tour. What year did the Space Center open? How many acres does the property occupy? How many guest visit the Space Center annually?

My head jolted forward as the rickety tram car began its way out of the parking lot. An overhead speaker, clearly broken, began sputtering partial words about what I could only assume was the necessary information to complete the first page of the packet. Annoyed, I observed other students beginning to write down answers to the obvious questions. Of course, my tram car had to have the only busted speaker. I glanced behind me, noticing Cyrus looking in my direction. I shook my head and shrugged my shoulders, pointing up to the broken speaker. He placed a hand over his face, exaggerating my situation. Laughing, I tossed the packet onto the empty seat next to me and closed my eyes, listening to the annoying crackle of the tour guide's voice as we slowly snaked down the paved path.

The ninety-minute tram tour – which felt more like four hours – finally ended at the Space Center Plaza. We were informed by Mr. Lawson that the answers to pages two-through-five could be completed inside the Space Center. The warmth of the building felt refreshing, as I unzipped the thin hoodie, admiring the vast room. Scanning the long list of empty blank spaces, I quickly learned that the questions were in order by exhibit. All one had to do was walk around and simply fill in the missing information. Apparently, I was the only one who had caught on to this little trick. I snickered, watching my fellow classmates zig-zagging back and forth, like mice in a maze. Satisfied with my diligent work, I decided to pass the time by exploring the large room.

I found most exhibits slightly boring, though my interests were perked up once I noticed a small, dark room tucked away in a corner. A tiny sign above the entry read, Eclipses, written in silver letters. Curious, I entered the dimly lit room, noticing several small benches all facing a large projection screen. Quietly, I sat watching a film begin to play on the dark screen.

The narrator's voice began speaking about a brief history of Solar, Lunar and Bi-Lunar eclipses. I shifted uncomfortably on the soft bench, and suddenly feeling very warm, I pulled the hoodie off my arms, laying it gently across my lap.

Mr. Lawson's voice called in the distance. I stood, knowing I better hurry if I didn't want to get separated from the rest of the class. Just as I turned to walk toward the exit, my vision blurred and blood rushed to my head, sending me to my knees. Grabbing my head with both hands, I shut my eyes, trying to escape the roller-coaster like sensation.

My field of vision exploded with imagery. Strangers I had never met, smiled at one another, then back to me. An odd-looking room with furniture not from this century filled the small space. Two familiar piercing blue eyes, shifted back and forth between the strangers and myself. My head began to feel as though it were being sucked through a pin hole. Just when I thought I couldn't bare another second, the phenomenon stopped as quickly as it had begun. I gasped, feeling instant relief as the strange visions vanished from my mind.

"What the heck was that?" I thought, feeling genuinely scared.

I spun my head around, checking to see if anyone had witnessed the strange fit. The overhead lights flickered softly from above and the large projection screen was black once more. I sighed, relieved I was still alone in the small room. Slowly, I climbed back to a standing position.

"ELARA DUNLIN!" bellowed Mr. Lawson.

I ran quickly out of the room to find my fellow classmates waiting together, appearing irritated by my disappearing act.

"I'm here!" I yelled, winded.

"Do NOT make us wait on you again Ms. Dunlin!" snapped Mr. Lawson.

I nodded in approval, catching Cyrus's eye at the opposite end of the group.

Looking concerned, he mouthed, "Are you okay?"

Noticing Hillary's glare, I gave a slight nod, moving my gaze quickly back to Mr. Lawson.

"We're going to take a quick thirty-minute lunch break and will then continue with a private tour of NASA's underwater training facility," he explained, pointing to the overhead sign that read, Dining Hall.

Students eagerly walked toward the dining area as I slowly followed behind, trying to piece together what I had just experienced.

"Maybe I fainted?" I asked myself. "It did feel really warm, but even if I did faint, who were those people and where was that random room? Why was *he* there?"

I found an empty table, carefully taking a seat on the red, plastic chair. Any appetite I previously had disappeared completely. I was too shaken to think about eating. Sighing, I laid my forehead on the cool wood table, closing my eyes briefly but opened them when my skin prickled with heat as Cyrus approached.

"Hey, are you okay?" he asked, pulling out a chair, taking a seat next to me.

"Yeah, I'm fine," I lied, forcing a smile. "I think I just had a fainting spell or something back there."

"Fainting spell? Do you want me to get Mr. Lawson? Do you need some water or something?" he asked, his eyes full of concern.

"No! I'm fine. I just need to sit for a few minutes," I reassured him.

Hillary, looking frustrated, stood in the distance eyeing us carefully. Her arms were folded tightly across her chest while her foot tapped loudly against the epoxied floors.

"I don't think your girlfriend likes you over here talking to me," I commented, nodding in her direction.

"I could care less," he quickly interjected. "She can't tell me who I can or can't hang out with."

"Good to know," I smiled.

"So, you really are okay then?" he asked, his mood relaxing.

I hesitated, unsure if I should share my experience with him but then surrendered once I met his gaze. I explained to him in the best way I could manage every detail about the strange phenomenon that had occurred back inside the small room. He sat quietly, listening to my explanation, lost deep in thought.

"I haven't a clue Elara. That is strange, but strange things keep happening to us lately so…" he began, his voice trailing off.

"So…what?" I asked anxiously.

"So…I don't know, add it to our list of the bizarre and unexplainable?" he laughed.

"I guess," I sighed, shaking my head.

It always amazed me how relaxed I felt around Cyrus. Even in stressful or uncomfortable situations he somehow had the ability to make me feel at ease, like everything would be okay.

It wasn't long before Kayle was sent to retrieve Cyrus. Looking annoyed, he slowly followed her, taking his seat next to Hillary. I eyed them carefully as they argued with one another while gesturing in my direction.

The last half of the day involved a private tour of the Space Center's Neutral Buoyancy Laboratory. Our class entered the enormous room, unsure of what to expect. A unanimous "wow" echoed throughout the vast space as our heads turned every which way. The largest indoor pool I had ever laid eyes on occupied most of the massive room. Taylor and Cliff, all too eager, began jumping up and down, keen to get a closer look.

Annoyed by their child-like behavior, Mr. Lawson violently shook his head side to side while pointing to the top of the room.

Bordering the top of the large room were walls of windows. NASA employees worked diligently on computers and other technical devices, mostly talking amongst themselves. A few men stood with their arms crossed, observing the arrival of our class. One side, resembling that of an air traffic-control tower was clearly where the underwater operations were observed. Men in uniforms, wearing head phones, communicated back and forth with one another. Large, gurgling bubbles surfaced in different areas of the pool. For some reason, I found the large body of water frightening. It was so deep that I could not see the bottom of the dark blue pool.

A tall, slender man in a bright blue NASA collared shirt strolled over to where our class stood, still admiring the vast space. He smiled and shook hands with Mr. Lawson, welcoming him to the lab. After a brief chat, the man casually walked to the front of our group and introduced himself as Nolan Leeds, Director of Operations for the Neutral Buoyance Laboratory. Mr. Leeds reminded us to stay close to the perimeter wall and to NEVER cross the brightly painted, yellow line that snaked its way around the pool.

"The pool you see here, is over half the length of a football field," he began, motioning to the blue water.

I noticed Cyrus out of the corner of my eye slowly begin inching away from Hillary and Kayle, heading in my direction. Curious, I followed his lead, meeting him halfway at the back of the crowd. Discreetly, he slid a neatly, folded piece of paper into my hand.

"I thought you might need this," he whispered, keeping his eyes focused ahead.

Glancing quickly at the crisp paper, I smiled, noticing it was the completed first page of the packet; the very same answers I had missed on the tram tour.

"You're the best!" I whispered back.

"Don't let Mr. Lawson catch you," he murmured, slowly side-stepping his way back to Hillary.

"Not only is this indoor pool one of the longest in the world, but it is over forty feet deep and contains full scale mock ups of International Space Stations, numerous ATV and HTV vehicles," resumed Mr. Leeds.

Continuing his speech, he began walking the length of the pool, forcing our small group to crowd closely together so as not to cross the dreaded yellow line. Taylor and Cliff knocked elbows with me while they pretended to push one another into the giant pool. Mr. Lawson was at the front of our group and completely unaware of their behavior as he continued to follow closely behind our guide. My skin prickled with heat, feeling Cyrus's proximity. Quietly, he walked directly behind me while Hillary chatted animatedly to Kayle about the latest gossip.

"She better be jotting down some of the answers to those questions," I thought, knowing it was her turn to complete the packet.

Deciding it was best not to leave my grade's fate in her hands, I slid my back pack off one shoulder, rummaging for the large packet. Quickly, I began filling in the missing answers to page one, thanks to Cyrus's generous offer. After a few minutes of walking the length of the pool, Mr. Leeds halted, allowing the class to observe an underwater platform holding an astronaut, slowing rising from the depths. Taylor, standing closest to the pool craned his neck to get a better look, while Cliff continued to pretend he was going to push him into the water any minute.

Hunched over, using my thigh as a writing desk, I took advantage of the break from walking to rapidly fill in the remaining unanswered questions. Cyrus popped his neck loudly, listening to Hillary continue to fill him in on the details of her already purchased prom dress.

"You already got a dress? Isn't prom like six months away?" Cyrus asked.

"Exactly, Cyrus! I didn't want all of the good dresses to be picked over before then!" she snapped.

I laughed quietly at their banter, continuing to fill in the missing answers.

The next few moments happened in the blink of an eye, but I experienced them as if in slow motion. Taylor, becoming irritated by Cliff's non-stop horseplay, gently shoved him, causing Cliff to lose his balance. Before I even had time to notice what was happening, I shielded my body by using both hands to soften the inevitable blow.

Everything slowed down as though I were outside of my body watching it happen on half speed. The packet of questions dropped quickly to my side as I stood, upright and alert with my arms outstretched. By the time Cliff began to lose his balance, my hands had already made contact with his back. The amount of force that left my hands was like nothing I had ever experienced before. It felt as though all the warmth in my body had gathered together, then surged out of my palms in a concentrated heat wave. I watched in awe as Cliff's body left my hands, slamming hard into Taylor. Taylor, looking as though ten men had pushed him, flew over the forbidden yellow line, crashing loudly into the deep, dark pool.

CHAPTER 11

The splash that was "heard around the world," as my fellow classmates so cleverly named it, caused every head inside the vast building to turn. Kayle and a few of the other students closest to the water's edge gasped as the splash soaked them.

An emergency siren rang loudly while uniformed NASA employees ran to the edge of the pool, followed closely by Mr. Leeds. A voice over a loud speaker repeated "All Stop!" as the suited astronaut now sat idled on the underwater platform. Taylor looked genuinely terrified as he quickly swam to the NASA employees' outstretched arms. As he grabbed a hand of each of the worried-looking men, he was pulled from the cold pool. Looking concerned, Mr. Leeds asked Taylor if he were injured. Taylor, still in shock, turned in circles assessing every part of himself, reassuring Mr. Leeds that he was unharmed. Slipping a hand into his pocket, Taylor frowned, cursing as he realized his cell phone was ruined.

"My damned phone is trashed!" he yelled at Cliff.

"Dude! It wasn't me, it was her!" Cliff pointed at me.

Annoyed by Taylor's lack of propriety, Mr. Leeds stormed over to Mr. Lawson who huffed and puffed as he hurried to the scene of the incident.

"Clearly your students are not mature enough to respect the rules of our facility!" he barked, wagging a finger at Mr. Lawson.

"Mr. Leeds, with all due respect, I do not tolerate this behavior. Please do not punish the rest of the group, for one's wrong doing," he said, glaring in my direction.

Taylor, Kayle and a couple of other students stood shivering, looking back and forth among one another.

"Jake!" yelled Mr. Leeds toward at a uniformed NASA employee. "Don't just stand there! Grab those kids some towels."

He turned, facing Mr. Lawson once more.

"Very well, Mr. Lawson, we will continue the tour with the other students but if anyone steps out of line, your group will be asked to vacate the premises."

"Thank you," replied Mr. Lawson, embarrassed by Mr. Leeds' patronizing tone.

"Students! You heard Mr. Leeds. Do exactly as he says, or all of you will be in SERIOUS trouble."

Still in shock over the incidents, I stood frozen, unable to move. The intense heat that had surged through my body moments earlier slowly faded to a gentle buzz. Nervously, I glanced down at my shaking hands.

Hillary consoled Kayle, attempting to dry her off with the towel handed over by one of the NASA employees, though she looked more concerned about the light mist of water that beaded on her own hair. Cyrus stood motionless, staring at me with an all-too-familiar expression; the same expression he had during football practice. Mr. Lawson walked over to the dripping wet students, informing them to head to the restrooms to use the automatic hand dryers as best they could to dry off, before catching up with the rest of the group. He then turned, walking faster than I had ever seen him move in my direction.

"Ms. Dunlin!" he barked.

"Mr. Lawson," I began. "Please, I didn't push Taylor into the water on purpose! It was just..."

"THAT IS QUITE ENOUGH!" he bellowed, his voice echoing throughout the huge room. "You completely disobeyed the rules! I clearly stated before we left that there was to be no horseplay," he chided, winded from his fast pace.

Tiny beads of sweat surrounded his furrowed brow, as he paused, wheezing.

"I know, it's just..."

"No excuses! You pushed Taylor into the water and that is unacceptable. You are to march back to the bus and sit there alone for the remainder of the day. As soon as we return to school you are to serve detention this afternoon and I better not hear another word out of you for the rest of the day! Do I make myself clear?" he asked, his voice still raised as several NASA employees stopped their jobs to watch.

"Mr. Lawson, if I may..." Cyrus began, slowly walking toward us.

"No, you may not, Mr. Lofton!" he snapped, holding up a hand in his direction.

Ignoring the gesture, Cyrus continued to approach.

"I saw the whole thing happen! She didn't push him in on purpose. She was only trying to..."

"Cyrus! I am warning you. If you want to participate in the playoff game tonight, I highly suggest that you turn around and catch up with your classmates."

"Just go," I mouthed, nodding in the direction of the now smaller group.

"I'm sorry," he whispered back.

Cyrus turned, slowly heading back to the group of students huddled around the suited astronaut.

"To the bus, now!" Mr. Lawson hissed, pointing to the closest exit door.

Feeling overwhelmed, I did not argue and swiftly made my escape from the Neutral Buoyancy Laboratory. The cool air hit my face like an arctic blast. My warm skin cooled quickly, but my blood still surged with adrenaline.

"Great," I thought, searching the enormous parking lot for the tram.

It was nowhere in sight. Far in the distance, I could make out the old, yellow school bus. I exhaled, knowing I would have to walk the entire way.

Tucking my hands into the thin pockets and securing the hood over my hair, I shuddered as the wind pushed against me while I made the long walk back to the bus. My mind raced, going over the events that took place only moments ago, again trying to find a logical explanation for another strange event.

I squinted as the frigid wind stung my face, continuing the long walk.

There may have been an explanation that sounded rational, but I knew what had really happened. The look on Cyrus's face after Taylor crashed into the water gave all the confirmation I needed. The exact same phenomenon that Cyrus had experienced on the football field had now happened to me. The super-human strength I witnessed Cyrus use on his teammate had just surged through my own body.

It was though my body reacted on its own, as though some defense mechanism had been turned on. Colors were brighter, sounds were louder and everyone around me moved in slow motion, while I stayed at the same speed. Without consciously making any effort, my body stood alert, ready to defend itself. Heat surged through my veins, concentrating in my hands the moment they connected with Cliff's body. Though it may have looked like I physically shoved him, I did not use any force to move him. The intense heat pushed through my hands, dissipating only after leaving his body. It was as though the heat itself moved Cliff, not my physical strength.

"What is going on?" I wondered, utterly perplexed. "Strange events are happening around Cyrus and I, left and right without any explanation."

The wind swirled around my already chilled body. I shuddered, clenching my fists in the hoodie's shallow pockets.

Tall pine and oak trees lined the perimeter of the facility, swaying in the strong breeze. The cloudy, gray sky above mirrored my deflated posture.

A loud crashing sound close by caused me to flinch. I slowed my pace, cautiously turning, afraid as to who I may see. Leaves danced along the quiet, gray parking lot as a crow took flight from a nearby tree. My eyes darted back and forth, desperately searching. As far as I could tell, I was alone but my heart still hammered in my chest. In the distance, a large pine tree rocked back and forth, battling the strong winds. A fat squirrel scampered around the pieces of a fallen limb in search of food.

"Relax," I pleaded with myself. "It was just a tree branch."

My nerves calmed once I reached the bus. The door swung open as the driver looked down at me, apparently confused.

"Your field trip already over?"

"No. I was just told to come back and wait here for the rest of the day."

"Well, hop on because you're letting out all the warm air!" he barked.

I climbed up the stairs and selected a seat a few rows back, tossing my back pack onto the floor board. The warm air felt nice at first, but quickly became stifling in a few minutes. Careful to not get caught by the large bus driver, who clearly preferred temperatures equal to that of a North African desert, I slowly cracked the bus window, allowing enough cool air inside to ease my discomfort. I rested my head on the cool window and closed my eyes, wondering how the day could get any worse.

My eyes shot open at the sound of students entering the bus, chatting loudly as they took their seats. I wiped a thin trail of drool from my chin. This was the second time I had fallen asleep in one day.

"I've got to start going to bed earlier," I thought, hearing my mother's disappointment voice.

I watched closely as Cyrus, Hillary and Kayle entered the bus. Hillary was complaining to Cyrus that her once perfect blonde locks were now frizzy due to the high chlorine content of the pool. Her eyes locked onto mine as she stressed the word, POOL, glaring angrily as she walked by. Cyrus kept his head down ignoring her whining.

Mr. Lawson appeared out of breath as he climbed the three steep steps onto the bus, landing hard onto the seat of the first row closest to the driver. I took a moment to eavesdrop, listening to the noisy gossip about the incident at the Buoyancy Laboratory, but quickly regretted it when I heard my name referred to in every other sentence. Desperately wanting a distraction from the incessant chatter, I reached into my back pack, removing the incomplete packet, deciding that now was a good time to complete the missing answers.

The bus pulled into the crowded school parking lot, only minutes before the final bell rang. I quickly texted my mother, lying, explaining that I had a project to work on in the library but assured her I would be home in time for dinner.

The sky appeared darker, even gloomier than when we left earlier that day. I was in no rush to exit the bus, considering I would spend the rest of the afternoon in detention. I stood, stretching my arms over head, then popped my neck before getting up. Mr. Lawson met me awkwardly at the door to the bus.

"Elara, I hope you haven't forgot about detention this afternoon," he began sternly.

"No sir," I replied, gloomy.

"Good. Then you can go ahead and make your way there now," he said, motioning toward the school campus.

I nodded in agreement and headed down the steps.

"Mr. Lawson," I called, turning toward the bus once more. "Where am I serving detention?"

"In Señora Lopez's class, of course," he responded.

I gulped. In a flash, this day had gone from bad to worse. Frustrated, I began the long walk to the portable buildings located at the back of the school.

"Elara."

Cyrus's voice caught my attention.

I swiftly turned, happy to see his face.

"Do you need a ride home today? I don't have to catch the bus for the away game until 4:30."

"What about Hillary?" I asked, trying to find her in the sea of students vacating the school grounds.

Cyrus paused before speaking.

"I told Hillary that we needed a break."

"I'm sure that went over well," I mentioned, finding Kayle and Hillary standing together, glaring furiously at us.

"She's really been wearing me out lately," he confided, running a hand over his bright blond hair.

"Really?" I asked playfully. "I can't imagine why."

He couldn't hide the large grin that crossed his face.

"Well, look who decided to be the comedian today?" he teased.

I laughed hard, amused by my own joke.

"So, do you want a ride?" he asked, his tone more serious. "I know you had a tough day. I figured you could use a friend right now."

"Cyrus, you have no idea how much I appreciate the offer, but I have detention for the rest of the afternoon," I groaned.

"Ah ... that's right. I forgot," he responded in an apologetic tone.

"I better go," I said, gesturing toward the portables. "If I'm late for detention, she will make my life hell for the rest of the year."

"Text me if you want to hang out this weekend," he added, raising his hand for a high five.

High fives always made me uncomfortable. I never understood the satisfaction of giving or receiving one. They reminded me of one of those corny trust exercises people do at team building camps, where someone falls into the open arms of others. The purpose of this exercise is to make one feel more confident, but in reality leaves everyone feeling awkward.

"Will do," I chuckled, reluctantly slapping his hand.

Our fingers interlocked briefly, causing me to blush. Releasing my hand from his grip, I felt his eyes follow me as I hurried toward the portable buildings. It was funny how one, seemingly insignificant moment, instantly lifted my spirits.

CHAPTER 12

It appeared that Mr. Lawson called Señora Lopez on the ride back from NASA, asking if she wanted to make my life miserable for the rest of the day. Not only was the room freezing cold, but she had both windows cracked, allowing the frigid late afternoon air to blow in.

Shivering, I stood next to the large black metal file cabinet that looked as though it had been thrown from a two-story building. I used both of my hands in attempt to pry open the top drawer. When unsuccessful, I placed a foot on the lower drawer bracing myself, then pulled with all my strength.

"If you break my file cabinet, you will be spending every afternoon with me for the remainder of the school year," she spoke, pronouncing each word as if she were speaking to a young child.

Rising from her desk, clearly irritated by my actions, Señora Lopez walked over to the beat-up file cabinet nudging the drawer gently with her hip. My jaw dropped watching the drawer open effortlessly.

"Oh…" I murmured.

Ignoring me, she casually walked back to her desk where she continued to grade papers.

I stood for the remainder of detention, attempting to organize the disaster of the paperwork in the file cabinet. Papers were stuffed every which way, crunched up together resembling miniature accordions. I sighed, frustrated with the job but happy she had given me quiet, busy work versus something that involved communicating with her.

"Elara," she called, not lifting her head from the large stack of papers.

"Yes," I responded quietly.

"It is after five, so you can go now."

Relieved that my punishment was over, I gently closed the middle file cabinet drawer before reaching down to grab my bag. Saying nothing, I tossed it over one shoulder and headed to the door.

The crisp, late afternoon air stung my face as the wind whirled around me, causing my entire body to shudder. Quickly I fumbled for the zipper of the thin hoodie, zipping it up as high as it would go. I tucked my long hair into the hood, pulling the drawstrings tight and tying them into a snug bow. I knew I looked ridiculous, but instantly felt warmer.

The sun was barely visible as the night sky began to make its appearance. Never had I seen the school grounds this late in the day. Round lights mounted at the top corners of the portable buildings began to flicker on one after the other. The main building looked empty. Only a few lights remained on, which I assumed were for the janitors who would eventually make their evening rounds.

I quickly made my way from the portable buildings to the main parking lot, still shivering from the cold. It was empty except for two older-model cars that were parked next to each other at the far end of the lot. I stopped to weigh my options. I could walk down the well-lit, main road where Cyrus and I had our accident or I could take the soon to be very dark, creepy trail, getting home in half the time. If I hoped to get home before dinner, I had only one option; the forbidden trail.

Turning away from the parking lot, I headed up the hill toward the vast football stadium. I came to an abrupt stop at the foot of the trail head. The last bit of sun slowly vanished from the horizon. I hesitated, wondering if I had chosen the best option.

"You can do this, Elara!" I encouraged myself, taking a small step forward.

The dry mulch cracked loudly beneath the weight of my shoes. Craning my neck as far as it would stretch, I looked down the long path.

"Impossible!" I said aloud, eyeing the trail suspiciously.

Looking up between the tall, vast trees, I desperately searched for the moon. It was nowhere in sight. I shook my head, rubbing my eyes.

"How could this be?" I wondered.

By now the trail should have been dark, but for some reason I could see everything clearly, as if it were lit with cool, white lighting.

Standing motionless, I took in my surroundings. A family of birds looked down from their nest. An enormous brown barn owl resting on a nearby branch searched for its dinner as the strong wind howled causing fallen leaves and pine needles to dance in circles around my feet.

"Well this is one to add to our book of strange events," I thought, taking another hesitant step forward.

One foot followed the other in an effortless attempt to make my way home, thanks to the newly acquired gift of night vision. I was making great timing until the wind blew so hard, I had to stop to readjust the hoodie that now hung half off my head. Cool air whipped through my hair, as I tried to quickly re-tie the drawstrings. Numb from the cold, my fingers fumbled to stuff my hair back into place.

"POP!"

My hands froze, letting the hair fall out of the hoodie and down my back, now at the wind's mercy.

I didn't have to look up to know that *he* would be standing there. I could feel his presence close to me, exactly as I had the first day on the trail. My eyes finally looked up and within moments met his gaze.

There he stood just a few yards away, motionless just like every other time I had seen him. Only his jet-black hair moved in the strong breeze. His eyes were focused and sparkled a deep, crystal blue. His fair skin was clothed in dark rugged pants and a tight-fitting, long-sleeved shirt that looked clean but worn.

My hair whipped around my face, hitting me in every direction, but I stood still, transfixed on him. He was handsome, gorgeous in fact, but not like the typical male model you might see in a magazine. He was rugged. Tiny scars covered his pale hands, which rested relaxed by his side. His hair was longer than most guys I knew and looked as though it hadn't been cut professionally in years. My observations halted as he took a step toward me.

Instinctively, I took a small, hesitant step backward, preparing to run, but froze once more. I was tired of running, tired of looking over my shoulder and tired of flinching at every snap and crack that sounded near me. I inhaled a large, cool breath of air, mustering up every ounce of courage I could find.

"Why do you keep following me?" I asked, my tone sharp and direct.

Planting both feet firmly on the ground, he crossed his toned arms, saying nothing.

Irritated by his silence, I took a step forward. My blood pumped quickly as my heart pounded.

"Why do you keep following me?" I repeated, my voice raised.

Slowly, he uncrossed his arms and took the last few steps toward me, defying the laws of personal space.

"I have my reasons, Elara," he whispered, the warmth of his breath close enough to feel.

He was easily a whole head taller than I, causing me to look up into his eyes as he spoke. His voice was calm, smooth, almost dream-like. Forgetting to breathe, I gasped, taking a step back.

"How do you know my name?" I managed, my confidence rapidly dissolving.

"I know a lot more than your name," he replied.

Chills crept up my spine.

"What is that supposed to mean?" I asked, my eyes scanning the trail for the quickest escape route.

"It means that I can finally give you the answers you've been searching for," he answered, pushing his dark hair out of his striking face.

"I'm not searching for anything," I lied, almost stuttering.

"You're not?" he asked, clearly not buying my previous response. "You aren't wondering why you keep seeing me or why strange things keep happening to you?"

"How could he possibly know any of this?!" I wondered, my mind racing.

I shook my head violently, trying to clear my mind as anger began to dissolve any fearful thoughts.

"No! You've just been stalking me! That's how you know these things!" I yelled, pointing at his chest.

"Yes, I have been following you Elara, but not for the reasons you think," he replied calmly.

"I'm sorry! I didn't know creepy stalkers followed people for reasons other than what I think!" I argued.

"That is what you think of me? A creepy stalker?" he grinned, never breaking eye contact.

"What else am I supposed to see you as?" I questioned, feeling angrier by the minute because of his nonchalant attitude.

"I'm not quite sure yet. Are you always so quick to judge someone?" he asked.

"Oh no! Don't go and try to make me feel like the bad guy, when you're the one who has been scaring me for months!" I snapped.

"I'm sorry, Elara. I have not been stalking you. I have only been … observing."

"Observing? That's what you want to call it?" I challenged. "Where I'm from, strangers that 'observe' people are called stalkers!"

"Well, I'm not from here and you and I are not strangers so I guess I'm off the hook," he countered.

My eyes looked away from his, shifting back and forth.

"So, you're from out of town?" I asked, confused.

"You could say that," he nodded, the small grin on his face growing into a large smile.

"How are we not strangers? This is the first time we've ever spoken, so as far as I am concerned we are strangers."

"Now that is a long story, but let's just say I knew you when you were first born."

I stared at him searching for age lines on his smooth, chiseled face. He looked only a few years older than I. How could he have known me when I was born?

"What are you talking about?" I pressed. "Were we like childhood friends and I just don't remember you?"

"I think the easiest way to explain all of this is to just … show you," he said, holding out his hand.

"No way!" I protested, gluing my hand to my side.

"I'm not going to hurt you Elara," he assured, motioning for me to take his hand.

I shook my head, disagreeing with his request while taking another step back on the empty trail.

"I promise this will all make sense, once you see for yourself," he said, quickly grabbing my wrist.

He was strong. Much stronger than he appeared. My efforts were feeble with any attempt to escape his tight grasp.

"You're hurting me!" I yelped, trying to free my wrist.

"Just hold on a minute," he commanded, unfazed by my escape attempt. "This will probably feel strange to you," he said, closing his eyes while sucking in a large breath.

"This is it," I thought, the gravity of the situation sinking in. "I will never see my parents, or anyone else ever again. My darkest fears about this guy have finally manifested."

CHAPTER 13

I closed my eyes, bracing myself for his next move. I waited for what felt like minutes for something horrible to happen, but to my surprise his hand let go of my wrist as quickly as he had taken it. My eyes shot open, taking a quick step backward. He stood quietly with a look of confusion crossing his face then turned his hand over, inspecting it as though there were something wrong with it.

"That was unexpected," he said, still looking at his hand.

Now was my chance to escape. He was distracted and this lucky break might give me the head start I needed to make it closer to the clearing, closer to home.

I sprang past him, sprinting down the trail and not looking back.

"Elara!" he called.

I could hear the ground crunch beneath him, as he took off after me down the long winding path.

Thanks to my night vision, my feet effortlessly dodged fallen tree limbs and over-grown roots. I had easily sprinted a half mile before noticing that something was very different about this escape attempt, compared to the first one I had experienced. Yes, I could see in total darkness, but it also felt as though I could run forever. I was running as fast as before, but my side didn't burn in pain. My lungs inhaled the cool air effortlessly, as my legs churned beneath me. The adrenaline was still present in full force; my senses sharp and aware. But I wasn't out of breath and my heart continued to maintain a smooth, relaxed rhythm.

"What is happening to me?" I wondered, dodging a low-lying tree branch.

I slowed my pace listening for the mysterious man. Relieved, I could only hear my own rhythmic footsteps.

"Maybe he got tired," I thought, feeling overly optimistic.

I knew I shouldn't look back, but curiosity overpowered my better judgement. Jogging onward, I briefly turned my head around, pleased to find an empty trail behind me. Not wanting to take any chances, I quickly returned to the sprint like-speed. The clearing couldn't be much farther. I had to be getting closer.

POP!

The young man appeared out of thin air only a few feet in front of me. His hands shot up, bracing himself as I slammed straight into him, knocking us both to the cool, hard ground. Unlike charming romantic movies where the girl trips gracefully, landing perfectly placed on top of the male lead, our current situation looked more like something out of a cringe-worthy, psychological thriller.

Stepping on him as I climbed to my feet, I got up as quickly as I had fallen. Mystery man, on the other hand was not so quick to recover. Still lying on the ground, he winced in pain, making it obvious as to the part of his body my foot had landed on. Knowing this would most likely be my last chance to escape, I took off down the worn path. That moment was short-lived though, as he quickly grabbed my ankle, taking me down to the ground once more.

I hit the ground hard. The palms of my hands braced my fall but unfortunately took most of the damage. Deciding I could seek medical attention later, I violently wiggled my leg trying to free my ankle.

"Stop running, Elara!" he barked. "I'm not going to hurt you," he said, holding my ankle uncomfortably tight.

"Let me go!" I yelled, still struggling.

"Just give me a chance to explain," he said, loosening his tight grip.

A strange sense of déjà vu washed over me as I caught his eyes while he spoke. Maybe I did know him from a time I could not remember. I knew my thoughts were irrational and most likely unsafe, but I had to get some answers. He had just appeared out of thin air right before my very own eyes. I knew myself well enough to know that even if I did make it home safe, I would forever wonder who he was and how he appeared out of nowhere.

"Okay!" I blurted, surrendering. "I will stop running and listen to what you have to say, but only if you let go of me and keep your distance."

"Agreed," he nodded, sounding relieved.

His pale hand gently let go of my ankle. He stood quicker than I, taking a few steps back, providing me the requested amount of space.

I stood, not quite as elegantly as he, brushing off my knees and rubbing my scraped palms. The cold stung the small cuts that covered my now bleeding hands. I shuddered as the wind whipped around us. Adjusting my hoodie, I attempted to tuck my long hair back under it, feeling colder than I had all day.

Seemingly unaffected by the weather he casually dusted himself off then crossed his arms, watching me intently. I took another step backward and planted both feet firmly on the ground, hiding my injured hands in the tiny pockets of the hoodie.

"Oh, and if you have any weapons on you, I want you to set them on the ground," I added, trying to sound tougher than I appeared.

"Fair enough," he agreed, pulling a large, folded pocket knife from his back pocket.

I gulped, my eyes never leaving his armed hand.

In one swift motion he opened the knife, exposing the sharp, four-inch blade. I flinched at the speed at which he hurled the knife through the air. It landed hard between the two of us, the blade sticking at least two inches deep into the cold, hard ground.

My eyes widened, looking quickly between him and the knife.

"Sorry," he added, smirking at my reaction.

"Do you have any other weapons?" I stammered in a quiet voice.

"No," he reassured, holding up his empty hands.

I exhaled, rubbing my cold arms while nervously looking around the empty trail.

"Let's start over," he suggested, sensing my discomfort.

I nodded, squinting from the icy breeze circling around us.

"My name is Jax," he said, pressing a hand to his chest. "Take comfort in knowing that I have not been stalking you over these past few months."

My eyebrows raised, skeptical of his statement but his hand shot up stopping me before I could speak.

"I have only been … observing," he continued, eyeing me carefully. "I promise that I mean you no harm. I only want to help you understand what you have been experiencing lately. I must warn you though, what you're about to hear may seem unbelievable and perhaps jarring to your nervous system." He paused, waiting for my approval.

"Uh … okay," I said, before having time to process his words.

"Elara," he began quietly, cautiously. "You are not from here and your parents are not the people you think they are."

"What?" I sputtered, trying to decipher his cryptic message.

Jax moved forward, slowly narrowing the gap between the two of us. My hand raised, making it clear I wanted him to keep his distance. Agreeing, he stopped in his tracks.

"What are you talking about?" I asked, shaking my head. "Of course they are and I know I'm not from here, I'm from Maine."

He exhaled, tossing his hair out of his blue eyes once more.

"No, Elara, you were not born in Maine. You were born in the same place I came back from right before you ran into me. The people you call your parents are actually your adoptive parents."

Jax spoke quietly, gently, as though trying to talk someone off the ledge of a tall building. Memories of my early childhood flashed through my mind like a slideshow. The only parents I had ever known were visible in every image.

"He's mental! Of course, they're my parents! I may look nothing like them, or have few, if any of their personality traits but they are my parents! Who cares if I can't relate to either of them? Every teenager feels that way," I thought, my mind racing.

Even so, doubt slowly crept through me, as the same light-headedness I had experienced earlier that day at NASA resurfaced. My mind shifted back to that vision, observing the three blurry faces once more. The more I focused on them the clearer they became. A woman with long black hair and deep-set blue eyes, smiled lovingly at me, and then to the man next to her. He was taller than she, with light colored hair. His kind, tawny eyes, lit up when he smiled his warm grin. A young, teenaged boy with dark hair and familiar, piercing blue eyes poked his head between the man and woman. His face was peaceful with an expression of certainty, knowingness.

"Breathe ... keep breathing," I thought, my head starting to spin.

Feeling faint, I reached out to grab something, anything to keep from toppling over. Jax was at my side in an instant. His hands moved instinctively, one taking my wrist, the other my waist.

"This can't be true," I said, shaking my head quickly back and forth, still gasping for air.

"Elara, you need to try to calm down. Slow, deep breaths," he encouraged softly, trying to steady me. "I understand I'm giving you a lot of information to take in right now."

Only after I was stable did Jax let go of my wrist and waist before taking a step backward, renewing the promise to keep his distance.

"A lot to take in? You just suggested that my entire life has been a lie and I am supposed to take that lightly?" I snapped, feeling anger begin to surge through me.

"There's no easy way to tell you this," he countered, making eye contact. "I wanted to show you where you came from, but when I wasn't able to jump, I realized this was going to be a lot trickier than I had originally hoped."

"What the hell are you talking about?"

"Here it goes," he said, tossing his head back. "Elara, you are not from Maine. You were born in a place called Aroonyx, the same place I come from every time you see me. The people you know to be your parents love and care for you but they are your *adoptive* parents. Your biological parents…" His voice trailed off as he quickly looked away. "They died, shortly after you were born."

There was a deep pain in his eyes as he spoke. Carefully he found my eyes once more, unsure as to my reaction.

I stood there motionless, suddenly feeling empty. The two adult faces I had seen in my memories just moments ago dissolved into a deep void. My heart, feeling colder than it ever had before, thumped in my aching chest.

He paused, allowing me to take in the painful words before continuing once more.

"Not only are you from a different planet…."

"Wait! What?" I stammered, instantly shaken from my somber trance.

"Elara, you have to let me finish."

"Fine," I replied, shaking my head at the absurdity of it all.

Jax sighed, frustrated with the frequent interruptions, then continued once more.

"I know it sounds bizarre telling you that you are from another planet, but it's the *truth*. Aroonyx is a planet much like Earth but different in many ways."

He paused, expecting an interruption but quickly continued when I remained silent.

"There are two types of inhabitants living on Aroonyx: Solins and Lunins. They each have certain attributes or 'powers' as you may call them, that can only…."

"Jax, just stop," I interrupted, waving both hands. "This is completely insane. First you follow me around for months appearing out of thin air. Then you tell me that not only am I adopted, but that I was born on another planet and now mention that people living on this planet have powers? Do you even hear yourself right now?"

"I warned you, Elara. I told you this would be alarming if not jarring to your system. I know you don't want to believe any of this but you *must* trust your instincts. You say you don't believe me? Then how do you explain this?"

Taking a step forward, Jax calmly closed both eyes. Within an instant, he had vanished faster than I could have blinked. I stood there, awe-struck looking like a child witnessing their first magic trick.

"Jax?" I called out, barely above a whisper.

J.M. Buckler

My arms shot out, feeling the cool air in front of me as if I were trying to find an invisible person. Feeling foolish, I lowered my arms but began walking in circles around the area where he once stood. I stumbled, my foot tripping over something hard. It was the knife, still stuck firmly into the cold trail. The only proof that Jax had ever been there. I bent down, pulling it out of the ground, then stood to inspect the blade. The knife was heavier than it appeared. The handle, gray in color, was worn and made from some sort of metal. The blade itself appeared sharp but looked as though it needed a good cleaning. Dark, rust-colored stains covered both sides of the knife. I shuddered wondering if the stains were in fact rust or dried blood.

POP!

The loud noise instantly caused me to drop the knife at my side. There stood Jax, only a few feet from the exact spot where he had vanished only moments ago.

I tried swallowing but was unsuccessful. My mouth and throat felt as though they hadn't tasted water in weeks.

"Where did you go?" I managed, still amazed that I had just witnessed a man disappear and then reappear out of thin air.

"Back to Aroonyx," he replied, calmly. "I thought if I showed you this, then you might actually start to believe me," he said, holding up a small object no larger than an index card.

Carefully, Jax stretched out his arm, offering me the item. I hesitated; every fiber within my body told me that what he was about to show me would change my life forever.

"Take it … please," he said, stepping forward. "After all, it's yours."

He held the small object, only inches from my quivering hand. I only had to lift my fingers to take it from his grasp. Slowly, I turned it over, petrified by what I might see. My free hand shot up to my mouth, attempting to hold in the loud gasp.

Warm tears filled my eyes as I gazed down at the frayed picture.

A hand-painted portrait of a handsome man with blond hair and dark, amber colored eyes smiled warmly. A woman, with long black hair and deep-set, crystal blue eyes looked down lovingly at two newborn babies which were wrapped tightly in pale colored blankets. The faces were a perfect match to those in the strange visions. The two infants were carbon copies of their parents. The boy lay carefree in the arms of his father. The girl, held tightly by her mother. My hand shook, as a single tear fell onto the old picture.

"I can only imagine how challenging this is for you to believe, Elara, but you must understand that everything I have told you tonight is true," he whispered, slowly stepping closer.

I took several paces back, holding the picture firmly in my grasp. Trying to compose myself, I used the back of my hand to wipe away the tears that fell.

"If that *is* a picture of my biological parents with me as a newborn then who is the other baby?" I asked, my voice cracking.

"I think you've had enough information for one night," he warned, cautiously.

I shook my head, disapproving.

"Tell me who the other baby is," I demanded, my voice still shaking.

Jax paused, observing my emotional distress.

"Elara...I don't think now...."

"TELL ME WHO THE OTHER BABY IS!" I yelled, my voice steadier than before.

Exhaling deeply, Jax adjusted his stance, making eye contact before speaking once more.

"The other baby in the picture is your twin brother."

I looked around the trail wondering if a camera crew from a reality show were about to hop out from behind a bush explaining that this was all some sort of cruel joke.

I scoffed, rubbing my hands over my face.

"So now, you're telling me that not only am I adopted, but that I also have a twin brother? What, did he die too?" I snapped, my emotions getting the best of me.

"No. He is very much alive and well," he responded, a small smile creeping over his face.

"What?" I demanded. "Why are you smiling?"

"I think over time you will find the humor in it as well," he stated, still smiling.

"I'm not laughing right now, Jax! Nothing about tonight has been funny."

"Give it time, you will," he continued.

"Enough with your predictions! If he is alive, then where is he?" I asked anxiously, crossing my arms tightly around my body.

"He is much closer than you think."

"Enough with the riddles, Jax! You show me a picture of my deceased parents and then tell me I have a brother, a twin brother who is alive and well but you won't tell me where he is? What kind of cruel game are you playing?"

"Elara, please understand that I never wanted to cause you any distress. This isn't easy information for me to share. I have waited nine very long years to make contact; now I am finally able to tell you the truth. I knew it would be challenging getting you to believe me, but it is my obligation to do so. I promise I will tell you anything and everything you want to know about your past, but I need you to fully trust me," he finished, speaking with more emotion than he had all night.

He paused, his eyes locking onto mine.

"I will tell you who your twin brother is, but fair warning, it will come as a shock."

Jax let out a deep, long sigh, shifting his weight while crossing both arms.

"Elara, your twin brother is...Cyrus."

CHAPTER 14

I felt my knees buckle. Once again, Jax was at my side steadying my uncooperative body.

"No, no, no," I repeated, over and over, shaking my head violently. "That's impossible," I inhaled, beginning to hyperventilate.

"Deep breaths in and out," he instructed me.

Holding my head between my legs, I closed my eyes. My time spent with Cyrus raced through my head like a dramatic video montage: the strong connection I felt with him, the ease at which we could talk about anything together, the same way we popped our necks, how we could look at one another and instantly know what the other one was thinking and to top it off, the strange things that kept happening to us.

I looked down at the tattered picture once more. The male child looked much like Cyrus, but the man in the portrait could have easily been Cyrus fifteen years from now. The muscular build, tan skin, blond hair, amber eyes and the same pearly grin. It was so obvious! How did I not notice it when first looking at the picture? All this time, I thought our connection was because....

A wave of nausea suddenly washed over me. My hand shot up to my mouth as I groaned loudly.

"It's okay Elara. It isn't like you knew he was your brother," Jax noted, as if reading my private inner thoughts.

"Have you been watching us this whole time?" I asked, feeling embarrassed while still gasping for air.

"Let me help you," he said, assisting me to an upright position once more. "Solins are known to be attractive and well liked. You didn't know he was your brother so it's only normal that you felt attracted to him."

"Stop, just stop!" I begged. "This is all absurd!"

Looking concerned, Jax backed off, taking several large steps away from where I stood.

"None of this can be real! You have to be making this up," I pressed.

"How could I make this up? I just vanished before your eyes, then reappeared with a picture of your biological parents and brother, which I have kept for nine years just so I could show you in hopes that you would believe me!"

"Well, you hoped wrong," I argued, turning my head away from his gaze.

"Why are you being so stubborn? You can't deny the things that have been happening to you and your brother. Don't you find it odd that you can now see equally as well at night as during the day? Do you find it strange that you feel as though you can run forever and never tire? What about Cyrus? Has he shown strength unlike any human can physically display?"

I exhaled, utterly speechless. I knew everything he said were true, but I couldn't wrap my mind around the reality of it all. My life was not supposed to be this confusing, jumbled-up mess. My life was steady, predictable. I always flew under the radar, not above it. Anger consumed my being. Everything had been easy before Jax showed up. I wanted him and everything he told me to go away.

"Just stay the hell away from me!" I demanded, stepping backward.

"You're serious?" he asked, bewildered by my response.

"Yes! Leave me alone and do NOT try to contact me again."

I turned away, walking toward the trail head. Feeling as though I were saying goodbye to an old friend, my eyes filled with warm tears. Jax followed me, quickly grabbing my hand.

"Elara, don't do this!" he objected.

I flinched as his rough hand grasped tightly around mine.

"Let go of me Jax! I never want to see you again," I muttered, my voice cracking.

Loudly, he exhaled, sounding defeated. Within an instant his hand was gone from mine. I turned, only to find empty space behind me. The wind whirled around where he once stood, blowing leaves in every direction. I shivered at the cold breeze, feeling more alone than I ever had.

I walked the rest of the way home feeling numb, not from the cold, but from my time with Jax. Leaves blew around my feet, as I solemnly marched back to our street. The fear of Jax lurking behind every corner vanished, as I began to second guess my request for him to leave me alone.

"Why was I so quick in telling him to leave? I wondered, regret showing its dark face. "It was too much. Tonight, was too much. He should have known better than to share these things, like he was reading off a simple grocery list. If he had been planning this encounter for nine years then he should have spent more time finding a graceful way of explaining everything to me. Jax was foolish to approach me on the trail at night alone. What was he thinking?"

Anger surged through my being. My hands ached, my nails digging deep into the fresh cuts as I closed my fists tightly. I took a deep breath, allowing myself to release on the uncomfortable feeling.

The porch light to our house was on, though it blended into my already bright surroundings. I didn't have an excuse for my late arrival. I would have to improvise, which I despised, because I was a horrible liar.

At the sound of the door opening, my mother and father darted around the corner of the kitchen. My mother's eyes were red and swollen from crying. Her expression went from relief to anger as she watched me walk through the door. My father, looking relieved as well, shook his head in disapproval.

"Where have you been!" my mother yelled, running over to me.

Frantically she searched me up and down, as if the answer she sought were written somewhere on my body.

"I just lost track of time," I replied in a dejected tone, looking down at the floor.

"Lost track of time?" she snapped. "It is almost seven o'clock! You didn't answer your phone or reply to any of my texts!"

Her voice, which I found to be extra irritating this evening, pierced my ears louder than ever.

"Sorry," I mumbled, refusing to look at her as I made my way toward the stairs.

My mother stood motionless, her mouth gaping, shocked by my response. My father, quickly took hold of my arm.

"Elara," he started, in the serious tone he rarely used "please don't walk away from your mother when she's speaking to you. You know how she worries. You should've at least called her and said you would be late. We didn't know where you were."

The word mother hit me like a dagger. I paused, feeling the old picture in the pocket of my hoodie. Twisting my arm out of my father's grasp, I continued toward the stair case.

"Elara!" called my father, his voice stern but full of concern. "What has gotten into you?"

"She was probably with that boy Cyrus again!" my mother sputtered.

I stopped in my tracks, my hand grasping the picture tighter than before. My encounter with Jax raced through my mind. His words repeated over and over like a broken record player. "… your adoptive parents, your twin brother … Cyrus." Anger, grief and confusion boiled in my veins, as I spun around to face my parents.

"I want to see a picture taken at the hospital the day I was born," I demanded, facing my mother.

"What?" she stuttered, caught off-guard.

Quickly, her eyes darted to my father, a look of urgency on her face.

"I want to see a picture of you holding me at the hospital right after I was born," I repeated, planting my feet firmly onto the wooden stairs.

Looking as though I had asked her to pull a rabbit from a hat she laughed nervously, still eyeing my father.

"Honey, where is this coming from?" she asked, twisting a lock of her short blonde hair. "You've seen plenty of pictures of when you were a baby."

"Yes, but I've never seen one of us at the hospital," I pressed, my nostrils flaring.

She shifted her weight uncomfortably, continuing to look between me and my father.

"I haven't a clue where that album would be. It's probably somewhere in the attic with the other boxes we never unpacked."

"Doubtful, considering you unpacked every item of this house two weeks before I started school," I replied coldly.

"This is ridiculous, Elara! You are just trying to change the subject about why you're so late coming home. Come on, let's just go eat dinner," she spoke casually, walking toward the kitchen, her arms moving equally as excited as her mouth. "It's already cold, but we can warm it up in the microwave. Your father and I are excited to hear all about your field trip to NASA."

My mother had a brilliant way of always changing the subject if there were something she was uncomfortable talking about. I watched as my father, deep in thought, stood his ground near the stairs.

"No," I said to my mother, insistent. "I want to see that picture or any picture for that matter from the day I was born."

She turned, facing me once more.

"The attic is a giant mess right now. We can look this weekend after I get your father to help move some of those heavy five-gallon paint buckets that he was supposed to put...."

"There isn't a picture, is there?" I interrupted, tears quickly forming in my eyes.

"That's ridiculous!" she began, nervously tucking her short hair behind her ears. "Of course, there is, we just have to find it – that's all," she stuttered, her voice cracking.

"Enough!" my father bellowed.

His fierce tone caused both my mother and I to jump. I had rarely ever heard my father raise his voice, much less yell. He was always the laid back, easy-going one in the family. He squeezed the bridge of his nose with his thumb and index finger, exhaling a long, deep breath.

"Emily, we made a promise that if she ever asked?" he began, looking at my mother.

"Asked what?" I quickly interrupted.

My heart pounded, already knowing the answer.

"Not now, Rog," she begged, walking quickly toward him.

"Elara," he began.

"Not this way, Roger," she pleaded.

My father's hand quickly shot up in her direction, silencing my mother.

"Elara," he started once more. "There is no picture of you at the hospital with your mother on the day you were born, because you were...."

"Adopted," I managed, finishing his sentence. Jax's words still echoed loudly in my ear.

My mother's face fell, as my father nodded in approval.

The room spun as the trail had earlier that evening, but this time Jax wasn't there to steady my uncooperative body. Everything he shared with me had sounded crazy, but now with this part of the puzzle verified, I felt trapped, imprisoned between two realities. The room spun faster than my eyes could focus. I exhaled a final breath as my vision began to fade.

"Elara!" my father gasped, reaching out to catch my falling body.

He was too late. Everything faded to black as I let myself fall.

CHAPTER 15

My eyes opened sluggishly, squinting at the morning light that poured through my bedroom windows. Rolling over, I watched the fan rotate slowly above my bed. The moment of peace instantly dissolved, as I recalled the events of the previous evening. I winced, touching the spot where the metal button of my jeans had dug into my lower stomach all night. Apparently, my parents had managed to carry me all the way upstairs to my room.

"The picture!" I thought, my mind now fully awake.

I reached for the pocket of my hoodie, sighing with relief when my hand grasped the portrait. Carefully, I pulled the picture from the thin pocket, pausing before turning it over. Nothing Jax had shared with me the night before made sense, but even in the midst of confusion I couldn't deny what I had seen in the strange visions.

"Their faces," I thought, turning over the picture. "These faces, were the faces of my real family. A past I had never known until now."

A lump formed in my throat, as I held the picture tightly. I flinched at the sound of footsteps on the stair well.

"Elara, are you awake?" my father called, his voice cautious, gentle.

Rolling off the bed entirely too quickly, I groaned. Every muscle in my body ached in pain. I had never sprinted as far as I did the night before and the after-effects were ever present. I limped over to the bedside table, sliding the old picture beneath the lamp before hobbling toward the door. Slowly, I cracked it open, enough to speak through the small gap.

"Yeah, I'm up," I replied, yawning.

"If you don't mind," my father began. "It would mean a lot to your mother and I, if you would meet us down stairs at the kitchen table so we can talk about last night."

You could have cut the tension with a knife. I didn't have to see his face to know he was hurting.

"Right. Let me take a quick shower and I'll be right down," I agreed, continuing to speak through the crack of the door.

"Great! We'll see you in a bit," he said, sounding relieved.

Realizing there was no escape from the inevitable meeting with my parents, I proceeded to the bathroom. I flicked on the light, gasping when I noticed my reflection. The entire right side of my face was a deep shade of purple. I winced as my hand assessed the damage.

"Apparently, my father did not catch me in time," I thought, reflecting on the blackout.

I shook my head, starring at the heaping mess that gazed back from the mirror. The windy conditions of the previous night had taken a toll on my hair, making it look as though an animal had tried to nest in it. I attempted running my hands through the black tangles, giving up when my fingers stopped only inches from my scalp. Large dark circles reflected back below my eyes. The palms of my hands were scraped and covered in dirt.

I undressed, taking the longest shower of my life, allowing the hot water to wash over me in hopes that it would also wash away the heavy burden I now carried.

Wiping the steam from the mirror, I smiled at the improved reflection. Yes, the bruise on my face was just as visible as before, but my once-knotted hair, now shiny and smooth, rested neatly over my shoulders, thanks to the half bottle of conditioner I depleted. The dark circles under my eyes looked a shade lighter and the dirty cuts on my hands were barely visible, now that my hands were clean. I dressed swiftly, trying to make up for the lengthy shower, then headed down stairs to face my parents.

The emotions of the previous night began to resurface, as I stepped off the wooden staircase. My blood pressure began to rise at a rapid rate as I neared the kitchen. Anger, frustration and confusion consumed me. I was ready to lay it all out on the table, telling my parents how I really felt about them keeping a secret of such magnitude from me for so long.

I rounded the corner with my guard up, ready to go to battle to prove my point, but paused when I saw my parents sitting across the table from one another. My mother gazed down at her coffee mug, looking as though she hadn't slept all night. My father stared somberly out the kitchen window, tapping his thumb quietly against the rim of his cup. In that moment, a quiet peace came over me. The anger and frustration I had felt so deeply suddenly melted away as compassion and understanding filled the empty space. The simplicity of it all struck me like a bolt of lightning.

"How could I expect my parents to show me compassion and understanding, if I refused to show them the same? Yes, I was hurt and angered by the secret they had withheld from me, but they were the ones who had kept this secret for eighteen long years. I had only known about it for less than twenty-four hours. They chose to keep this information from me for a reason. They did what they thought was best. Who was I to judge?" I thought, walking into the kitchen and making my presence known.

"Elara," my father said, clearing his throat.

He stood smiling, then gestured for me to take a seat.

"Sweetie, how's your face feeling?" my mother asked, grimacing at the purple bruise.

"It's felt better," I replied, pulling out a chair. "What exactly happened last night … after I blacked out?" I asked, taking a seat at the square table, my muscles protesting every movement.

"You don't remember anything after you fell?" my father asked, eyeing my mother carefully.

"No! Everything started to spin, then went black. I only remember waking up this morning," I explained.

My mother and father exchanged worried glances.

"What is it?" I asked nervously, looking between the two of them.

"It's just that after you fell, you started rambling on and on about planets, and running, and someone named Jack or something," my mother began.

My face flushed.

"It didn't make any sense, so we got pretty worried," my father added. "We were going to take you to the emergency room, but then you quieted down and said you just wanted to go to sleep, so I carried you upstairs and put you on your bed," he continued.

"I was afraid you had a concussion, so I stayed awake to check on you every twenty minutes," my mother noted, looking down at her hands.

The sincerity in which she spoke was comforting. Though she constantly drove me crazy, I could not deny the fact that she truly cared about my well-being.

"Gosh, I don't remember any of that," I replied, feeling a bit confused. "I just remember everything going black, then falling."

"Well, last night was a bit …." my father stammered, his voice trailing off.

Turning toward the window once more, I watched as large tears began to form in his eyes. Seeing my father like this was heart-breaking. I had only ever seen him cry once and that was seven years ago when his father suddenly passed away.

"Dad, mom … listen," I began slowly. "I don't know why you chose to keep this secret from me for so long, but I'm sure you had your reasons. Though I may not fully understand these reasons, I want you both to know that I forgive you."

My parents stared at me, both with equally shocked expressions.

"Elara, we assumed you'd be really upset with us," my father began, looking relieved.

"You're not angry with us?" my mother asked, reaching out a hand; my father following suit.

Taking both of their hands into mine, I smiled as I looked into their eyes.

"I know people are only capable of choosing what they think is best at the time. I understand if you thought keeping this secret from me for so long was the right decision."

My words tasted bitter, remembering how harshly I lashed out toward Jax the night before.

"When did you grow up so quickly?" my father asked, letting go of my hand.

"Ha!" I laughed. "Let's just say that yesterday was a *very* interesting day."

"Honey, all we can say is that we *did* make the best decision we thought at the time. That decision was to bring a beautiful baby girl into a home that would love and support her," my father beamed, looking over at my mother.

"Do you mind if I ask a few questions?" I asked hesitantly, shifting my weight on the wooden chair.

"Of course not! Fire away," he nodded, leaning back in his chair.

"I would like to know where I came from?" I asked in a more serious tone.

I'm not sure why I asked them this question. It wasn't like they were going to tell me they hopped on a spaceship and flew to another planet to pick me up from some alien adoption agency, but still, I needed to hear their version of the story.

"Very well," my father began. "Your mother and I desperately wanted children, but after years of trying we ran out of options."

My mother's face fell as he spoke.

"It was me, not your mother," he said, pointing to his chest. "The reason we couldn't have children, that is," he continued awkwardly. "After over a year of waiting, our local adoption agency called us with the good news. They had a newborn girl that had recently come into their custody. After years of patiently waiting, we eagerly accepted their offer and within three days you were ours to take home to raise as our own."

"I understand," I said, nodding. "I guess what I'm trying to ask, is where exactly did I come from? Did they say why my parents had given me up for adoption? Do they even know who my biological parents are? Do you?"

My father and mother glanced at each other, unsure of what to say next.

"What?" I asked, my heart beginning to beat loudly in my chest.

"No one knows who your biological parents are, Elara," my mother started. "The agency told us that they found you on the steps of their door early one morning with a note attached."

"A note?" I interrupted. "What did it say?"

"This child's name is Elara and she was loved," my mother answered, looking down as she spoke.

I let out a deep sigh as the portrait Jax had given me appeared in my mind once more. Uncomfortably I swallowed, forcing the large lump of sadness back down into the pit of my stomach.

"The adoption agency in . . .?"

"Maine," interjected my father.

"Okay, so the adoption agency in Maine told you I just showed up on their doorstep with a note saying my name, but no explanation as to where I came from?" I asked, irritated by the lack of information.

"Yes," my father proceeded, eyeing my mother nervously. "I know it sounds strange, but please know that you have always been *our* daughter. From the moment they let us hold you, we never looked back. Never once, has a day passed that I don't count my blessings that you are in our life," he gushed, tears forming in his eyes once more.

"I believe you both; I do," I began, quick to recover. "It's just a lot to take in right now."

"Is there anything we can do to make this information ... easier to digest?" he asked.

"No. I think I just need some time alone to process everything."

"That's fine," my father nodded, eyeing my mother. "We understand. Take all the time you need."

I winced as I stood and slowly made my way back up the stairs to my room. I collapsed onto the bed, feeling helpless. Everything Jax had told me about my biological parents the previous night was proving true. My parents had confirmed the fact that I was adopted and no one knew who my biological parents were. I had so many questions I needed answers to and the only lifeline to my past was now gone because of my knee-jerk reaction.

"Why did I over-react like that and tell him to stay away from me?" I scolded myself. "Even if I wanted to see Jax again, I have no way of contacting him. Maybe if I went back to the trail and waited he would appear? Not likely," I corrected myself.

My thoughts were interrupted by a buzzing noise coming from my cell phone. Wishing I had the power to levitate objects, I groaned, reaching for the vibrating phone on my bedside table. A ball of anxiety hit my stomach when I noticed the text message was from Cyrus.

"Hey trouble maker! How did detention go?"

Even though the thought of Cyrus and I being related seemed absurd, I couldn't help but now look at him differently. Feeling guilty, I placed the phone back onto the table without responding. Cyrus and I had always been honest with each other so it pained me to keep this giant secret from him.

"I surely am not going to be the one to break the news to him," I thought, as I rolled over onto my stomach, planting my face into soft bed.

"Jax?" I whispered quietly into the comforter.

Some naïve part of me hoped he would hear my call. Frustrated, I rolled off the bed, deciding to head to the trail in hopes of finding some way to contact him. Before heading down stairs I lifted the lamp, verifying the fragile picture was still secure and out of sight.

"I'm going for a walk!" I yelled through the house, limping down the last few steps.

To my surprise, both of my parents appeared around the corner within an instant.

"Where are you going?" my father asked carefully.

My mother stood close by, her face full of apprehension.

"I just need to get out for a while, you know. Do some thinking," I replied, trying to downplay my urgency to get back to the trail.

"Okay, well don't forget your phone," my mother said.

"Actually," I began, avoiding eye contact. "I'm going to leave it here. I don't want any distractions right now."

My mother began to protest, but was quickly silenced by my father. I could tell he was feeling guilty and would have likely let me get away with anything that day. I knew I was using the circumstances as leverage but in that moment, I didn't care. I needed to get to the trail. I *needed* to find Jax.

CHAPTER 16

I took off toward the trail, as fast as my sore legs would carry me. I ran for the first block, but was stopped abruptly by my cramping side. Irritated, I slowed my pace to a brisk walk, recalling the effortless attempt of last night's sprint.

"Who am I kidding?" I thought, feeling deflated. "I told him, rather rudely, to stay away from me. Could I really expect him to be waiting for me with open arms?"

In the distance, I noticed the trail head come into view. Once ominous and fearful, it now looked inviting, beckoning to me as though it had all the answers to the questions that raced through my mind. The cool wind blew gently, soothing my sore face. I took a small step onto the trail, the dry mulch crunching loudly under my shoes.

Minutes turned into hours, as I aimlessly searched the trail for Jax. I retraced every step trying to find the exact spot he had appeared. I tried running for as fast and far as I could, over and over, in an attempt to recreate the previous night's effortless movement only to be humbled with exhaustion and even more frustration.

I squinted, searching for the once vivid bird's nest high in the trees, only to feel my eyes water from the sun's intense rays. My once detailed, power of sight had seemed to return to its normal 20/20 vision.

Desperate, I tried yelling for help, curious to see if a distress signal would call him back to me. This effort was short lived when a jogger swiftly came to my aid. Looking concerned she asked what was wrong. I quickly lied, informing her she must have been hearing things. Unamused, she shook her head before continuing her quick pace. Plopping onto the hard ground, I began questioning my sanity.

"This is crazy! What am I doing? Running, calling out for help? He's not coming back and it's all my fault. I should be thankful he's gone and out of my life, instead of acting like a mental person chasing after a shadow," I thought, tossing my head up to the sky.

Sighing, I pulled myself to my knees, feeling my sore muscles protest with every movement. Placing a hand on the ground to steady myself, I was surprised to feel a cool, hard object. My heart nearly leapt out of my chest when I noticed it wasn't just any object, but an old knife: Jax's knife! My mind raced, recalling how I had removed the knife from the hard ground only to drop it when he had reappeared.

"I guess he never came back for it?" I thought, my mood suddenly lifting. "Maybe there's a slight chance that this knife is special to him and he will have to come back for it," I thought, feeling re-energized.

I smiled, feeling victorious for the first time in weeks. I now had something of his; something tangible. Carefully I folded the sharp blade into the handle and slid it uncomfortably into my pocket before heading back to the entrance of the trail.

My parents greeted me as soon as I came through the door. I was taken aback by their cheerful mood, but they seemed equally as taken aback by mine. It was funny how finding a simple object could change my entire perspective. Just having something that belonged to Jax suddenly made me feel not alone, and that was a relief.

"Well, you seem in better spirits," my mother grinned.

"Yeah … I guess I am," I smiled, popping my neck.

My mother began to protest this behavior, but was cut short by a gentle nudge from my father.

"Your mother and I were thinking of taking you out to dinner tonight; anywhere you'd like."

I exhaled, unsure how to decline the kind offer.

"Mom, Dad, I see what you guys are trying to do here, but it isn't necessary. I just need some time alone to digest all of this ... new information."

"I understand," my father said, looking disheartened.

"Why don't the two of you go out?" I suggested. "I mean how long has it been since you've gone out on a date?"

"She has a point, Rog," my mother added, looking up at my father.

"I don't know if we should leave you alone right now."

"Dad! I'm fine. I'll just order a pizza and catch up on some homework," I lied.

"Hmm ... well only if you're sure. I guess it would be good for your mom and I to get out of the house and talk everything over."

"See! It's a win for everyone," I said, a little overly excited as I headed toward the stairs.

"You'll call us if you need anything?" he asked, resting a hand on the wooden banister.

"Promise," I assured him, smiling.

It was odd how nothing, but at the same time everything, had changed between my parents and me. There remained a comfortable, familiarity about their presence but now a strange, empty void occupied the space as well. I still looked at them as my parents, but with all this new information, how could I not see them differently?

I spent the rest of the afternoon sprawled across my bed feeling exhausted, falling in and out of sleep. I would wake, startled, forgetting where I was, then doze off yet again dreaming of random people at my school and never-ending trails that ran in circles.

Something hard poked me in the ribs as I attempted to roll over. Groaning, I removed Jax's knife from beneath me, examining it once more. Carefully I opened the large blade, curious to see if the stains were in fact rust – or blood. It was hard to tell. I brushed my finger across the smooth metal. Whatever it was had been there for a while and was un-phased by my finger's presence. Shuddering at my own thoughts, I tried folding the blade back into the handle with one hand. Profanity escaped from me, as the gray handle twisted awkwardly. The sharp blade slammed down on the side of my index finger, immediately exposing a deep gash.

Running to the bathroom, I quickly opened the bottom drawer to find a limited stash of bandages. Sifting through the old, discolored box, I managed to find one small circular and one large knuckle bandage.

"This has to suffice," I thought, quickly ripping open the thin paper of the knuckle bandage.

Warm blood began trickling down my wrist.

"Ah," I protested, hurrying to the sink to wash away the blood that now dripped down my forearm.

The oddly shaped bandage did the job and fortunately the bleeding stopped as suddenly as it started. Leaving the bathroom, I flipped the light switch out of habit only to be taken aback when more light filled the small space. I looked through the bathroom door toward my bedroom windows, noticing the sun was no longer visible in the evening sky. My hand, still resting on the switch flipped it back to the off position. I gasped. The only noticeable difference between the light switch being on and off was the color of the light being displaced. When switched on, the light in the bathroom glowed a warm, yellow hue and when switched off, instead of total darkness, it now looked as though someone had replaced the bulbs with cool, white light.

I stood motionless; the only movement coming from my hand switching the light on, then off again. Amazed, I remembered back to the previous night on the trail. I could now see perfectly clear in total darkness, just as I could then.

Walking around my bedroom like a visitor, I inspected my night vision eye sight. I opened drawers, looked under the bed, ran back to the bathroom and walked around the closet; my mouth open in awe.

I walked out of my room and down the hallway, relieved that I no longer had to run to turn on lights. Whatever this new talent was, I felt grateful. My fear of the dark was no longer an issue. Feeling awake and refreshed as I did every night, I bounded down the stairs, relieved that the soreness in my legs was gone.

I made my way to the kitchen, noticing the time of half-past six displayed on the microwave clock. My parents wouldn't be home for hours, which left me plenty of time to investigate this new talent, uninterrupted. I smiled, grabbing a protein bar from the pantry. The usually dim space now glowed brightly. Leaning against the cool granite island, I thought back to Jax's words on the trail.

"What exactly did he mean by powers?" I wondered curiously. "The trail. Night on the trail!" I thought excitedly. "Maybe he will appear again, if I'm back on the trail at night."

Shoving the last bite of the card board-like protein bar into my mouth, I ran to the coat closet, grabbing a khaki canvas zipper jacket, then slipped my feet into an old pair of boots. I shut and locked the door behind me before jogging to the trail head once more.

I smiled gleefully as I took in the sights around me. Raccoons rummaged for food near curbside trash cans, while birds sat quietly high up in their nests. The wind was still and the air temperature felt significantly warmer than the previous night. I could see the trail head coming into view. I stopped suddenly, realizing that I had run the entire way. My breathing was slow and rhythmic. My side was void of any pain and my once sore muscles now felt limber and rested.

"Amazing," I thought, continuing my jog-like pace.

Before, I wondered if adrenaline was the cause of these super-human like powers, but now I could see that something had changed. Something inside of me was different. I didn't stop running until I reached the area where Jax had appeared. Slowing my pace to a walk, I began scanning the thick woods around me. He was nowhere in sight. Shutting my eyes tightly, I strained my ears for the familiar popping noise. Apparently, my hearing had not improved along with my new eye sight. Desperate, I began calling out his name.

"Jax? Jax? Okay, I sort of believe you. You can come back now!" I yelled toward the motionless trees.

A shuffling sound nearby, startled me. My heart leapt as my head whipped around, only to be let down when I noticed a family of opossums congregating near an old rotting log.

"Who am I kidding?" I thought irritated. "He isn't here. Why did I think tonight would be any different from earlier today? Why did he listen to me? If all of this was so important to him, then why hasn't he come back? He said he waited nine years to contact me? Does he just give up that easy? He was right about my parents adopting me and obviously right about some sort of strange super-human power, but being born on another planet, that was insanity. Right?" I asked myself aloud, nodding in agreement.

I turned my head back and forth looking between the tall pine trees.

"Oh man, now who's the crazy one?" I thought, giving up the search and deciding to turn back home. "I'm the one who is talking to myself alone in the woods at night."

I jogged the remainder of the way home, delighted with the newly found stamina. My eyes shifted back and forth, admiring the sights.

"Why was I so afraid of the dark before?" I wondered.

The trees, the birds, everything that was seen in the day was still present at night. The darkness was truly just the absence of light and nothing more.

The house was as quiet as I had left it. I bounded up the stairs, never reaching for the light switch. Tossing the worn coat onto my bed, I noticed my cell phone glowing on the night stand. I paused before picking it up.

There was a small, red "1" above the voicemail icon. I had missed a call from Cyrus. My stomach churned, as my finger pressed the play button.

"Hey Elara, it's Cyrus. My dad is driving me crazy about my college applications so I'm going to get out of the house for a while. Text me if you want to hang out later."

I collapsed onto the bed, letting the phone fall from my hand.

"How will I ever face Cyrus? Everything is so different now. I have this huge burden of information that I hardly believe myself. How could I share that with him? What am I supposed to do? Waltz up to him and say, "Hey Cyrus, sorry I couldn't hang out this weekend but I got held up by that stalker guy. Turns out he knew us when we were born and told me that not only are we adopted, but we are twins! Oh wait, there's more. He also said we both have super powers and are from another planet! Anyway, so how was your weekend?"

I scoffed, rubbing my eyes. The entire situation sounded even worse when played out in my mind. My head turned, hearing keys unlocking the front door. I could hear laughing as my parents walked into the house. I glanced at the time, surprised to see it was only 7:56 p.m.

"Elara?" my father called.

"Upstairs," I answered, quickly heading down to meet them. "You guys weren't gone long." I noted, sitting on the middle of the stairs.

"We just grabbed a quick bite," my father answered while helping my mother with her coat.

"We didn't want to leave you alone for too long tonight," she added, tossing her fingers through her short blonde hair, then stopped suddenly as if seeing a ghost.

"Honey, why are all of the lights off?" she asked, squinting in my direction. "What are you doing sitting in the dark? It's pitch black in here," she continued, deeply concerned, looking over at my father.

"Oh," I stuttered, feeling as though my secret had been outed.

A small smile slowly crept across my face.

"I … guess I didn't notice."

CHAPTER 17

The ear-piercing sound of the alarm clock caused my eyes to shoot open. I groaned, stretching uncomfortably to reach the entirely too small off button. My stomach churned with anxiety. I dreaded the thought of returning to school.

The past two weeks had been a disaster. The weekend of freedom I spent looking for Jax and exploring my new powers was short-lived after my parents came home early, only to find me sitting alone in the dark. Concerned for my well-being, they refused to leave me alone and began treating me like a fragile person in need of constant supervision. Weekends were now labeled "family weekends" and involved running errands with my mother, lunch outings, dinners at home and game nights on Sundays.

I had hoped school would be an escape from this absurdity, but unfortunately it had the opposite effect. Unsure of how to face Cyrus, I decided it was best to avoid him every way possible. Knowing his schedule made it easy for me to dash from class to class, taking different routes to prevent any contact. The most challenging part of the day was Astronomy, where he was impossible to avoid.

The first Monday back at school after the long weekend of ignoring Cyrus's text and calls was brutal. I sat in Astronomy, anxiously awaiting his arrival. His reaction when he saw me was nothing less than alarming.

"Elara! What happened to you?" he asked, tossing his bag on the floor before examining my bruised face.

I had tried concealing the injury with some old makeup that I rarely wore, but my efforts were ineffective. The once purple and blue bruise had changed colors to an unflattering greenish brown.

"I'm fine," I lied, letting my hair casually fall over my discolored face. "I just tripped and fell onto our stair railing," I continued, refusing to meet his gaze.

"Is that why I didn't hear from you all weekend? I had a feeling something was wrong, but I didn't want to just show up at your house uninvited."

"I was busy," I replied, opening the Astronomy text book.

"What's wrong?" he demanded, trying to make eye contact. "Something's off – you're not yourself."

"Nothing is wrong!" I snapped, slamming the book shut.

Cyrus paused, surprised by my harsh response.

"You're not a very good liar, Elara," he stated, taking his seat and facing forward.

Warm tears began to form in my eyes. I blinked, trying to force them away while turning my head to look out the classroom window. I hated treating Cyrus this way, but I didn't know how to act around him anymore. Keeping a secret of this magnitude was physically painful.

The remainder of the week followed the same agonizing pattern. Every day after school I bolted from my seat past Cyrus, hoping to avoid any further communication and headed straight to the library. Once there, I would find a dimly lit back corner where I would finish my homework and wait until dark, so I could take the trail home in hopes of finding Jax. I lied to my parents, telling them I was swamped with school assignments and found it easier to focus while working in the library. This plan was successful only if I got home no later than 6:00 p.m., which usually gave me no more than thirty minutes to look for Jax.

I was frustrated beyond belief and had never felt so alone in all my life. My parents were driving me crazy; Cyrus, my only true friend and supposed twin brother, had to be avoided at all costs; and then there was Jax, who I was convinced was gone forever and may as well have been a figment of my imagination.

I sighed, looking up at the ceiling of my bedroom. I dreaded getting out of bed, but was practical enough to know that I couldn't spend the rest of the day sulking without my mother finding me.

I pointed and flexed both feet. My calf muscles ached. The countless nights running the trails searching for Jax had taken its toll. Every morning my body protested the previous evening's routine.

"Note to self," I thought, swinging my sore legs slowly off the bed. "Stretch before and after running escapades."

Grunting loudly, I hobbled into the bathroom like an elderly person, pausing to take note of my reflection. The bruise, once painful and discolored, was now barely visible. Only a small yellow spot no larger than a dime was a vanishing reminder of my time with Jax.

I opened the small bathroom drawer to the left of the sink. There lay Jax's knife looking alone and forgotten. Taking the knife from the drawer, I walked to my bedroom and tossed it carelessly, into the bottom of my back pack. I wasn't exactly sure why I decided to bring the knife to school that day, but for some strange reason I found comfort having it near me.

Grateful it was the last day of school before winter break, I quickly made my way into the main building, shivering from the frigid air. Another unexpected cold front had blown in the night before, leaving everyone unprepared for near-freezing temperatures.

For the past week, I had hiked around the entire school building to avoid running into Cyrus, but with the day's bitter cold weather, I decided to take my chances. I rapidly regretted my decision once I was inside the warm rotunda. No sooner had I attempted to round the corner of the main hall, did my skin began to prickle, warning me that Cyrus was near. I skidded to a stop when I saw him leaning against a locker, distracted by a fellow classmate. Just as I began to turn to head in the opposite direction, his head snapped toward me. Our eyes locked onto one another's for the first time in over two weeks. I froze, unsure of my next move then quickly turned and sprinted back toward the school's front door.

I squinted as the icy wind pierced my eyes, causing them to water. Swiftly, I jogged the remainder of the way around the main building to the portables. My side cramped and the frigid air burned my lungs as I was forced to slow my pace.

"This is ridiculous," I scolded myself. "I can't keep avoiding Cyrus like this. He has done nothing to me, yet I avoid him like the plague."

My thoughts dissolved as the familiar warming sensation moved throughout my entire body once more.

"Elara!"

My head turned toward the sound of my name, already knowing who I would find.

There stood Cyrus, only a few feet away from the portable buildings. His arms were folded tightly across his broad chest. The cold wind whipped around us as the first bell sounded, ringing loudly across the school grounds. I shut my eyes, wishing myself away from the confrontation. To my disappointment my powers did not mimic the disappearing act that Jax had displayed that night on the trail. When I opened them, there, only inches from my face, stood Cyrus.

"You can't keep avoiding me like this."

I sighed, finally surrendering.

"I know," I replied, looking at the ground.

He nodded for me to follow him behind the portable building where we were out of view of the overly zealous hall monitors.

Cyrus leaned his muscular back against the aluminum framed building, his arms still crossed.

"So…" he began.

"So … what?" I asked, finally meeting his gaze.

He laughed loudly, his pearly teeth glowing.

"So … what did I do to make you avoid me like you avoid Hillary?"

I smirked, acknowledging his little joke.

"Cyrus, you didn't do anything," I began in a more serious tone.

"You're not giving me the 'it's not you, it's me speech' are you?" he asked, still smiling.

"What?" I stuttered.

"Elara, I'm going to give it to you straight. Lately you are the only person I can be myself around. My parents are driving me nuts and how I ever put up with Hillary and all of her craziness, I'll never know. When I'm around you I feel centered … relaxed. I can tell you anything. You …" his voice trailed off.

"You what?" I asked, cautiously.

"You can't say you don't feel something," he said, resting his tan hand on mine.

"Oh no!" I began, shaking my head quickly side to side.

"I see. So … this is what rejection feels like," he said, taking a step back while lifting his hand from mine.

"Ah," I laughed nervously. "No, it's not what you think," I said, hiding my face in my cold hands.

My stomach tightened and mind raced as I tried to decipher a way to explain what Jax had told me that night.

"Remember my stalker?" I began.

"You sure do change the subject fast," he stated, sounding hurt.

"I'm not trying to change the subject! Please, just let me finish," I said, holding up a hand. "Do you remember him?" I repeated.

"Of course, I remember him. I almost hit him with my car," he replied, sounding irritated.

"Well … I ran into him on the trail the other night while walking home. You know, the day I had to stay after school for detention."

"Wait a second," he started, taking a step closer. "Is he the reason for your bruised face?" he asked, his voice raising as he spoke.

"What? No! Gosh no! I really did fall and hit the stair railing," I replied defensively.

Cyrus paused, looking unconvinced.

"Continue," he nodded, uncrossing his arms.

"Okay, so I ran into him on the trail and at first I was totally freaked out, but then he explained the reason why he had been following me. He also gave me some information about my past that no one would have known about. I didn't even know about it. I thought he was completely mental, until I got home and asked my parents and they confirmed most of it."

"Confirmed what?" he asked.

I paused clenching my jaw tightly.

"Confirmed … what, Elara?" he repeated, this time sounding even more agitated.

"That I'm adopted. My parents adopted me only days after I was born and decided to never tell me."

Cyrus's eyes widened.

"Wow! I don't know what to say. No wonder you didn't want to hang out that weekend," he exclaimed, looking relieved.

I nodded anxiously, knowing Cyrus was completely oblivious to the emotional bomb I was about to drop.

"That's crazy that they kept a secret like that from you for so long! I'd be furious," he continued. "But, I don't understand why that would make you avoid me? Why didn't you just tell me? I don't care that you are adopted. That doesn't change how I feel."

The knot in my stomach enlarged, as I shifted my weight nervously.

"And that guy?" he asked.

"Jax?"

"Yeah, how did he know you were adopted? What is he, like a private eye or something?"

"Something like that," I breathed hard, letting the air rush out of my lungs. "He also informed me of another ... important detail of my past."

The bitter taste of bile slowly crept its way up my esophagus, causing me to clear my throat louder than necessary.

"What's that?" he asked.

"Cyrus, there is no easy way to say or try and explain this to you, because honestly, I'm still trying to figure it all out. You'll probably think I've lost my mind, but here it goes ... our birthday's being the same day are not a coincidence."

His eyebrows rose, creasing his tan forehead.

"I'm not following you."

"The reason I've been avoiding you these past two weeks is simply because, I know how to act around you as my friend, but I don't know how to act around you ... as my brother."

I paused, feeling some relief that I had not blown chunks all over the both of us.

"You're not making any sense, Elara," he said, looking uncomfortable.

"Listen, I know this sounds completely insane and trust me, I thought the exact same thing when Jax told me everything, but it is the truth."

Cyrus stood motionless, still trying to process what I had just told him.

"Here's the part where it gets interesting; not only are we brother and sister but we are ... twins. Apparently, the adoption agency didn't have a problem splitting us up," I continued, my voice slightly shaking.

"Wait a second," he laughed, shaking his head. "You're wanting me to believe that I'm adopted and you and I are not only brother and sister, but twins?" he asked, rolling his eyes.

"I understand how you feel right now. I felt the exact same way, but you have got to ask your parents!"

Cyrus crossed his strong arms once more, his eyes narrowing with frustration. The heat radiating throughout my body intensified, as he spoke.

"What? You want me to just stroll up to my parents, and say hey mom and dad, what made you want to adopt a baby eighteen years ago?"

"I'm not saying to do it like that," I said, the heat continuing to build.

"You don't have any proof, Elara! What, some random dude shows up on the trail and informs you that both of us are adopted and you actually believe him!" he barked.

"No! I didn't believe him at first! It wasn't until he vanished and then reappeared out of thin air did I finally stopped to listen to what he had to say."

Cyrus scoffed, shifting his weight.

I continued quickly, feeling as though I were running out of time with my poor attempt at explaining.

"When he came back, he handed me an old picture of two babies and their parents. When I looked at the man in picture, our *father*, it was as though I was looking at you, only older.

Cyrus rubbed a hand over his blond hair, shaking his head, reminding me of myself when Jax had attempted explaining all of this.

"This is insane! Maybe you hit your head harder than you thought," he snapped.

"That was low," I remarked, looking away.

"Elara, I'm sorry that you have had a rough couple of weeks finding out you're adopted and all, but trying to pull me into the middle of it is just bizarre. I mean I thought Hillary was crazy but...."

"And, that was even lower," I muttered, hurt by his harsh words.

We stood silently, awkwardly looking away from one another. My skin continuing to surge with heat in waves, like electricity flowing through a wire.

"I have to go," he said, turning toward the main building.

"Cyrus, please don't leave, not like this!" I begged. "I didn't know how to tell you. There isn't an easy way...."

He whipped around, his face only inches from mine.

"Then maybe you shouldn't have told me!" he hissed.

My hands buzzed and shook violently. The heat, now so intense, felt as though it may burst through my skin at any moment. I should have been frightened, but somehow felt energized and more awake than I had in weeks. I stood my ground, not backing down from Cyrus.

The muscles in his jaw tightened, as his hands closed into tight fist.

"I had no choice but to tell you," I argued. "Strange things are happening to us, Cyrus. We can't pretend that the car accident, the crazy strength you showed on the football field and the incident at NASA were all just random events. You know something is going on, something we both can't explain! Then the very same guy who has been following me for months, appears out of thin air...."

"Just stop, Elara!" he yelled.

"No! I'm not going to stop until you listen to me and...."

"THAT'S ENOUGH," he shouted, loud enough for the entire school to hear.

Cyrus breathed hard, as every muscle in his body tensed with anger. I was silent, but continued to stand my ground.

"Stay away from me, Elara!" he warned, his voice barely above a whisper.

I stood motionless, watching Cyrus storm off toward the parking lot, never once looking back. The warm, buzzing feeling slowly drained from my body as Cyrus disappeared down the steep hill.

My brave, stand-up-for-myself posture quickly dissolved as tears stung my eyes. Instantly, I felt the reality of the situation sink in; I was now completely alone. The relationship between my parents and me would never be the same; Jax was gone; and now Cyrus. I had single-handedly managed to isolate myself from everyone in my life.

I wiped a warm tear from my cheek with the back of my hand. The idea of walking into Señora Lopez's classroom late and in my current condition wasn't a viable option. Without giving it further thought, I began jogging back to the main building toward the parking lot. I made it down the steep hill, just in time to see Cyrus's car speed out of the lot.

Never had I seen Cyrus so upset. He had perfect attendance and for him to skip class like this was completely out of character.

I groaned aloud, feeling responsible.

"I should've never said anything," I thought, irritated.

Just then, Mr. Leeland, our school's truant officer, walked out of the main building, turning his collar up to shield himself from the cold. I had only moments to hide before he would surely find me out of class, standing at the bottom of the hill.

I looked toward the school's main road, knowing I would be spotted almost instantly if I tried that route. My only hope of getting off campus and out of sight was the trail. I sprinted up the hill and past the football stadium, not stopping until I was a few hundred yards inside the wooded trail.

Breathing heavily, and rubbing my aching side, I slowed to a casual walk. I shifted the heavy backpack uncomfortably. Something hard from inside the bag poked at my ribs. I paused, reaching awkwardly to retrieve the unwanted item.

"Jax's knife," I remembered, pulling it from the bag.

The dull sky made the worn handle look even more gray than it had this morning. Carefully, I exposed the sharp blade. I gently turned it over in my hand, noticing a small engraving etched along the bottom of the knife blade. I squinted, running my fingers across the fine print. It was barely visible and looked as though someone had attempted to scratch out the tiny letters.

"For..." I said aloud, trying to decipher the small words. "For my..." I continued.

I paused, unable to read the last word.

"For my son," clarified the familiar, silky voice that filled the empty space around me. I gasped, dropping the knife.

CHAPTER 18

My mouth gaped. After weeks of his absence, no more than five feet away stood Jax looking as though he never left. Feeling as though the air had been siphoned out of my lungs, I gasped for more oxygen. Unable to move, I watched Jax casually walk toward me, seemingly unaffected by the freezing weather. He bent down slowly to retrieve the knife that lay at my feet. As he stood, I marveled how his scarred hand effortlessly closed the knife blade in one quick flick. Acknowledging our proximity, he cautiously took two steps backward before slipping the knife into his back pocket. Jax's warm breath left his mouth in small white clouds. The shock that had come over me quickly changed from frustration to anger.

"How dare he just show up out of thin air after weeks of searching," I thought, my posture shifting.

Intuiting my frustration, he looked down, running a pale hand through his dark hair.

"Elara…."

"No," I interrupted. "You don't get to speak right now. Not until I've said what I have been wanting to say for days!" I said, taking a step forward. "Do you realize what I've been going through the past few weeks? First you chase me through the trail, nearly frightening me to death and then you tell me the most bizarre story I have ever heard in my life. Next, you disappear only to return with a picture of my biological parents who happen to be dead and then really push me over the edge by telling me that Cyrus is my twin brother!"

"Elara, I…"

"No! Not until I've finished," I yelled.

The wind blew my hair around my face, making me look more comical than serious. Quickly, I tried taming the wild strands that were now blowing in every direction. I sighed, giving up, continuing with my speech.

"Then you disappear, leaving me without any answers. My parents, or adoptive parents for argument's sake, now feel like strangers in my home. I am forced to lie and avoid my only friend, who just so happens to be my twin brother. I have never felt more alone in my life, and where were you Jax? Nowhere! Did I mention I have spent every day searching this trail looking for you, acting completely mental in hopes that you would reappear once again out of thin air? Oh, and let's not forget these 'powers' that I now possess. Here Elara, take these new powers and figure them out all on your own. ALONE!"

I was winded after the long outburst, but felt relieved that I finally got the opportunity to get everything off my chest.

Jax stood unmoving from his position on the trail. He breathed slowly and calmly, listening intently to my tirade.

"I told Cyrus he was my twin brother today. You can imagine how well that went," I added sarcastically, throwing up my hands.

Jax's blue eyes focused carefully on mine as I continued to speak.

"You know what he said? He told me that I was crazy and to stay away from him. So, thanks a lot, Jax! Now my only friend never wants to see me again."

An unexpected tear glided down my cheek. I brushed it away, looking at the ground, allowing my long hair to hide my face.

Letting out a long, deep breath, Jax closed his eyes briefly. The mulch path crunched loudly under his boot, as he took a small step forward. I stood rigid, arms folded tightly across my chest.

"May I be permitted to speak now?" he asked cautiously.

I shrugged my shoulders, refusing to meet his gaze.

"Elara, *you* were the one who told me to stay away, remember?"

His words felt like a punch in the gut.

"If it were up to me, I would have never left you alone with all of this new information to digest," he continued.

His silky voice was calm and soothing. The anger that boiled through my veins slowed to a simmer as I continued to listen to his side of the story.

"As soon as I jumped back to Aroonyx, I regretted leaving you but then and only then did I realize the severity of the situation."

"And what exactly is the situation?" I interrupted.

"The simple fact that I had to see if you were strong enough. I had to see that you could take a blow and keep moving forward. That you wouldn't give up and just fall apart the second things weren't working out the way you intended them to."

My jaw slowly opened.

"So, this was all some sort of stupid test?" I barked. "Jax, I have spent weeks searching for you so I could get some answers to the million questions that occupy my brain 99% of the time…"

He scoffed, shaking his head.

"Weeks? You are upset because you've waited weeks to see me again? Nine years, Elara. I have patiently waited nine, very long years to contact you and then when I finally get that moment, you tell me you never want to see me again!"

His voice was still calm and silky, but also had an edginess to it that was alarming.

165

"So, forgive me, Elara," he continued, "if I don't sympathize with your sadness about Cyrus's reaction to the truth."

I stood, unmoving once more. His words sliced through my soul, causing me to reflect on my behavior. I had never thought of anyone besides myself during these last few weeks. Not my parents, not Jax, not even Cyrus. I had been selfish, only concerned for my own feelings and comfort.

"Okay...." I began, looking down, feeling like a child who had just been scolded.

"Forgive me, Elara." His tone was milder. "For I am not a sensitive or emotional person. I have spent a lot of time on my own, which has led me to have a somewhat... detached personality."

His eyes never left mine as he spoke. He never shifted his stance or looked the slightest bit uncomfortable, standing there in the freezing weather. I swallowed, attempting to collect my emotions before speaking.

"Jax, I don't know what to say. Yes, I'm angry because these last few weeks have been physically painful to get through. Yes, I'm angry that you left, even though I told you or yelled at you, for that matter, to stay away and I haven't a clue what is happening to me or why you have come to find me. I feel alone and honestly, I feel...scared."

I sighed, feeling the tension slowly dissipate from my body. I took in Jax's appearance for the first time that day. His eyes, exactly as I remembered them, mirrored my own. The bright, sapphire blue color sparkled vividly against his pale skin. His clean-shaven face was youthful but hardened. His jet-black hair, unlike mine, seemed to obey the wind by blowing every strand in the same direction. His clothes, rugged and worn, looked as though he had them for years. He hardly flinched as a long gust of wind whipped through the trail, sending a shiver down my spine.

Jax paused, turning his head slightly to observe me before speaking.

"I can understand that the information I gave you that night must have felt overwhelming."

I raised my eyebrows.

"But I had my reasons for staying away and please remember that it was you who initiated my banishment."

I nodded, feeling scolded once more. My arms tightened around my body, as I shifted my weight uncomfortably.

A small smirk crept over his face.

"What?" I asked irritated.

"It's just that I notice your posture changes quite drastically when you get upset," he answered.

I paused, amazed by his detailed observation.

"And yours doesn't change at all!" I snapped back.

A big grin crossed his face as he shook his head, taking another step forward.

"Truce?" he asked, extending his right hand.

My hand shot out as a habit, but I hesitated before allowing our hands to meet.

"Promise me you won't disappear again?" I questioned, my hand still outstretched.

"Promise me you won't ask me to?" he quickly responded, still smiling.

"Deal," I nodded, taking his hand.

"Deal," he said, grasping mine in return.

CHAPTER 19

His hand was cold and rough, looking much older than his general appearance. Jax's eyes never left mine as he shook my hand firmly, then casually let go, crossing his toned arms.

"So…" he began.

"So now what?" I interrupted.

He laughed, tossing his ebony hair out of his eyes.

"You don't have much patience, do you?" he asked, lifting his eyebrows.

"Not when it's freezing cold and my life has been turned upside down," I replied, shivering.

"Well, then where would you like me to begin?"

"Uh…let's see. I don't know, maybe the part where you left off about me being from another planet? That seems as good a place as any," I replied sarcastically.

Jax paused before speaking, as if weighing his options.

"You and your twin brother Cyrus were born on a planet called Aroonyx."

"Aroonyx? What kind of name is that?" I asked, making a face while trying to pronounce the unfamiliar word.

"What kind of name is Earth?" he countered.

Once again, I was left stumbling over my words and once again a smirk slowly crept over Jax's face.

"Shall I continue?" he asked.

Annoyed, I waved a hand in acceptance before once again folding my arms tightly across my chest.

"Aroonyx is a planet much different than Earth. One of the main differences between the two planets…."

"Jax," I interrupted once more. "I'm really trying to be patient, but honestly I could care less about the history of Arinyx…."

"Aroonyx," he corrected.

"Right. Aroonyx. I really just want to know how I got here," I said, bobbing up and down in attempts to stay warm.

He was quiet as he took in every word I said before speaking once more.

"Okay, fair enough. Why don't we try it this way? You ask the questions and I will do my best to answer them for you."

"Perfect!" I agreed, feeling accomplished for the first time that day.

My mind raced, examining every question that had gone through my mind over the past few weeks. I popped my neck, feeling anxious as though I were on a game show with a strict time limit.

"Try to relax, Elara. There is a lot of information to cover, so don't feel pressed to ask every question today," Jax began, taking note of my nervous posture. "We have some time, though not as much as I would like."

"What are you a Sphinx with a riddle or something?" I asked, feeling even more anxious than before. "We have time but not much? What is that supposed to mean?"

"I'm unaware of the term 'Sphinx,'" he stated.

"What?" I asked, completely bewildered.

"You said a Sphinx with a riddle?" he answered, looking equally as confused.

I shook my head from side to side.

"Clearly, he wasn't from here," I thought.

"It's just an expression of sorts," I clarified. "But, that's beside the point! What do you mean we don't have much time?"

Jax smiled, amused by my overly anxious attitude.

"Well, if you would've let me finish explaining the history about the planet where you were born then you would understand why I said we have time, but not as much as I would like."

Tossing my hands up, I gave in.

"Okay, fine. I don't need information about the weather patterns or topography of the planet, but can you please explain the time reference you just referred to."

Sighing, Jax ran a hand through his dark hair before continuing.

"Time passes on Earth much differently than on Aroonyx. On Earth, time moves twice as fast, so for every year that passes on Aroonyx, two years pass on Earth."

"Wait," I interjected, holding up a hand. "When we first met, you told me that you knew me when I was born."

"Yes," he responded quickly.

My sharp mathematical mind suddenly came to an abrupt stop.

"I was thirteen when you were born," he added, as if sharing a clue.

"Two years for every year," I said, counting childlike on my fingers. "I'm eighteen now so that would make you...twenty-two?" I asked, my fingers quickly double-checking the math.

"Correct," he replied, sounding impressed.

"Eighteen years have passed here on Earth but only nine on Aroonyx? How is that possible? Why did you wait so long to come back and find me?" I asked, my mind attempting to put together the missing puzzle pieces.

"Elara, your calculations are accurate but unfortunately I am unable to answer the second part of your question. The reason for the drastic time differential between the two planets has yet to be discovered."

I sighed, disappointed with his response.

"Now, to answer the last part of your question," he continued. "I didn't wait nine years to come back and find you. I've kept a very close watch on you and Cyrus for your entire lives. It's only now, after you and your brother have come of age, that I can finally share this information with you."

"Why did everything Jax say seem to have some sort of cryptic message hidden in the wording?" I wondered.

"What do you exactly mean when you say come of age?" I asked, still shivering from the cold as I bounced my knees up and down trying to get warm. The frigid wind swirled around us, causing my eyes to squint. I exhaled, annoyed at how unaffected Jax was by the cold. He stood there calmly as though it were a comfortable 70 degrees outside.

"Would you like to continue this conversation somewhere warmer?" he asked, taking note of my less than subtle body tremors.

"That would be fantastic!" I rejoiced, hopping up and down. "Oh." I thought aloud, still bouncing to keep warm. "There's slight problem."

"What's that?" he asked.

"We can't go back to my house. My mother would…well let's just say, that isn't an option," I said, thinking of my mother's expression when she found out I skipped school only to bring home a rugged-looking older man.

"Somewhere else, then?" he asked, uncrossing his arms.

"There's a Starbucks not too far from here, if you don't mind walking?" I asked hopefully.

"What's a Starbucks?"

I laughed aloud.

"Wow, you really are from another planet."

Jax, clearly unamused by my humor, waited for my answer.

"It's just a place that sells coffee and tea," I replied my voice trailing off, confused by the fact that never in my life had I described a Starbucks to anyone.

"You are familiar with coffee and tea?" I asked, unsure of his response.

"Yes, but we only have tea leaves on Aroonyx. No coffee beans exist," he stated firmly.

"Right," I sighed, feeling more and more confused by the minute.

I motioned for him to follow as I walked past him.

"I hope you don't mind walking. It's about a mile or so from the entrance of my neighborhood. I don't have a car, so unless you brought one back with you from your planet we're out of luck." I stated, looking over my shoulder.

"Like I mentioned before," he began, finally moving from the spot where he had been standing for so long. "Aroonyx is very different from Earth. We do not have cars, or any transportation, for that matter."

"How do you get around?" I asked. "Horse and buggy?"

He smiled, brushing the hair out of his eyes as we walked side-by-side, our strides falling into a smooth rhythm.

"We get around...like this," he said, pointing to our feet as we walked.

"You walk everywhere!?" I asked, utterly shocked.

"You make it sound like such a bad thing," he replied.

"No! It's not that I don't like walking or anything. It's just that everything these days is so spread out. It would take forever to get anywhere."

"You must understand that Aroonyx has a very small, condensed population. The villages are close together. We do not have the same large mammals that roam here on Earth. Horses, cows, donkeys, oxen; none of them exist on Aroonyx."

"Wow!" I exclaimed, stopping to let this new fact settle.

I turned to look at Jax, now only inches from where I stood. He looked even taller standing next to me and his eyes looked as though they had seen a lifetime more than my own.

"Something wrong?" he asked.

"No, it's just really challenging for me to imagine another planet where people exist and thrive. My whole life I've been taught that there are no other life forms on any planets. I just...." My voice trailed off as a sudden feeling of disillusionment washed over me.

"Elara," Jax began softly, sensing my discomfort. "I told you when we first met that the information I was going to give you would be a shock to your nervous system and that you would have a hard time believing it. I don't expect you to accept this information with open arms or open eyes, for that matter. It will take time, but once you see Aroonyx for yourself it will start to all make sense."

"See Aroonyx?" I asked stuttering.

"That *was* the plan," he added, continuing down the trail. "I tried to show you the first night we met. Do you remember when I grabbed your wrist right before you ran off?"

"Uh yeah, I definitely remember that part!" I exclaimed, rubbing my arms to keep warm.

"I knew if you could see Aroonyx with your own eyes then you would believe me, but obviously, it didn't work.

"Why didn't it work?" I asked nervously.

"I was unsure at first, but once I returned back home it suddenly came to me and everything made sense."

A large branch snapped from a tall pine tree above, crashing loudly only inches away from Jax. I flinched, startled by the loud sound, but Jax on the other hand, took a defensive stance with his knife ready at his side. I laughed nervously, unsure of what to make of the situation.

"I don't think that branch will attack you," I whispered, teasing him.

In one smooth motion, Jax flipped the blade of the knife back into the handle, returning it to his pocket once more.

"Forgive me," he started, exhaling quietly.

I observed Jax as he stood silently, rubbing his thumb over a deep scar that covered the palm of his hand.

"How did you get that scar?" I asked curiously.

Ignoring me, as though he never even heard my question, he continued his explanation while walking down the winding trail.

"I first jumped to Earth with both you and Cyrus, so it would make sense that I would only be able to return to Aroonyx with the both of you. I believe that's why I couldn't jump with you alone."

"What is this jumping thing you keep referring to? Is that what you call it when you go back and forth from Earth to Aroonyx? Also, why do I hear that popping noise when you appear?" I asked.

"Popping noise?" he questioned, as we continued our walk together down the trail.

"I hear this loud popping noise right before you appear. It's how I always know I am about to see you. Except for that first time I saw you outside my window. Maybe you were too far away for me to hear it?" I wondered aloud. "It's like a weird warning or something. I even heard it right before Cyrus almost hit you with his car, but you were really close to us, so...."

He laughed aloud.

"Yes, that day I jumped a little too close, didn't I?"

"You were lucky Cyrus was so quick to react. Had I been driving, you would've been a goner," I smirked, looking over at him.

He smiled, his eyes remaining focused on the empty trail.

"I don't have an answer as to the strange noise you are referring to. I've never heard a noise when jumping to or from Earth."

I sighed, wishing he had an answer for the strange noise, but was eager to learn more about his vanishing act.

"Okay, but can you at least elaborate on the whole jumping thing?" I asked, pointing to the exit of the trail.

"Elara, I know you're not interested in a history lesson about Aroonyx, but there is some information you need to know for everything to make sense. I believe once you have a better understanding of how things work on Aroonyx, the context will change and perhaps you will be able to see the situation differently from the way you are currently seeing it."

I halted, turning to look up at Jax. An idea had formed in my mind and though it sounded crazy I knew it had to be done.

"Jax, I understand your point and I do agree with everything you just said, but before you begin can you do something for me?" I asked.

"What's that?" he questioned, crossing his arms.

"Could you go…or jump, back to Aroonyx and bring me something?"

"What do you want me to bring you?" he asked, curiously.

"I don't know…something you can only find there. I think I need a visual conformation that life exists on another planet," I stated, unsure of his response.

Jax paused, observing me carefully.

"I'm very much alive and you witnessed with your own eyes that I have the ability to travel to and from Aroonyx, also, I brought you the picture of your…."

"I know," I interrupted, feeling a familiar cold spot in the pit of my stomach.

"I just want to see something that I've never seen before. You look like any other human here on Earth and we have plenty of painted portraits of people. I need something new, something different that will convince me that I'm not just imagining all of this."

"I see," he said nodding, fully understanding my request. "It means that much to you?"

"It really does," I pleaded.

"Okay, I'll try but I can't guarantee that I can bring something back," he stated, uncrossing his arms.

"Thank you," I said, looking up at his bright blue eyes.

"I'll be right back."

In an instant, Jax vanished. I gasped, still taken aback by his disappearing act. Anxiously, I looked around, curious as to where he would reappear. I fished my cell phone out of my back pack and watched as the clock ticked away the minutes: five minutes, ten minutes, fifteen minutes dragged slowly by. I paced back and forth, wondering why it was taking him so long. Irrational thoughts occupied my mind as I impatiently waited.

"What if he couldn't get back?" I thought nervously. "Don't be foolish Elara! He has gone to and from Earth for nine years now! He wouldn't...."

POP! The familiar sound that once sent chills up my spine now sent relief. There, no more than five feet away, stood Jax covered in a light dust of snow. In his hand, he held something I had never seen before.

"You look freezing!" I said, moving to his side.

Amazed, I gently touched the frost that quickly began melting from his forearm.

"I wasn't gone too long, was I?" he asked, shaking the remaining snow dust from his hair.

I glanced at my phone.

"Twenty minutes or so," I replied.

"Sorry, I tried to hurry," he said, holding up a small item in his hand.

"What is it?" I asked, my hand gesturing to touch the unique gift.

"Elara, this is a Moon Drop. It is a rare flower found on Aroonyx, he proclaimed, gently placing it in the palm of my hand.

I marveled at the strange but beautiful flower. It's long, curvy black stem was soft to the touch, reminding me of silk. At the end of the delicate stem was a large, round tear-drop shaped bloom that was so white in color it appeared to glow. I turned the magnificent flower over in my hand as Jax continued to speak.

"The Moon Drop is not only rare but has unique qualities. Not only does it thrive in Aroonyx's harsh climates, but it will only bloom during the full moons."

"Moons?" I interrupted, my eyes never leaving the delicate flower.

"Yes, we have twin moons on Aroonyx," he smiled, watching me admire the fascinating gift. "This small flower spends its entire life growing into this perfect specimen. Once the full moons reach their highest point in the night sky, its petals will then slowly unfold, revealing a dust-like center that glows brightly in the moonlight. It will stay glowing until the sun breaks at dawn, but then crumbles to the ground into black ash, blowing away in the winds, never to be seen again."

Jax paused, watching me turn the flower over and over in my hand before speaking once more.

"Some find the story of the Moon Drop disheartening. They wonder about the purpose of this flower's life. To depend on our sun to grow and survive for its entire existence, but once mature that very same light that gave it such strength destroys it entirely. I don't agree with this theory, though. I don't believe the Moon Drop is ever destroyed by the sun. I believe it only changes form."

Time stood still as Jax spoke. A tear rolled slowly down my cheek, as I stood transfixed on the stunningly beautiful flower.

I wasn't sure if it was an emotional build-up from everything that had happened over the past few weeks, or the simple fact that the story of the Moon Drop hit a nerve that resonated deep within.

In that moment, something shifted. The stack of doubt that had been so heavily weighing on my shoulders disappeared entirely as I looked from the Moon Drop to Jax and back again.

I was ready. I was ready to know where I had come from and not only that, but I *wanted* to know. I wanted to know everything. The frustration about Jax appearing in my life, then disappearing, had vanished. The frustration with my adoptive parents, now gone completely. When I thought of Cyrus, I no longer felt sad or alone. I felt compassion and understood his reasons for feeling angry with me. My head snapped up. My mind was alive, refreshed, awakened.

"I'm ready," I said firmly.

"Are you sure?" he asked, a smile slowly crossing his handsome face. "Your life as you know it will change forever."

I exhaled deeply, accepting his terms.

"It already has," I replied, returning the unique flower to him.

He nodded, resting a hand on my shoulder.

"Then let's go back and start from the beginning."

CHAPTER 20

I felt warmer than I had all day as we continued our walk out of the trail and onto the wide sidewalk that wound to the edge of our community entrance. My mind felt sharp and ears alert, as Jax began his story.

"Let me take you back to a time when Aroonyx was ruled by a strong leader named Arun. Arun, a young Solin, was only…."

"Jax, I don't mean to keep interrupting, but I have no idea what you're talking about. What is a "young Solin?" I asked, stepping over a large crack in the gray sidewalk.

"Let me explain," he said, his posture relaxing more and more with every step we took. "Elara, there are two types of inhabitants living on Aroonyx: Solins and Lunins. Solins are born during the day and Lunins are born at night. They differ drastically both in their physical appearance and emotional qualities."

I nodded, rubbing my arms to keep warm.

"Physically, Solins have blonde, almost white hair and their eyes are vivid shades of orange. Also, they have a distinct, bronze complexion and are very muscular."

The image of Cyrus popped into my mind, as Jax described his features perfectly.

"Lunins are quite the opposite with their fair skin, black hair and eyes that vary from light to deep blue in color. Though less muscular than Solins, their bodies are well-toned," Jax continued.

I eyed Jax wondering if he had made an error in his description of Lunin's physiques. It was apparent his arms were well defined as his biceps showed easily through his tight-fitting shirt. My arms on the other hand, looked as though I had twigs stuck inside my sleeves.

We paused our quick pace, allowing a car to pass in front of us before starting across the busy street. Engaged in Jax's description of me and Cyrus's physical traits, I looked down at the pavement watching one foot follow the other, completely lost in thought.

My head popped up as Jax's arm shot out, grabbing my arm firmly. I stopped dead in my tracks, startled by his quick reaction time. An electric-powered car, which I never heard coming, had slammed on its breaks and stopped only a few feet from where we stood. My mouth gaped at the near miss as I looked up at Jax. The driver of the car, irritated by my lack of caution, blew the horn twice before speeding off through the busy intersection.

"Thanks," I said, watching the car drive off.

"Always keep your head up while walking," he noted, letting go of my arm.

I nodded in agreement and looked both ways before proceeding to the other side of the street, as Jax continued his description of Aroonyx's two types of inhabitants.

"Emotionally, Solins are relaxed and keep calm during stressful situations. They are charmers, strong-minded and will easily be chosen as the leader of a group."

"Well that explains a lot," I thought, remembering how calm and collected Cyrus was when he almost hit Jax with his car.

"The downfall of a Solin is their temper. If cornered or angered, they can become explosive, which can be dangerous during the day."

I frowned, thinking of Cyrus's reaction to my attempt at explaining our past. He was angrier than I had ever seen him but I never felt physically threatened. Maybe Cyrus was different from other Solins.

"Lunins are trustworthy and loyal but can also be stubborn and impatient," Jax smirked, looking at me over his shoulder. "Typically, Lunins are reserved, but can become argumentative if challenged. When angered, a Lunin tends to let emotions cloud their better judgment which can lead them to over-react to a situation."

I swallowed, feeling embarrassed as though Jax had peered into my soul, describing me perfectly.

"So, that means...." I began, slowing my pace as we approached another intersection.

"Yes," he interrupted. "Your brother Cyrus is a Solin and you, like myself, are a Lunin."

"But how's that possible?" I asked, feeling confused once more. "If we are twins, then why are we not both Solin or both Lunin?"

A car honked its horn loudly, attempting to get our attention. Clearly irritated by our delay, the woman driver motioned animatedly for us to cross the street. Jax casually looked over at her and nodded, acknowledging her request. The woman's frustrated posture melted away as she smiled back at Jax, her eyes glazing over as she took in his appearance. I snickered as we ran side by side across the street to an even wider sidewalk that curved up a steep hill toward the local Starbucks.

"That is the interesting thing about you and your brother," he continued, oblivious to the woman's reaction.

I laughed, shaking my head.

"I'm sorry, I just can't get used to hearing Cyrus referred to as my brother."

"I knew you'd find the humor in it one day," he teased.

I rolled my eyes, shaking my head.

"Your births were unique because you were born during a bi-lunar eclipse. One evening right before dawn, the twin moons aligned perfectly, blocking out the morning sun completely. This type of bi-lunar eclipse had never happened before and lasted for more than fifteen minutes. This was when you and your brother were born."

"So that's the reason why one of us is a Solin and the other a Lunin?" I asked, my mind spinning.

"There have never been twins who have differed from each other like you and Cyrus. Also, there is no record of this specific type of eclipse ever taking place. Eclipses are very rare on Aroonyx. In fact, there have only ever been two recorded. I do not have a definite answer to your question, Elara. I can only put the facts together and assume that is why the two of you are different."

"I see," I said, huffing up the never-ending hill.

"Do you need to rest?" Jax asked, noticing my distress.

"No," I huffed.

"If it were night...." he began.

"How have I let him speak this long without asking about the powers?" I wondered excitedly.

"Can you explain how these powers work?" I asked, motioning for him to talk while I continued to climb the steep hill.

"Every Solin and Lunin are born with specific traits, or as you may call them, powers. These 'powers' become active once a child has come of age. Eighteen years of age, to be exact. When a Solin becomes active they can show incredible strength and their vision can extend to depths far beyond the limitations of the human eye. Lunins have the ability to see at night equally as well as during the day and can perform any type of cardiovascular training such as running, swimming, walking...."

Smiling, Jax paused, noticing my slow pace.

". . .and never feel tired or short of breath."

"Well that explains a lot!" I exclaimed, holding the stitch in my side.

"I would imagine that by now you have figured out that these abilities only last for so long. A Solin's powers last from sun-up to sun-down, while a Lunin's powers are active only during the night," Jax explained.

"Yes! This is all making sense now," I said, feeling relieved to know that I had not been going crazy over the past few weeks. "The night vision thing is cool, but I'm not sure what the Olympic runner-like stamina is helpful for, though I guess right now it would come in handy," I finished, breathing heavily now, at the top of the hill.

"It has its benefits," Jax added under his breath.

I surveyed a bridge that blocked our passage. Unfortunately, the sidewalk stopped, discouraging pedestrians from crossing the dangerous two-lane bridge.

"Hmm...." I thought aloud, surveying the bridge. "I didn't think this walk-to-Starbucks plan over very well. We can't safely cross this bridge unless you feel like playing Russian-roulette with the oncoming cars."

"What about just going under it," Jax said, pointing to the steep ravine that led to a small creek which flowed under the tall bridge.

"What?" I gasped, looking down toward the rocky creek bed.

"Elara, you can't tell me you're afraid to hike down and back up that small hill, are you?" he asked, shock lingering in his voice.

"I'm not scared, it's just cold and I'm tired from walking up one hill already. I don't particularly feel like repelling down this one and risk slipping and falling to my death."

Jax laughed, loud and deep. Clouds of warm breath left his mouth, as he shook his head smiling.

"Then let's just say that this starts your training," he said, beginning to side-step his way down the steep hill.

"My training? What are you talking about? Jax...wait!"

"Come on, try and keep up!" he called, not looking back.

Sighing, I tried following his lead down the steep ravine, stumbling every other step. My hands braced myself, as I scooted down the cold, rocky slope trying to catch up.

"How are we doing back there?" asked Jax, as he casually walked at a brisk pace down the hill as though he were on a flat plane.

"Just perfect," I mumbled sarcastically.

After a few more minutes of the painstaking journey down the hill, we finally reached the creek bed. The small creek was full and flowing, courtesy of the rainy season. The cool, gray sky made the water look shades darker than that of a clear day. The tall pine trees that surrounded us bent gently in the wind as the rush of cars overhead echoed loudly under the bridge.

"See, that wasn't so bad," Jax said, observing the surroundings.

"Yeah, but now we have to climb up that one!" I exclaimed, pointing toward the equally rocky hill ahead of us.

"And get across the creek," he noted.

I hoped up and down, shivering from the cold.

"I'm already freezing! I don't want to walk through the cold water."

Jax let out a long exhale before taking a seat on a large rock next to the creek. He looked like a model from an advertisement for an outdoor sporting goods store. All he needed was a tent somewhere in the back ground with a fishing pole to complete the shot.

Rubbing my arms in hopes of warmth, I cautiously walked over to where he sat, keeping my distance.

His thumb moved over his scarred palm once more, his eyes lost deep in thought.

"Does your scar hurt?" I asked.

"Only when I think about it."

"Did you cut it on something?" I pressed, my curiosity getting the best of me.

"You see those rocks over there," he pointed, ignoring me for the second time that day.

"Third times a charm," I reminded myself silently.

"Yes Jax, I do see those rocks in the water that are spaced out very far apart from one another."

"We can cross there," he said, hopping to his feet.

I groaned, watching him walk to the edge of the flowing creek. Reluctantly I followed when he waved his pale hand for me to join him. I stood silent next to Jax watching the cold water part around the algae-covered rocks.

"You go first," he motioned at the slippery looking rocks.

"No way!" I started.

"That way, if you fall I can catch you," he interrupted.

"Oh…okay then," I agreed, feeling foolish.

I spread my arms out as if walking a tight rope, praying I wouldn't slip off the slimy rocks. One step after another, I stretched my legs to reach the next slippery stone. Only three rocks left and I was clear of the icy water that flowed beneath me.

A small, awkward sounding squeal left my mouth as my foot slipped, causing me to lose my balance. My arms shot out behind me hoping to brace the fall into the frigid creek, but to my surprise Jax's hands were around my forearms in the blink of an eye. He balanced perfectly on his rock while now holding my entire body weight, effortlessly with his strong hands.

Gently, he rocked me back to a standing position where I was once again stable on my own rock.

I rejoiced, wanting to look back at Jax but was afraid I would lose my balance once more.

"Thanks for the second save today!" I exclaimed, hopping off the last rock, relieved to be on the other side of the creek bed.

"Anytime," he said, effortlessly stepping next to me.

"These night-time powers of ours don't give us balance or coordination, do they?" I asked, starring up at the large hill.

"No, I'm afraid not," he answered. "This Starbucks place is just up that hill?" he asked, tossing his black hair out of his eyes.

"Yep. As soon as we climb up there we will be moments away from a nice warm place with even warmer coffee," I replied excitedly, bobbing up and down as the wind blew hard around us.

"After observing your... comfort level with the outdoors, allow me to give you a few pointers on climbing."

"Okay," I replied, my eyes focused and mind ready to take in this new information.

"Never attempt a climb, if you don't have to," he said, pointing to his right.

A manicured trail that was lined with soft mulch wound its way up the steep, rocky hill. My jaw dropped, when noticing the very same trail crossed a small bridge just a bit farther down the creek, then led up the very same hill that we had just hiked down.

"Are you kidding me right now?" I snapped. "Did you know that was there this whole time?" I asked dumbfounded.

A large grin crossed his rugged face.

"Jax! You made me hike down the hill and hop over those rocks for no reason?"

"I was hoping to teach you a lesson," he said, crossing his arms.

"And what lesson was that?"

His smile faded, as he began speaking in a more serious tone.

"Elara, Aroonyx can be a very dangerous place. I need you to be aware of your surroundings. You can't approach a new situation and just follow someone's lead. I need you to be smarter than that. You must observe every angle and every aspect of a new environment. That trail was not hard to miss. The only reason you didn't notice it was because you were only looking at what was directly in front of you: the steep descent, the creek bed, then the steep ascent. If you take a moment to get outside of your immediate focus, you will open yourself up to more options, and possibly safer ones."

Feeling scolded, I looked down at the ground.

Taking a step closer, Jax rested his cool hand on my even colder shoulder.

"Elara, I am not reprimanding you. I'm here to help you; to prepare you the best way I can for what lies ahead. You may find my techniques unconventional, but I have my reasons."

We stood silently together for an awkward amount of time. My eyes remained focused on the cold, hard ground but I could feel Jax's eyes never leaving mine.

"Come on," he encouraged, lowering his head to meet my gaze. "Let's get you to that Starbucks place."

CHAPTER 21

The short walk up the mulched-lined path was a breeze compared to the earlier descent. We walked side by side silently, each unsure of what to say next. The green and white Starbucks sign glowed like a beacon of hope, as we made it through the last part of the trail.

"Finally!" I cheered.

I sprinted to the door, eager to feel warmth as Jax followed slowly behind me. My cold face welcomed the warm air that now surrounded me as the familiar sounds and smells put me at ease. Norah Jones belted out an overplayed song, as the baristas busied themselves filling customer's orders. I turned, watching Jax enter the building.

"What's that unique smell?" he asked, sniffing the air.

"Coffee!" I grinned, clapping my hands like a child. "I thought we could get a cup and you could finish my history lesson on Aroonyx," I offered, motioning for him to follow me to the counter.

"Sure, if that's what you'd like."

Relaxed, and now feeling warm, I stepped up to the counter to order two Grande drip coffees from the overly friendly cashier, but quickly found myself irritated by her flirty behavior toward Jax.

Every question she asked was directed toward me, but for some reason she only looked at Jax when I answered. She smiled, tossing her hair, then practically drooled into my cup as she handed Jax both coffees while letting her hand linger on his just long enough for me to notice. Jax, unfazed by her behavior, looked at me, confused, when I rolled my eyes, then walked away to find an empty table.

I sat quietly at the small wooden table wondering why it bothered me if she flirted with Jax. It wasn't like he was mine to claim. I hardly knew him. I couldn't blame her for finding him attractive. He was handsome, rustically handsome, for that matter and looked nothing like the other guys around here. I felt better only momentarily, until I noticed that Jax had not made it to the table because now another woman, who was significantly older, had stopped to flirt with him. I rolled my eyes once more, as Jax finally took his seat across from me.

"Everyone is really friendly at this Starbucks place," he said, taking a sip of the hot coffee.

"I bet they are," I said under my breath, looking away.

"The coffee is nice," he smiled, turning the cup round in his hand. "What do these numbers mean?" he asked, showing me the phone number the cashier had written on his cup.

"Doesn't mean a thing," I lied, feeling a slight satisfaction.

My hands tingled, as I rubbed them together, feeling heat return to my frigid fingers.

"Before you get back to the history of Aroonyx do you think you could explain one more thing?" I asked, trying to shake the heat that now surged through my hands.

"Sure," he answered, taking another sip from his cup.

The warming sensation moved throughout my entire body, causing me to shift uncomfortably in my seat.

"Everything okay?" Jax asked, resting his cup on the table.

"I think so," I sighed, feeling the heat intensify.

I glanced over Jax's shoulder, noticing a table in the back corner of the small room. My heart skipped a beat as my eyes found Cyrus. He sat alone, staring out the large window, lost deep in thought.

I froze, unsure of what to do next.

"Elara?" Jax whispered, beginning to stand, but quickly I motioned for him to sit back down, not wanting to draw attention to our table.

"Cyrus," I mouthed silently, pointing over his shoulder.

Jax, resembling a well-trained solider, quietly stood up and made his way to the double doors we had entered. Turning around gently in my chair while holding our two coffees, I tip-toed toward the door.

In the highest pitched voice imaginable, the overly friendly cashier yelled, "Have a good day!" as she noticed Jax's departure.

I cringed at her impeccably poor timing, afraid Cyrus would turn around to investigate the strange sound and find me standing there, mid tippy-toe. Deciding to take my chances, I darted out the door only to find Jax nowhere in sight. I hurried around the back of the building, remaining hidden from Cyrus's view, hoping to find Jax. As soon as I rounded the corner of the building I found him standing near a large green trash bin, looking relaxed and once again completely unfazed by the icy weather.

My skin prickled from the cold, as the wind blew around us.

"And you were just getting warmed up," Jax teased, smirking once more.

"Of all the places, he could have gone to sit and think!"

"Why didn't you just go up and talk to him?" he asked.

"Oh, I don't know Jax, maybe because the last time we spoke he told me to stay away from him," I snapped.

"You told me you *never* wanted to see me again but eventually came around," he added, his voice lingering on the word never.

I scoffed, irritated by the simple fact that he was always ten steps ahead of my every move.

"I'll talk to Cyrus again, just not today. I think I need to give him some time to cool off before I try to approach him."

I shivered, motioning for Jax to take his cup of coffee from my freezing hand.

"Thank you," he said, taking the large cup. "Well, since you are unwilling to go back inside, where would you like to go next?" he asked, taking another large sip of coffee.

"I haven't a clue. There are only markets and retail stores within walking distance."

Jax's eyebrows raised.

"Within my walking distance," I corrected.

"I could build us a fire," he mentioned casually, as if this were something he did daily.

I laughed aloud, not wanting to fall for his little joke.

"Yeah, because that won't send the fire department right over," I said, rocking to keep warm.

"I could easily build one under the bridge. The fire will be hidden by the large overpass and with such heavy winds, the smoke will dissipate long before any crossing cars would notice."

Jax spoke with such authority on the subject, I found myself suddenly speechless.

"You're serious?" I managed in a small voice.

"Quite serious," he nodded.

"This has been a very weird day for me," I added, feeling as if I were stuck in a never-ending dream.

Jax exhaled, his deep blue eyes finding mine.

"I can imagine. Have you had enough for today? We can always continue this tom…."

"NO!" I interjected. "Yes, I'm freezing and tired and confused, but I really want to learn about Aroonyx and where I came from and all the details in between. Just be patient with me, Jax. My mind is racing, trying to catch up, but it seems as though you are always a lifetime ahead of me," I sighed, looking away as I spoke.

Jax stood observing me as if listening to my inner thoughts.

"I think a fire will make you more comfortable. I know the cold can be somewhat of a distraction," he remarked.

"All right," I said, still unsure of how he would conjure a fire out of thin air.

"Shall we?" he began, taking one last sip of coffee, before tossing the cup it into the large green trash bin.

I nodded in agreement, starting to walk back around the building, then stopped abruptly when Jax cleared his throat.

"We need to go around this way," he said, pointing in the opposite direction.

"Why?" I asked.

"Have you forgot what I told you about Solins?" he interjected.

I racked my brain wondering how Cyrus's super human strength would prevent us from reaching the trail.

"If we go the obvious route around the building, Cyrus will have a clear view of us through the windows."

"Yeah, but we'll easily be forty or so feet...." I stopped mid-sentence. ". . . but Solins have the power to see in great detail at far distances," I finished, remembering what Jax had explained earlier.

"You'll get it," he said reassuringly, nodding for me to follow as we made our way around the building through the back of the parking lot.

"Hey, Jax...," I said, quickening my pace to catch up.

"Yes?" he answered, not slowing his brisk walk.

"You're a Lunin, right?"

"Correct," he stated.

"But, you also have other powers," I said, sipping the warm coffee.

"I'm not following," he said, lifting a low-lying tree branch out of the way, as he walked through the wooded area.

"You have powers at night but you can also disappear and then reappear on Earth."

"Ah … now I see what you're getting at," he said, beginning the hike down the smooth trail.

"Yes, you and I, like every other Lunin, have the same abilities but I am also what is known on Aroonyx as a Seeker."

"I'm sure you can guess what my next question will be?" I asked, following him down the trail.

Jax laughed, softly side-stepping his way down the steep path.

"A Seeker is a Solin or Lunin who also has the ability to jump, as it's called, to and from Earth. These days, Seekers are very rare on Aroonyx but this wasn't the case many decades ago. Seekers are extremely intuitive. They can get an accurate feel about a person or situation instantly. It's hard to explain but when a Seeker gets a strong intuition it always proves true."

"Can you go to other planets?" I asked, excitedly.

"Not that I'm aware of," he stated. "I've only ever been able to jump to Earth and as far as I know, so were the others."

"So how does it work? Do you just visualize a place in your mind and you appear there?" I asked, unsure if my question were foolish.

"I wish it were that easy. I can only tell you from my own experience and no, it does not work that way. Honestly, I'm not exactly sure how it works. When on Aroonyx, if I want to jump to Earth, all I must do is think about you or your brother and within an instant I am somewhere in your vicinity. When I decide that it is time to go back to Aroonyx, almost instantly I return and for some reason I'm always back in the exact same spot where I left."

"Wow!" I exclaimed, taking the final step off the trail, back onto the edge of the creek.

"That must be amazing to travel like that. Can you jump to and from different places on Earth? Like, could you leave right now and end up in China or Paris?" I asked, feeling more excited by the minute.

"Not unless you or your brother were there," he answered. "Elara, you have to remember that for these past nine years I have only spent time checking in on you and your brother. It wasn't until you both came of age that I started jumping more frequently. Shall we cross using the bridge this time?" he asked, nodding toward the small wooden bridge.

I nodded, still processing this new information.

We crossed the bridge together in silence. His words resonated in my mind, as I tried grasping the concept of Jax having another life. We walked side-by-side, until we reached the large bridge.

"I'll be right back," he said, motioning for me to take a seat on a large rock.

"Okay," I said, my mind still preoccupied.

I wasn't sure how long had passed before Jax returned. Branches filled his arms, and he tossed them onto the ground next to where I sat perched on the cold rock. Within moments Jax had arranged the branches into a teepee-like formation. He reached into his back pocket, removing the grey knife. I marveled for the second time that day, as he effortlessly flipped open the sharp blade. He then began striking the blade back and forth on his pant leg. A small ball of fuzz began to appear in his hand. After placing it underneath the teepee, he reached into his other pocket and removed a dull, metal-like piece of material. He turned his body, shielding the branches from the strong winds, then struck the knife blade against the metal. I jumped, startled by the large spark that landed directly onto the ball of lint. Immediately it caught fire and then spread its flames to the dry branches.

I sighed with relief, feeling the warm heat travel up to my cold face. I placed the empty coffee cup on the cold ground, then reached out my hands, attempting to thaw out my numb fingers.

"I'm impressed," I said aloud, smiling at the crackling woods.

"You've never built a fire?" he asked, sounding concerned.

"Only in our fireplace back in Maine."

Jax sighed, shaking his head.

"We're going to have a lot of information to cover," he said, taking a seat on the rock next to me.

"Sorry," I replied, feeling like a tremendous burden.

"Don't apologize," he stated firmly. "It was never your decision to come here," he said, his voice trailing off.

I paused, unsure of how to phrase my next question.

"About that," I began, swallowing uncomfortably, as a large knot formed in my throat.

"Right," he said, running both hands through his hair looking uneasy. "Are you warm, comfortable?" he asked, looking me directly in the eyes.

I nodded in agreement, as the fire burned brightly under the dark bridge.

"Then once again, let me try starting from the beginning."

CHAPTER 22

The small fire crackled loudly, as the warmth slowly enveloped me. I exhaled a long deep breath, allowing my body to relax for the first time in hours. I sat quietly, focused on the glowing embers as Jax spoke softly, thoughtfully.

"Unlike Earth, the number of people living on Aroonyx is incredibly small. For the first hundred or so years the population was sparse, but over time it has grown to around two thousand."

"Whoa..." I commented, looking up at Jax.

"Yes, it is quite the contrast to Earth," he continued. "Around fifty years ago, a Solin by the name of Arun was nominated as the first leader of Aroonyx. He was young, only twenty years of age."

"Why only then, did they nominate a leader?" I asked, gathering my long hair together before tying it up into a tight bun.

"There was never a need for one," Jax answered. "Aroonyx's population had been so small, that for the most part everyone lived in harmony. It wasn't until the population grew that people began having different opinions and ideas of how the world should work."

"I see," I nodded, holding my hands over the warm fire.

"Arun was brave, smart and being a Solin, a natural leader. The citizens of Aroonyx were thrilled to have someone they could trust to uphold the simple laws they created.

"For the first few years, Arun did exactly as promised. He upheld the laws, gathered the most intelligent Lunins he could find to design better plans for crop growth and slowly began to better the planet as whole. As I mentioned earlier, Seekers are very rare on Aroonyx though during Arun's reign, this was not the case.

"The Seeker's power was first discovered on the day a young man named Saros came to Arun, explaining that he had just been to another place, another time, and had seen amazing things. At first, Arun was unconvinced by these claims and dismissed the young man, but when Saros began drawing Arun pictures of the things he had seen, Arun's interest was ignited. He asked Saros if he could go back to the place he had visited and learn how to build one of pictures he had drawn. The young man said he would try – and then vanished right before Arun's eyes. Unsure of what he had just witnessed, Arun waited curiously for Saros's return. Hours turned into days, as Arun began to question if what he had seen were real. To his surprise, Saros appeared once more with detailed drawings of how to build a windmill. Elara, you must remember that Aroonyx is a much less developed planet than Earth, so at the time the idea of being able to use wind power for grain mills and water pumps was life-changing."

I nodded, fully engaged in Jax's history lesson. I glanced up at the bridge, listening to the cars pass overhead. Jax's prediction was correct as I watched the white smoke vanish before ever reaching the top of the bridge. I resettled myself on the cold rock listening intently as Jax continued.

"Saros apologized to Arun for his lengthy visit to the foreign world. Confused by this, Arun informed Saros that he had only been away for a few days. It was then that the drastic time difference was discovered. Elated with Saros's ability to travel to and from a more advanced civilization, Arun gave Saros the title Seeker of Time and kept him close to his side as his most trusted advisor."

"So that's why you're called a Seeker!" I exclaimed, finally catching on.

Jax nodded, before continuing.

"Arun and Saros worked closely together for years helping Aroonyx mature and grow as a planet. Saros continued jumping back and forth to Earth, gathering new information that quickly advanced Aroonyx at a rapid rate. It wasn't long before other Seekers came forward, showing that they, too, could jump to and from Earth.

"Arun was delighted that he now had an exclusive group of Seekers who were working together to benefit the people of Aroonyx. Arun's Seekers were treated like royalty. They were given land, houses, and fancy titles.

"Years passed and new inventions were built every day. With this amount of growth, conflict began to rise to astounding proportions. Desire, greed, and jealousy took control over the once peaceful citizens of Aroonyx. Crime rates began to grow as the people desired more and more from their leader.

"One day a young Seeker returned with new designs for a tool. The Seeker's intention was pure; to assist the people of Aroonyx by making hunting more efficient. Simple handmade knives that had always been used for hunting now had the potential to be precisely formed into much more effective tools. Arun was fascinated by this concept and desired to learn more. Being his closest friend and advisor, Arun asked Saros to return to Earth to learn everything he could about these new designs. Saros, accepting Arun's request, jumped to Earth – but never returned."

I flinched, startled by the loud crackling noise of the burning wood. Jax paused, watching my reaction.

"What happened to him?" I asked.

"No one knows. He was never seen again."

"So, then what?" I asked, anxiously leaning forward on the uncomfortable rock.

"Arun, deeply concerned for his friend and advisor, believed that Saros had somehow managed to get trapped on Earth. Out of caution and for the safety of his selective group, Arun prohibited any Seeker to travel back to Earth, afraid they would be trapped as well.

"Years passed without any communication from Saros or the return of new information. Aroonyx, once thriving, was now faltering. Its people grew angrier with every passing day, consumed by their greed and desire for new inventions. The citizens demanded that Arun allow the Seekers to return to Earth so they could learn more about Earth's advanced ways. Arun was unable to give the people what they wanted and feared an uprising. Feeling physically threatened, he suddenly viewed the new designs for tools as weapons. Arun, a once calm and caring leader, quickly transformed into a fearful, disillusioned dictator. As you can imagine, with any paranoid dictator, he became desperate. Arun began *insisting* that the Seekers return to Earth with strict instructions only to find designs for weapons that he could use as a defense in case of an uprising. As soon his intention shifted, the Seekers were no longer able to return to Earth."

"Wait, I'm not following. Why couldn't they jump back to Earth?" I asked, my senses feeling more alert than they had all day.

"There has never been a conformation as to why. It is only with my personal experience, that I've come to this conclusion. The shift that I speak of is that of intention. I believe a Seeker is only able to jump, if the intention is pure and completely selfless. Arun's Seekers were able to bring back helpful information to Aroonyx because it was benefitting others, not just themselves. When Arun demanded that they return for destructive reasons, they were no longer able to jump to Earth. I have had my own experience with this."

"Really, how?" I asked, intrigued.

Jax paused watching the fire, his blue eyes sparkling vividly.

"Let's just say, I know it to be true," he stated, continuing to watch the burning logs.

"Okay...." I murmured, feeling as though that topic was off limits.

Jax rubbed his hands together over the warm fire, turning to face me.

"When the Seekers informed him that they were no longer able to return to Earth, Arun assumed they were plotting against him, along with the people of Aroonyx. His downward spiral continued as he now felt frantic and began threatening the Seekers, telling them if they did not jump to Earth, he would jail them. His threats proved true for every known Seeker. Desperate to calm his fears of an uprising, Arun took matters into his own hands, killing every jailed Seeker one-by-one."

Shocked, I looked at Jax with wide eyes, as a chill crept up my spine.

"He killed...all of them?" I stuttered, pulling my knees up to my chest.

"Every last one he could find," Jax said, turning his gaze back to the fire. "Word of these killings quickly spread throughout the villages. Any known Seeker left their families and homes to hide out in the woods, hoping to escape the Collectors."

"The Collectors?" I asked, inching closer to Jax.

"Arun, still desperate in his desire for a Seeker to jump back to Earth, created a selective group known as the Collectors. They consisted of impressionable adolescent boys and young men, ranging in age from twelve to early twenties. Criminals, outcasts, and orphans, all flocked to Arun in hopes of joining the ranks. He made them feel special, justified their destructive behavior and accepted them into this highly exclusive group. They had one purpose, and one purpose only; collect as many Seekers as possible."

I inhaled deeply, noticing I had been holding my breath. Jax turned, facing me once more, pushing his black hair out of his eyes.

"The Collectors brought Arun many Seekers, all of them incapable of jumping back to Earth. Every Seeker delivered to him was eventually killed. Arun's twenty-year reign came to abrupt end when his paranoid delusions ultimately led to him take his own life. He was forty years old."

My head snapped toward Jax, as he suddenly stood.

"Where are you going?" I asked, overly anxious.

He laughed, dusting off the back of his pants.

"Just to get some more fire wood," he said, amused by my response.

"Of course," I replied, trying to play it cool.

I watched as Jax scanned the side of the creek bed for fallen tree limbs. Every move he made was calculated, well thought out. He moved with a purpose, unlike me, who just drifted from one place to the next. The way he conducted himself reminded me that of a special-forces-solider. His feet moved quietly, cautiously, beneath the weight of his boots. Nothing outside of himself seemed to faze him – not the weather, the terrain, or my naiveté on everything he had shared with me thus far.

Jax returned, carrying a few branches under one arm, then dropped them gingerly onto the nearly empty pile. He bent down slowly, selecting a thick branch and tossed it carefully onto the burning fire. He brushed off his hands over the orange flames before taking a seat once more on the large rock.

"So, where were we?" he casually asked.

"Where were we?" I mocked. "You kind of left me on a cliffhanger there, Jax!"

"Right. Okay, let's see...Arun's body was found alone in the bedroom of his fortress-like dwelling. The Collectors, no longer having a leader, disbanded and went back to their lives before Arun. Aroonyx went for many years without a leader after Arun's dictatorship."

"You mean to tell me that the people let Arun control Aroonyx for that many years and never did anything to try and stop him?" I asked, feeling my emotions begin to stir.

Jax paused, a slow smile crossed his face.

"This bothers you?" he asked.

"What? Of course, it bothers me Jax. I hate to think of one person controlling the lives of others. Especially, when that someone is a murderer!"

"Good," he replied, nodding his head in agreement.

"Why is that good?"

"It's good, because I will remind you of those words later, when you begin to disagree with me," he stated, smirking.

"Well that didn't make any sense," I said, shaking my head in bewilderment.

"It will," he chuckled quietly, shifting his weight on the gray rock.

"After Arun's death, the people of Aroonyx refused to nominate another leader. They felt betrayed and did not want to risk the chance of another dictator taking control of the planet. Time passed and Aroonyx's growth appeared to stop altogether.

"Yes, inventions that had been found on Earth remained, but nothing new was produced. It was as though time had stopped. People moved on, forced to let go of the strong desire they once had, now knowing these new ideas and technologies were no longer available. Crime rate went down slightly, but

Arun's reign left the people of Aroonyx jaded. The once gentle, patient and trustworthy citizens of Aroonyx had now transformed into a mixture of what you find here on Earth. Aroonyx had gone twenty years with a leader and even though it ended badly for both parties involved, the people had grown accustomed to having someone to rely on and someone to blame. About eleven years passed, before the citizens of Aroonyx were ready to give a new leader a chance."

"Who was it?" I asked anxiously.

Jax didn't answer as he watched the fire burn brightly, his pale skin reflected in the warm light. The wind blew hard, sending smoke directly into his face. He sat there unaffected, clasping his hands together, lost deep in thought. His face, only twenty-two years of age, looked wise and mature.

"Jax?" I asked quietly, wondering if I should interrupt his intense concentration.

"Forty-one years ago, another rare eclipse took place on Aroonyx. Not as rare as the one on which you and your brother were born, but a rare one, nonetheless. There was a child born during this unique solar eclipse. Different in appearance, he did not fit into one category, but seemed to share traits of both Solins and Lunins. His skin had a bronze complexion, but his hair was jet black. He had one amber colored eye and one bright blue. It wasn't until he came of age, that he learned of his ability to have both Solin and Lunin traits."

"Wow," I replied intrigued.

"Once this became known, people began flocking to his side, amazed by the multitude of his abilities. He was well liked by all, thanks to his charming Solin side, but also highly intelligent, courtesy of his Lunin traits. He quickly used this to his advantage by lying and cheating his way into the hearts of the citizens of Aroonyx.

"Rumors began to spread about the desire for a new leader. These rumors were all planted by his close circle. The same people who once followed him out of wonder, now followed him out of fear. No one had ever seen a person with both Solin and Lunin traits. Some thought it only natural that he would be the new leader, others feared a repeat of Arun's reign. The naysayers were quickly silenced and by the age of twenty-five, Zenith was the new leader of Aroonyx."

"Zenith? His name even sounds intense," I thought aloud.

Jax, apparently not wanting to be interrupted, quickly continued.

"Zenith was given the position under the strict agreement that he would step down after serving for five years, allowing a new leader to be nominated. I'll let you guess what happened when the time came for him to step down."

I frowned, not liking the familiar way the story was sounding.

"He refused?" I asked.

Jax nodded in conformation.

I sighed, frustrated by this news.

"And no one would challenge him?" I asked.

"No one dared. By that time, Zenith had the Collectors lurking around every corner."

"I thought they disbanded after Arun's death?" I asked, feeling even more frustrated with the way the story was heading.

"Zenith never planned to step down once taking control. Unlike Arun, he never had intentions of bettering Aroonyx. His first five years of doing 'good' was all a façade to gain the trust of the people. Zenith, knowing his true plans for Aroonyx, reassembled the Collectors to protect him from any uprising that could occur. The Collectors are now responsible for completing Zenith's dirty work. They are his enforcers, informants, and act as his personal body guard. Zenith, in some bizarre way, idolized Arun. He wanted everything he had and more. Reassembling the Collectors was like a twisted homage to Arun's reign."

"How many are there?" I asked, as my heart thumped loudly in my chest.

"I can't say exactly how many there are now, but there are enough, that is for sure," Jax answered. "You see, this was another clever move by Zenith. The Collectors are unmarked and wear no uniforms so the people never know where, or who, they are. This forces the citizens of Aroonyx to feel paranoid, always looking over their shoulders as if someone is watching. If there is an altercation and a Collector comes forward, Zenith will remove that member from duty for an extended period of time so people forget his identity. They are constantly being shifted in and out of the villages. They report news, rumors, and any talk of treason back to Zenith."

"Jax," I started.

A strong gust of wind blew, sending smoke into my face. I waved my hand frantically trying to clear the thick cloud.

"How do you know so much about Arun, Zenith and the Collectors?"

"Elara, I have lived a solitary life for many years now. During this time, I've kept my eyes open, as well as my ears."

"I see," I nodded, squinting through the heavy smoke, attempting to see Jax. "Is there any chance he would step down?" I asked, hopefully.

"It has been sixteen years that Zenith has ruled over Aroonyx, I do not see him volunteering to step down any time soon."

I gulped, imagining what life must be like on Aroonyx. I recalled the ruthless dictators I learned about in school, feeling my heart ache for people that I never knew existed until now.

Jax stood, reaching for another log to add to the crackling fire. He grabbed two thin pine branches and tossed them, this time carelessly, onto the burning pile. Hot embers danced around the scorching flames, forcing me to move away from the intense heat. I watched Jax's face harden as he stared deeply into the fire. His blue eyes were more focused than I had seen them all day.

My stomach growled loudly, acknowledging the fact that it was well after lunch time. I reached over to my back pack, searching the front pocket. Relieved, I found a half-eaten protein bar wrapped loosely in a foil wrapper.

"Do you want any of this?" I asked, sounding unsure of my offer.

He shook his head disagreeing, never taking his eyes off the glowing flames. We sat in an awkward silence for long minutes. My eyes shifted from the fire, to Jax's worn boots, then back again until finally he broke the silence.

"Zenith is the reason you and Cyrus must return to Aroonyx."

CHAPTER 23

"Excuse me," I coughed, nearly choking on the dry protein bar.

"It's the only way he will step down," he stated with a certain finality in his tone.

I shook my head frantically, disagreeing with Jax. I swallowed painfully, wishing I had a bottle of water to wash down the bark-like substance now left in my mouth.

"Jax! Do you even hear yourself right now? What do you mean it's the only way he'll step down? You were the one who said that you don't see him volunteering to step down anytime soon!" I snapped.

Slowly, Jax walked to the rock that sat beside my own, taking his seat once more. He quietly clasped his hands, interlocking his fingers together tightly as he spoke. For the first time since meeting Jax, I noticed him looking nervous, uncomfortable.

"Elara, the night I jumped to Earth with you and Cyrus changed my life forever. I mentioned to you before that Seekers cannot only jump to and from Earth but also have a strong intuition. That night when I saw you … and your brother for the first time, a strong sense of peace came over me. You must understand that I had a very troubled childhood and it was only after seeing you that I realized there was still hope. Not only hope for myself, but for the people of Aroonyx. I have a challenging time trying to articulate what I felt that night but the entire experience was more than just an intense feeling, it was a knowingness. I *know* that you and Cyrus are capable of defeating Zenith."

"What?" I asked, still attempting to swallow the last bite of protein bar.

Jax turned his head toward mine, his eyes focused, unblinking.

"Jax, I have been very willing to listen to the history of the planet I come from and yes, I find it frustrating if not infuriating that the people of Aroonyx have had to endure not one but two ruthless dictators, but what you are telling me sounds completely crazy. You can't expect me to believe that you had some 'feeling' that Cyrus and I would defeat Zenith. Two people, who haven't been to Aroonyx in what, eighteen years? You think I would just volunteer to go to a place I know nothing about, and try and take down its leader?"

I felt my heart begin to beat faster in my chest as I tried to wrap my mind around Jax's request. Everything he had told me thus far had sounded like a history lesson, nothing more. It felt as though a teacher were explaining the reign of Hitler, Stalin or Leopold II of Belgium, and then suddenly asked if I wanted to jump back into time and single-handedly try to defeat them. The thought of going back to Aroonyx and seeing Zenith and his Collectors up close and personal sounded like something out of nightmare.

Jax sighed, rubbing the scar on his hand, clearly frustrated by my response.

"Elara, now is the time when I will remind you of your earlier words. I believe you said, it made you angry to think of one person controlling the lives of others?" he asked, one eyebrow raised.

I scoffed, "Yes, I said that Jax, but that doesn't mean I'm going to jump back with you to Aroonyx and become a vigilante!"

Jax stood and began pacing back and forth in front of the fire, resembling a caged lion.

"I know it sounds crazy to risk you and your brother's lives based on a 'feeling' but you have to understand that this was much more than that. You and Cyrus are from Aroonyx and you were born during the rarest of all eclipses. Who knows what your powers are capable of?"

Hearing these words, my mind flashed back to the car accident with Cyrus and then to the buoyancy lab at NASA.

"Exactly, Jax!" I barked. "*We* don't even know what our powers are capable of! For all we know, Cyrus and I could be just like every other Lunin and Solin on Aroonyx. Why would we leave our perfectly safe and modern homes, to go back in time to a world we know nothing about? Oh, and let's not forget Cyrus! I hope you have some grand plan up your sleeve as to how to convince him to believe any of this! I'm sorry, Jax, but the answer is no. No, I'm not going back with you to Aroonyx."

"Elara, you have to trust me…" Jax began, still pacing.

I stood, no longer willing to stay seated. My heart raced as my mind surged with fear and anger.

"No, Jax! It's not my fault that *you* chose to wait eighteen years to tell me any of this. Maybe if I would have been taught about Aroonyx and where I came from a little earlier, than this would not have come as such a shock."

"Come on, Elara!" he countered, stopping his pacing to face me. "You think that would have been appropriate? I appear out of thin air in front of the eyes of a child? You would have thought I was a figment of your imagination, or worse ran and told your parents. I couldn't risk it! You do NOT understand the gravity of this situation!"

"Oh, I think I do Jax! You are telling me that Cyrus and I must return to a foreign planet and single-handedly defeat its leader! Cyrus won't even talk to me right now. How do you expect him to believe any of this or even agree to go back to Aroonyx?" I snapped, waving my arms animatedly.

"I didn't say any of this would be easy," he pressed, his jaw tensing as he spoke.

"No, but you thought it would be appropriate to leave out the part about us risking our lives?" I interrupted.

The cold wind sliced between us as we stood facing one another. Jax's posture was strong, unmoving. I swayed back and forth, caught off guard by the slightest breeze.

"You don't understand Elara, Zenith...." Jax added, his voice raising.

"I understand perfectly well, Jax! I am not going back with you and that is final!" I yelled.

"Zenith is the reason your parents are DEAD!" he shouted.

The harshness of his tone matched that of his voice.

I gasped, hearing those painful words. Suddenly, I felt colder than I had all day. The familiar empty feeling in the pit of my stomach resurfaced, as grief took its strong hold. I felt my body go weak as I slumped back onto the uncomfortable rock.

A look of regret crossed Jax's face, as he closed his eyes while shaking his head.

"I apologize, Elara. I've said too much."

He spoke quietly, walking slowly to where I sat motionless, unable to speak.

Minutes passed, as Jax and I sat silently, listening to the fire crackle and the rumble of cars overhead.

"I didn't want to tell you this way," he continued, his voice barely above a whisper. "Could you find it possible to forgive my lack of sensitivity?"

"It doesn't even matter," I answered, feeling more lost than ever.

"Of course, it matters," Jax said, turning his head quickly to face me.

"I forgive you Jax, if that's what you want to hear, but it doesn't matter about my parents. I didn't even know them," I said, deflated.

"But I did."

Curious, I turned to find Jax's gaze once more.

"I only knew them for a few hours, but in that short amount of time it was easy to see that they were good people and loved you and your brother very much. So much, in fact, that they would risk their own lives to make sure you were safe.

"Elara, I had been an orphan living on my own for quite some time when I met your parents. One night they caught me trying to steal food from your home. Your father made it very apparent that he was upset by my behavior, but it was your mother who showed me true compassion. She told your father that I was young and even though my actions were foolish, that people are only capable of making the best decisions they know how to at that time. Elara, this was the first time in a very long time I felt genuinely cared for. To see such a selfless act performed by your mother was ... exactly what I needed. It was only then that I realized what had been missing from my life for so long: kindness."

I exhaled, remembering how easily I found it to forgive my parents the morning after Jax had told me I was adopted. Her words, my mother's words, mirrored my exact thoughts on forgiveness. My heart fluttered, recalling how on that day a quiet peace came over me when I saw my parents sitting at the table. Even though I had no conscious memory of my birth mother, somehow I felt like a part of her was with me.

"Elara?" Jax asked, pausing.

"I'm sorry, that was just ... never mind, please continue," I motioned, nodding.

"After hearing my story your mother suggested to your father that I leave with them and start a new life."

"Where were they going?" I asked, moving from my slouched position to a more upright one.

Jax looked away, locking his hands tightly together for the second time that day. His jaw muscle flinched, as his teeth clenched firmly together. He was uncomfortable and uneasy, looking as though he either wanted to escape the situation or pull out his knife and fight it.

"Just tell me, I can handle it," I reassured, inhaling a large breath.

"Elara, your parents were leaving because Zenith had sent the Collectors to kill both you and your brother."

Only air escaped my mouth, as I struggled to breathe.

"Why?" I managed.

"News of your births quickly traveled back to Zenith. Remember, the only reason Zenith had remained in his position for so long is the simple fact that no one would challenge him. There had never been a person on Aroonyx who could share both Solin and Lunin traits. The thought of not one, but two children born during the rarest of all eclipses immediately threatened his position."

"But he didn't even know if we had any special powers! We had just been born," I interrupted.

"He didn't want to take that chance. He assumed that the two of you would be unique, special. Those two traits alone, he found as a significant threat and being completely paranoid, he immediately acted when he heard the news. He sent the Collectors to handle the situation. Your parents were planning on leaving the village that night, but the Collectors made it to your home before they were able to execute Zenith's plan."

I swallowed, forcing the large lump which sat in my throat down to the pit of my stomach. My leg nervously bobbed up and down, not wanting to hear the rest of the story. Jax, intuiting my reservations, proceeded cautiously.

"I'm not going to discuss the details of that night with you, Elara. All I will say is that before the Collectors entered the home, your parents handed me you and your brother, along with two notes. They looked me directly in the eye and instructed me to hide in the pantry and to keep you safe at any cost. Shortly after, a Collector found me hiding with the two of you, but before he could grab me, I miraculously jumped to Earth. I had only been to Earth one other time and never knew how to get back until that moment. Once back on Earth, I was shocked to find myself standing directly outside of a dwelling, which I learned later was called an adoption agency."

I nodded, confirming where Jax had been.

"It was mid-morning and I could see there were people working inside of the building. I placed you and your brother at the foot of the door with the notes your parents had left. It was only minutes before a middle-aged woman opened the door, surprised to find the two of you lying there together. I stayed close the remainder of the day to watch and observe their level of care toward you and Cyrus. Only after I was convinced that you were both safe did I return home. It was then that I discovered the time difference between the two worlds to be true."

My mind raced like a television switching through different scenes, scenarios of my parent's death. I wanted to turn it off, but felt the desire to know. I needed closure.

"When did you know that my parents were...gone?" I asked Jax, letting my hair down out of the tight bun. My head ached, as I massaged my temples and closed my eyes tightly.

Jax looked down. A sadness took over him as he spoke quietly.

"That was a very challenging day for me. I really don't find it appropriate to discuss the physical details about their death. To quiet your mind, I will confirm that yes, your parents were

217

murdered by the Collectors. I wish I could say they left without a struggle, but it was obvious they fought to protect you. I buried them next to the windmill near your home. If you choose to go back, I will take you and your brother to visit the grave site if you desire."

Jax stood, looking taller than usual as he crossed his arms. He watched as I continued to sit stationary on the cold, gray rock. Reaching out a hand, he motioned for me to stand. I took his hand as he gently pulled me to an upright position. Carefully he placed both hands on my shoulders, his eyes locking onto mine.

"Elara, I can only imagine what must be going through your mind. I am afraid that I have said too much, too soon. I have known about these events for years and have had the time to process this knowledge, one day at a time. I have given you fifty years of information in only a few hours, and most of it has been jarring if not disturbing."

Jax sighed, trying to find the right words.

"I'll go," I stated decisively.

"What?" he asked, sounding utterly shocked.

"I will go back with you to Aroonyx. I can't promise you that I'll be able to physically take on someone as powerful as Zenith but...."

Jax was quick to interrupt, grasping my shoulders tightly.

"Elara, I need you to listen very carefully to what I'm about to say. Zenith, is NOT powerful, he is quite the opposite."

My head turned, confused by his words.

"Zenith is a selfish, paranoid, delusional dictator. Yes, he displays unique 'powers' but that does not make him powerful. He looks at compassion, kindness, and love as a weakness and rules over others by the forces of fear and guilt. Zenith is nothing more than a confused, insecure person who is anything but powerful."

Jax squeezed my shoulders firmly with his strong hands, forcing me to focus on his words.

"A truly powerful person does not try to control others. They stand up for the truth and lead selflessly. They do not let their personal emotions cloud the view of the greater good. A powerful person looks at the situation for what it is, not at what they desire it to become. You and your brother are more powerful than Zenith will ever be."

A strong wind dimmed the remainder of the small fire. Only gray smoke swirled around the now black ashes.

I stood unblinking, staring into Jax's deep blue eyes. Only moments ago, I was convinced that his plan was irrational, if not insane, but now I found a strange desire to return to a world I never even knew existed.

An entire life, which was now part of me, felt unfinished. My old life here on Earth was complete, as though there were nothing left for me to accomplish. I had always felt that I was living my life on pause, waiting for something to happen. It was as though Jax had pressed my life's play button and for the first time ever, I felt as though I were no longer waiting. I knew that returning to Aroonyx was crazy and highly dangerous, but even if the odds were against me, I was convinced that going back was the right decision.

I sighed, nodding my head.

"I'll go," I repeated, still feeling dazed from my sudden change of heart.

"I'm glad you see the situation differently than you first did," he said, squeezing my shoulders once more.

"Now what?" I asked, feeling as though I had just run a mental marathon.

Jax removed his hands from my shoulders, crossing his toned arms once more. A large grin crept slowly across his handsome face as he spoke.

"Now we just have to convince Cyrus."

CHAPTER 24

I awoke the next morning, feeling rested for the first time in months. My eyes widened as I read 10:41 a.m. displayed on the clock on the bed side table. I rarely slept past 9:00 a.m. on the weekends, so this was a shock, but not a surprise after the previous day's events. I stared at the slowly spinning ceiling fan, recounting my history lesson with Jax. Thoughts of Arun, Zenith, my parent's death, and agreeing to return to Aroonyx flashed through my mind.

"How would we ever convince Cyrus to go back?" I wondered, stretching my arms overhead.

After our interesting afternoon under the bridge, Jax walked me back to the trail, informing me that he must return home but agreed to meet me the following day. Remembering this, I quickly jumped out of bed and headed to the closet to dress for the day. After staring aimlessly at the poor selection of clothes that hung from the metal racks, I finally selected an old pair of jeans, a long-sleeved shirt and a warm wool coat. I refused to let the cold affect my focus.

While brushing my long, black hair I glanced out the window to check the wind conditions. The trees barely moved; a stark contrast to the previous day's strong gusts. Feeling confident my hair wouldn't get in the way, I left it down but slid a hair tie onto my wrist out of habit. I bounded down the stairs, excited to start the day. I wasn't sure what time Jax would jump back to Earth, but I wanted to be there when he did.

"Hey honey!" My dad shouted from the kitchen. "You sure did sleep in."

"I was about to go up there and wake you," my mother added.

I turned the corner of the kitchen to see my father and mother, both still in their pajamas.

"At least I'm dressed," I replied, nodding at their attire.

They laughed, looking down at their colorful pajamas.

"Where are you going on this chilly Saturday morning?" my father asked.

"I thought I'd swing by a friend's house and maybe grab a movie," I lied, refusing to make eye contact.

"What friend?" asked my mother quickly.

"Hillary," I stuttered, completely shocked by my own answer.

"Well, don't be gone too long," she added. "You seem to have forgotten that it's 'family' weekend."

"About that," I started. "Since it is winter break, I was hoping we could also take a break from 'family' weekends?" I asked, my voice sounding higher than usual. "I just really want to spend some time with my friends," I quickly recovered.

My parents stared silently at one another as if speaking telepathically. My father nodded at my mother, who then sighed loudly.

"Fine, go and spend some time with your friends," she said, shooing me off with her hand.

"Do you need to borrow the car?" asked my father, as I headed toward the front door.

"No!" I shouted back. "I like walking," I replied, thinking of what Jax would say.

"But it's freezing," my mother yelled.

"I dressed warm," I called back, slipping my feet into the only pair of boots I owned.

Swiftly, I slid out the door, wanting to avoid any further delay. The crisp air surrounded me as I inhaled a large, deep breath. White clouds left my mouth, as I exhaled and began walking toward the trail.

It wasn't long before I was back on the familiar trail. As I looked around at the tall pine trees, it seemed quieter than usual. The chirp of birds and scuttle of squirrels were absent. Even the few dedicated joggers that I saw so frequently were missing. I shivered at the bitter cold, concluding that I was the only one who found it appropriate to be outside.

My observations were halted by a hand that had come out of nowhere, which now covered my mouth and right nostril. My attacker was fast, so fast that I never heard or saw him coming. I tried pulling his hand away from my face, but he somehow managed to hold both of my arms behind my back, leaving me helpless.

My eyes darted around frantically, searching for anyone who would come to my aid. I couldn't even turn my head to see my attacker. I struggled, barely able to move from his uncomfortably tight grip. The pine trees around me spun quickly, as my heart raced and knees buckled. He was strong, too strong.

But then he released his firm grip, letting me fall to my knees. I gasped as I inhaled large breaths. My lungs burned from the lack of oxygen. Utterly shocked, I turned my head quickly to meet the person responsible for this cruel behavior. There, standing above me with arms crossed, was Jax.

"What the HELL was that?" I yelled, bewildered by his behavior.

"I'm sorry," he started.

"You're sorry!" I bellowed. "Jax, you just attacked me!"

"Elara, that wasn't an attack. I was just trying to assess your defensive skills," he stated nonchalantly, reaching out a helping hand.

Slapping his hand away, I pushed myself back up, rubbing my sore jaw.

"Did I hurt you?" he asked, sounding genuinely concerned.

"Well that didn't feel good!" I snapped.

"You're upset, I can see that now," he continued.

"Good thing you're so intuitive," I countered.

He stood there smiling, shaking his head.

"Don't be smug!" I said.

"Listen, now that you have agreed to return to Aroonyx, I need to teach you certain skills that will keep you safe."

"Right, so you thought attacking me would work better than just showing me how to defend myself?" I asked, rubbing my aching arms.

"As I said, I did not attack you, Elara. No weapons or brutal force were used. You were put into a simple, locking hold. If I warned you about what I was going to do, then you would have been prepared. I needed an honest account of how you react to a surprise, physical altercation."

Once again, I was left feeling childlike in the presence of Jax. Every time, he somehow managed to make me feel tens of years younger than he. I sighed, taking in his appearance for the first time that day. Though now in different clothes, Jax looked more rugged than ever. His pants, dark gray in color were covered in patches, obviously not placed for the latest style; his shirt, perhaps once white, was beige in color. His unshaven face looked as though he could grow a full beard within a week while his dark hair hung in his face as he spoke.

"Are you sure you're okay?" he asked, walking over to my side.

"I'm fine," I replied, turning my face away from his.

His cold, rough hand, touched my chin gently moving it side to side as he examined my face thoroughly.

"I think you'll live," he whispered, letting go of my chin.

I scoffed, rolling my eyes.

"Don't be upset. I only did this so I know how much training you will need," he stated.

"And how much is that?" I asked nervously.

"A lot," he answered, beginning to walk down the trail.

I groaned aloud, turning to follow him.

"Where are we going?" I asked, hurrying to catch up.

"Nowhere," he replied. "I just thought you would stay warmer if we walked, rather than stood in one place."

"I know of one place we can walk," I began, feeling both excitement and nervousness wash over me.

"Where's that?" Jax asked, continuing his quick pace.

"Cyrus's house. I thought about everything we discussed yesterday and I don't want to wait any longer. Let's just go over there right now and talk to him," I began, pumping myself up for the task.

"Well, you're going to have to wait a little longer," said Jax, his eyes remaining focused on the trail.

"What? Why?" I asked deflated.

"Because he's on vacation with his family and won't be home until next Saturday," he stated, as though everyone was privy to this information.

"How did you know he was on vacation?"

"I check in on both you … and your brother," replied Jax, as though reminding me.

I felt my face redden.

"Yeah, of course you do," I managed, trying to recover.

"Don't get discouraged Elara. You may want to take some more time to think about how you want to approach Cyrus. Especially if you plan on doing it during the day."

I shook my head, disagreeing.

"Why does it matter if I tell him during the day?" I asked, stopping to look at Jax on the empty trail.

"Cyrus would never intend to hurt you, but you need to be on guard during the day if he were to become upset," he answered, nodding for me to keep moving.

"You make Solins sound unstable," I remarked.

"Elara, you couldn't even escape a basic locking hold position with *my* strength. There's no way you could possibly escape that of a Solin."

"Cyrus isn't violent! He would never hurt me and trust me, the other day when I tried telling him about being adopted, he looked as though he wanted to throw me across the school grounds, but restrained himself." I replied. "Also, it isn't like I'm telling him alone. You will be there so…."

Jax laughed, keeping his eyes focused on the trail ahead.

"You are mistaken on that note," he replied.

"What?" I asked, halting once more.

Jax stopped, looking me straight in the eye as he spoke.

"I will not be telling Cyrus with you," he stated, firmly.

"Why? He won't believe me unless you're there. I was hoping you would jump back to Aroonyx in front of him to prove all of the craziness is real!" I cried.

Jax stood smiling, shaking his head in disapproval.

"I'm sorry, Elara, but you must tell Cyrus on your own."

"I don't understand why," I replied, now feeling grateful Cyrus wouldn't be home for another week.

"Two reasons: firstly, Cyrus is your brother, not mine. You now have a personal account of what it feels like to receive such information, so I am confident you will find an appropriate way to present it to him," Jax finished, the smile on his face growing.

"And the second reason?"

"I just feel like sitting this one out."

Feeling more frustrated with Jax by the minute, I curled my fist into a tight ball, swung my arm back and punched him as hard as I could in the shoulder. Immediately I regretted this decision, as my knuckles throbbed in pain. Jax remained standing in the exact same spot, completely unfazed by my action.

"Geez," I exclaimed, jumping up and down shaking my hand at the intense pain.

Jax chuckled loudly as he stood shaking his head, disapproving of me for the third time that day.

"We are definitely going to have to work on your combative skills," he proclaimed, taking my injured hand into his.

Slowly he turned my hand over examining each knuckle and finger bone carefully. I winced as he squeezed firmly between the joints.

"You didn't break anything," he stated, letting my hand fall to my side.

"Well, thank goodness for that," I replied smartly.

"You tucked your thumb under your fingers. That's why your hand is hurting," he remarked casually.

I sighed, looking down at my throbbing hand.

"Watch," he said, moving my uninjured hand up to a halt-like position.

"You must align the first two knuckles with the bones of your forearm while keeping your wrist straight. This will keep you from making contact with only the ring and pinky knuckle," he said, slowly moving his arm back then allowing his fist to hit my hand softly. "You risk breaking your hand if you continue to punch the way you just did," he stated firmly.

I nodded approvingly.

"Try again," he encouraged, holding up his palm, motioning me to strike.

"But my hand is so...."

"Use your left hand," he interrupted.

I shook my head, as though he were asking the impossible.

"You're going to have to learn to use both," he spoke, intuiting my reluctance.

227

"Fine," I agreed, feeling foolish.

Awkwardly, I slowly pulled back my left hand back and struck Jax's hand equally as gently as he had struck mine, making sure my entire fist made contact.

"Try again," he nodded.

"Like for real?" I asked.

"Just think about how I snuck up on you earlier," he added, smirking.

That was all the encouragement I needed. I quickly pulled my arm back and hit Jax's palm as hard as I could. Surprisingly, my hand did not throb in pain, but once again Jax stood there, completely unaffected by my efforts. He lowered his hand and crossed his arms, while taking a wider stance.

"You did better by making the appropriate contact, but we are going to have to start with the basics," he began. "Never close your eyes when throwing a punch. You need to always be aware of which direction the counter-attack will be coming from. Keep your arms level with your shoulders. Your left arm was higher, which caused you to lose some momentum. Keep your chin down, not up, this way the punch comes out straight. Also, your stance was incorrect. Since you are right handed, let your left shoulder face your opponent. Keep your feet hip-distance apart in a triangular stance," he continued.

I stood there confused yet amazed, while watching Jax demonstrate the moves effortlessly as though he coached at a boxing gym.

"You must stay balanced between both feet and always start by slightly rotating your hips. This will give you a more powerful punch. Jab quickly then always return back to guard position," Jax finished, completing the motion.

"What, is Zenith some sort of world champion boxer or something?" I asked, bewildered at Jax's detailed knowledge.

"No, but his combative skills are highly advanced and his Collectors are well trained," he stated in a more serious tone.

"If you're saying this is going to be a strictly physical battle, then I may need to rethink my decision," I said, feeling slightly sick to my stomach.

Jax sighed, tossing his hair out of his eyes.

"I never said it would, but I need you and your brother to be prepared for whatever he throws at us. Zenith will not step down without a fight. I want both of you to be ready."

"You make Aroonyx sound like a place where there are dangerous, bad guys lurking around every corner, Jax," I said, rubbing my sore hand. "I don't know if I can handle that. I don't know if I want to," I murmured.

"Elara, your everyday citizen of Aroonyx is not a threat. For the most part, it is still a peaceful place to live. It is only in meeting Zenith and his Collectors that we must observe caution. When we do return, your identities must be kept secret, otherwise we will be fighting off the Collectors around every corner."

"Jax it would take months, if not years, of serious training to prepare me for what you speak of," I started. "Even then, I don't think I could hurt someone, much less kill anyone!"

Jax looked away, breaking eye contact. The subtle breeze blew quietly around us. His posture shifted as he exhaled loudly. I gulped, thinking about the day I found Jax's gray knife and the stains I had hoped were rust. I felt as though I had spoken out of turn. It was obvious Jax was well-versed in combat. I was foolish to think he hadn't seen his fair share of battles.

"I will do everything in my power to keep you and your brother safe. I would never send you on a suicide mission. I will only take the two of you back to Aroonyx once I know you are ready and capable of defending yourselves. We have some time to train and prepare for what lies ahead. You must remember that you will advance much quicker in your training than the average human here on Earth. We will train at night when your powers are strongest, that way you will not tire, though I can't promise you won't feel your progress the next morning."

"Ah…" I interrupted, "so that's why I was so sore the next morning!"

"Typically, human's muscles need time to repair after strength training, but with you, like every Lunin, your muscles will repair by the next evening."

"Well that's a perk!"

"This won't be easy Elara, but if you stay focused and listen to exactly as I say then you will be ready," he said, making eye contact once more.

"What about Cyrus?" I asked.

"Cyrus has the benefit of being a Solin. Strength is not something we will have to focus on. I will have him direct his efforts on stamina and combative exercises," Jax answered.

I thought back to the strange phenomena that continued to happen when in the presence of Cyrus. I wondered if now was a good time to inform Jax of those strange occurrences, but quickly changed my mind. I already felt foolish around him most of the time. The last thing I needed was him asking questions I couldn't answer.

"Elara," Jax began, his worn boots moving forward once more, "I hope your sudden desire to return to Aroonyx is not strictly out of vengeance," he stated firmly.

"What?" I asked, confused by his question.

"It's a valid concern. Nothing positive ever comes out of revenge. You were adamant about staying here on Earth until I told you that Zenith was responsible for your parent's death," he continued.

"No! It isn't like that," I said.

Jax turned, looking unconvinced by my answer.

"Yes, Jax, it angers me that he sent the Collectors to kill Cyrus and me, but instead ended up murdering our parents. In fact, many emotions come up when I think about his actions. I feel hurt, betrayed, and sad that I will never get to meet the people who were responsible for our birth, but rest assured that my decision to return is not one of vengeance.

"I find it disturbing that the people of Aroonyx have had to endure two horrible dictators. When you told me the story about my parent's death, something struck a chord, but that chord wasn't necessarily personal. It now feels as though I have an actual account of how horrible life can be on Aroonyx with Zenith as its leader. I can't bear to think of life going on any longer like the way you described it. If you say I can help, then I want to be of service any way I can. Even if that means learning how to throw a punch," I finished, holding up my injured hand.

Jax smiled, satisfied by my response.

"I'm glad you see the situation as so. Forgive me, I misjudged your intentions."

I smiled, feeling relief wash over me. For the first time ever, it felt as though Jax and I were equals. I didn't feel the usual ten steps behind, running to catch up.

"Confidence is a good look for you, Elara," he remarked, continuing down the trail.

"Thanks," I smiled, feeling accomplished.

"Since you are unable right now to tell your brother everything you are so eager to share," he started, a small smirk crossing his face once more. "Perhaps there is somewhere else you would like to go?" he asked. "Did you want to go back to Starbucks? You won't have to worry about Cyrus being there this time."

Immediately the face of the overly friendly cashier popped into my mind.

"No!" I interrupted. "I don't want to go there."

"Okay, I only asked because you seemed so keen on it yesterday," replied Jax, sounding confused by my answer.

"Uh, I just don't feel like coffee right now," I lied.

"Well, this is your world, so what would you like to do?" he asked, stopping to face me.

"You mentioned we need to start training – so let's start training," I responded, overly confident.

"Yes, but I was planning on starting once the sun went down. I don't think you'll be able to handle it otherwise," he said, crossing his arms.

"Thanks for the lack of confidence Jax! That's really helpful," I replied.

"I only say that Elara because of your, how do I say it, lack of … experience back there," he said, nodding at the trail behind us.

"Well, you won't know until I try, will you?" I asked, attempting to stand taller.

Jax placed a hand under his chin thinking quietly, then walked in circles around where I stood, leaving me feeling both awkward and vulnerable.

"You're going to need to take that jacket off," he said stopping while motioning for me to remove the warm coat.

"Why? It's freezing!"

"You're not going to be able to move freely with all of that extra material weighing you down," he pressed.

"Is that why you never wear a jacket?" I asked curiously.

"No. I just don't find it cold here," he laughed.

"What?!" I exclaimed, my mouth opening at his response.

"I tried to give you all of the details about Aroonyx, but you were the one who said you didn't want to hear about weather patterns," he replied.

I shook my head, feeling irritated that I was once again trailing behind Jax's every move.

"We're going to get back to this," I answered, beginning to unzip the warm wool coat.

"I figured," said Jax, pushing up his sleeves.

Grimacing, I took the only article of warmth from my body. I shivered while placing the coat gently on the trail. I hopped up and down like a boxer in a ring attempting to get warm. Jax, unaffected as usual, stood unmoving, directly in front of me.

"You sure you want to start your training now?" he asked.

"Yes," I answered as my warm breath turned into white clouds as I exhaled.

"Okay then, let's start with some basic self-defense skills. You may not be the strongest person in a fight, but I can teach you how to block and protect yourself," he started.

"Great!" I replied, continuing my hopping motion.

"You're going to have to stand still," he said toward my bouncing feet.

"Right," I said, gluing my arms to my side.

"Let's go back to the locking hold I had you in earlier," he began.

I groaned aloud.

"Elara, either you want to learn or you don't," he stated firmly.

"I'm sorry. I do want to learn," I responded, feeling less confident by the minute.

"Typically, when someone is put into this position," started Jax, as he stood behind me sliding his arm between the two of mine, effortlessly pinning them both behind my back. "It is either by a surprise attack, as you witnessed earlier, or if someone has already been apprehended and the attacker needs to hold them in place."

Jax's rough hand covered my mouth, this time thankfully leaving my nostrils unblocked so I could breathe. I felt my heart begin to pound, protesting the uncomfortable position that I found myself in once more.

"Elara, I can feel your muscles beginning to contract. This response signals me to use more force to keep you from struggling."

Jax tightened his grip as I felt my legs begin to twist beneath me, trying to escape.

"Now I know you are trying to escape," he continued.

Jax moved his hand just so slightly, so that his thumb now covered my right nostril.

"I can maneuver my hand so that in a matter of minutes you will lose enough oxygen, rendering you unconscious."

At these words, I felt myself begin to panic. The more I wiggled, the stronger his grip became and the less amount of oxygen entered my body. I attempted twisting my hands out of his but only winced in pain, as he tightened his hold. I tried shaking my head but this only encouraged him to now cover both nostrils, restricting any further air flow. I felt myself begin to gasp for air, but was unsuccessful. I tried screaming into his hand, but my efforts were ineffective as he continued his tight grasp. Feeling light-headed, I once again felt my knees buckling. Just as before, Jax released his grip, but this time caught me before I hit the ground.

Gasping, I spun around.

"We need like a safe word or something," I said catching my breath. "I almost passed out."

"You had a few more seconds to go," he remarked.

I rolled my eyes at his lack of compassion.

"I tried to warn you. We really should wait until this evening so you don't tire as easily," Jax said, pushing his sleeves further up his well-defined arms.

"I'm not tired, I just freak out when I'm incapacitated like that," I replied, rubbing my wrist.

Jax stood, looking as though he were debating whether to continue with the lesson.

"Maybe just start less aggressively?" I asked.

Disagreeing with my suggestion, Jax shook his head.

"Elara, I wish I could go easier on you but we don't have time to be lackadaisical. I want you to know what it feels like when someone restrains you. We can't just go through the motions."

I found myself getting more and more anxious every time he mentioned the words "prepare" or "get ready," as though I were being deployed to a war I knew nothing about. I sighed aloud, feeling completely out of my element.

"Think about your reasons for wanting to return to Aroonyx," Jax continued. "They were all selfless. Not once did you mention returning for your own sake. Fighting for a selfless reason has a completely different effect than fighting for a selfish one."

I nodded, letting out a long exhale. Jax was right. I wasn't returning for a vacation or to visit my parents' grave site. I was returning, because I was committed to helping the people of Aroonyx rid themselves of Zenith and his Collectors.

Taking the thin hair tie off my wrist, I flipped my head upside down, wrapping my hair into a messy bun. I rolled and popped my neck facing Jax once more.

"Okay, I get it. I understand the point you're trying to make."

"You sure?" he asked, his eyes never leaving mine.

"Yeah, let's do this," I said, pushing up my sleeves.

CHAPTER 25

The next couple of hours flew by, as Jax instructed me how to successfully escape a locking hold. Over and over we practiced until he was confident with my progress.

"That's it!" he praised, as I broke free for the third time in a row. "Much better."

"I think the hardest part is getting the first arm free," I huffed, rubbing my throbbing arms.

Jax nodded. "Yes, that's exactly right. Once you get your right arm free just remember to pull down the attacker's arm, then bite hard and move your...."

"Left hand to the groin, while slipping out under his arm, leaving you behind the attacker," I finished confidently.

"I'm impressed," replied Jax.

I smiled, trying to mask the pain.

"Are your arms okay?" he asked, walking over to my side.

"They're fine," I lied, pulling down my sleeves.

Before I had time to react, Jax reached for my right, most injured arm. He gently pulled up the sleeve, grimacing when he saw the deep purple, rug-burn type marks that occupied my entire forearm.

"You should take a break," he stated.

"I'm fine. You said so yourself, it needs to ... feel real ... we can't just go through the motions," I said, in my best impression of Jax's voice.

He laughed at my pitiful attempt.

"I did say that, but I also don't want your parents thinking you've joined a gang, so let's take a break until this evening. You'll feel like a new person once the sun sets," he said, pulling my sleeve back down over my arm.

I was tired, exhausted for that matter, and my arms ached, but I couldn't tell him that. I wanted to appear stronger than I felt.

"Well, if *you* need a break than I guess that's fine with me," I said.

"I think I do," he smiled, obviously not buying my new can-do attitude.

Jax retrieved my coat, then helped me move my arms into the tight-fitting sleeves.

"Better?" he asked, lowering his head to look me in the eyes.

"Much!" I sighed, letting go of my tough façade.

"You are a horrible liar," chuckled Jax, as he began walking down the trail.

"You're not the first person to tell me that," I replied, thinking of Cyrus. "Are you by any chance hungry?" I asked hopefully, feeling my stomach protest the skipping of breakfast and lunch.

"I could eat," he answered.

"There's a pizza place not too far from here," I suggested.

"I've never eaten pizza," he commented, as though I had implied it was a delicacy.

"What? First coffee and now pizza? Well, we're going to fix that," I replied. "There's a place not too far from the high school. We can cut through the campus to save time," I said, pointing farther down the path.

He nodded and began to walk down the deserted trail.

"Elara," Jax began.

His voice was rigid and more serious than I had heard it all day.

"Yeah," I replied, feeling concerned.

"I want you to understand the reason behind why I teach the way I do,"

"No, you don't have to explain," I interjected. "I totally get it and you're right. I need to be trained as if it were actually happening."

"I'm glad you understand that aspect of my teachings, but what I'm trying to say is that the only reason I have you do these exercises repeatedly is simply for one reason…."

Jax stopped, turning to look me in the eye.

"Elara, you can never let them take you," he stated firmly.

"What do you mean?" I asked, feeling a chill creep up my spine.

"Yes, I want you to be able to defend yourself from an attack, but more importantly, I want you to be able to escape unharmed. If you are to fall unconscious, or become injured to the point where you are disabled, the Collectors will apprehend you and if this happens your chances of ever escaping alive are unlikely."

I gulped, feeling my eyes widen.

"I need you to understand that I will do my upmost to keep you and your brother safe, but regardless of whatever happens to me, you and Cyrus must keep moving forward and find a way to defeat Zenith," Jax finished, never breaking eye contact.

The thought of Jax being injured in a fight seemed surreal. He was strong, smart, and obviously skilled in the art of combat. He was my only window to a world I knew nothing about. Fear consumed me, as I contemplated the three of us returning to Aroonyx, only to be left alone in a dangerous and unfamiliar world. The thought of Jax not being there made our entire plan seem irrational.

"Why would you say something like that?" I asked.

"I say it because it's true. I feel confident in what the future holds for you, Elara, but I do not know that of my own," he said looking away.

"But Jax, you're obviously skilled and experienced in combat," I began.

"To someone like yourself I may be, but to Zenith and his Collectors I'm afraid you are mistaken," he mentioned, continuing down the path.

The air felt colder, as we walked silently the rest of the way to where the trail opened to the high school. I didn't know what to say. Small talk seemed irrelevant at this point. Jax's focused but positive attitude seemed to shift to a more somber tone, making me feel tense and unsure of our future.

"Hopefully, once Cyrus was up to speed and on board with everything I would feel less dependent on Jax for emotional support," I thought, walking close to his side.

I was completely comfortable and at ease with Cyrus. Maybe it was the simple fact that he was my twin brother, but just being around him made me feel calm, serene. I eyed Jax carefully as we approached the end of the trail. He was lost deep in thought with his eyes fixed on the winding path in front of him.

"What did I expect from him?" I wondered. "He's already informed me that he has lived a solitary life for many years and is emotionally detached. It's obvious he's guarded about something from his past. He's so serious, restricted, and careful, even when he speaks. Every word he utters has a distinct purpose that's meticulously timed and phrased. I just wish he would relax and try letting his guard down sometimes," I thought, burying my hands deeper into the warm pockets of my coat.

I thought of veterans who returned from war permanently changed by the things they had witnessed and experienced. I wondered if their behavior mirrored that of Jax's. My thoughts were cut short when he finally broke the long silence.

"Do you enjoy school?" he asked casually, stepping off the trail while pointing to the vast campus.

Slightly stunned by his change of tone, I paused before answering.

"It's okay," I remarked, stopping to admire the empty school grounds.

"What subjects do you prefer?"

"Uh…Science and Math, I guess," I added, confused by his now chatty behavior.

"That would make sense," he mentioned, motioning for me to lead the way.

I stepped off the trail, bypassing Jax while heading toward the parking lot.

"Does Cyrus prefer English over Science?" he asked in an upbeat tone while following me down the sloping hill.

"Jax," I said, turning in my tracks. "I'm having a very difficult time trying to figure you out. One minute you seem cheerful and talkative, then the next minute you seem distant or upset. Is it me? Is it my lack of knowledge with … everything that is frustrating you?" I asked.

He looked away, clearly irritated by my comment then turned, making eye contact once more.

"Elara, my behavior has nothing to do with you so don't waste your time trying to figure me out. I told you before, I have a challenging time connecting with people on an emotional level. I will spare you the details of my childhood, but I can tell you that for the most part it was the furthest thing from pleasant," he finished.

"I'm sorry," I whispered, feeling as though I had pushed him into a corner. "I didn't know."

"No, you didn't know and you don't need to know, so let's stay focused on the task at hand; preparing you and Cyrus for your return to Aroonyx, nothing more. Please do not hang onto every word or take anything I say personally. I'm aware that you find me closed off and perhaps guarded."

My eyes darted around nervously, as though he could read my every thought. I felt embarrassed, as if my privacy had been invaded.

"And you are correct in thinking so. I am closed off and guarded. I have my reasons, none of which concern you," he finished, walking past me down the hill.

I stood there regretting my decision not to answer his question about whether Cyrus liked or disliked English. It was obvious I had misread the situation, thinking Jax and I were friends. Frustrated, I walked quietly down the hill, wishing Cyrus were here to confide in.

It wasn't long before we had made our way to the empty parking lot. The steel-gray sky overhead, hung like a heavy shadow above the two of us. Jax stood in front of me with his hands resting rigidly next to his side.

"I know I made you uncomfortable Elara, and I apologize," he remarked, still facing forward.

"Don't worry about it. I understand how this relationship is going to work. I was mistaken earlier, but now I totally get it. You're here on a mission, strictly to bring Cyrus and me back to Aroonyx. You didn't come here to make friends," I added, my tone sounding colder than I had anticipated.

Jax whipped around, his face full of disappointment. He rubbed his rugged face with both hands as he shook his head, trying to rid his mind of my words.

"Elara, you just don't get it," he said, sliding his hands slowly down his face. "Of course, I want to be your friend. I obviously care about you and your brother, or I wouldn't be here. I'm aware that you question my behavior and overall demeanor. It's just that...."

Jax paused, as if not wanting to finish the sentence.

"It's just what?" I asked, throwing my hands up, exasperated.

"It's just that I'll never be able to give you want you want!" he exclaimed, his blue eyes never leaving mine as he spoke.

My face flushed, as the blood quickly rushed to my cheeks.

"And what exactly do you think I want?" I stammered.

Jax hesitated, folding his arms tightly across his chest, then spoke quietly as if not wanting the empty parking lot to hear our conversation,

"I'm not a sensitive, stable, or an emotionally invested person, Elara. I'm unsure if I will ever be. I don't want you naively believing that I will change for you, or for anyone for that matter."

I scoffed, feeling the frustration inside boil over.

"Jax! You are my only outlet to this world that I know nothing about. First you show up in my life and completely turn it upside down. Then you inform me that I must prepare both physically and mentally, as if deploying for war and finally, somehow in my free time manage to figure out a way to convince Cyrus that any of this is real! What do I want, Jax? I want a friend. I want someone I can confide in, someone I can trust won't leave me to figure this out alone. I'm not asking you to change who you are, I'm just asking that maybe you put forth some effort to show me that you aren't this distant person on auto-pilot just going through the motions. Obviously, we're going to be spending a lot of time together. It would be nice if you could let down your guard just enough so I could see you for who you really are."

Warm tears filled my eyes as I suddenly began to feel my emotions get the best of me. I blinked hard, turning my face swiftly away from Jax, wishing he would lower his gaze.

Observing my discomfort, Jax quickly interrupted.

"I understand what you are asking. Rest assured that you can trust and confide in me as a friend. I can promise you that I am here for you and I will not disappear and leave you or Cyrus alone on this journey. I'm sorry that I'm not the person you *want* me to be right now, but this is all I have to offer," he said, motioning to himself.

Continuing to look away, I nodded, feeling frustrated that he hadn't given me the answer I had hoped to hear.

"It wasn't like I had asked him to change who he was...or had I?" I questioned myself.

Jax stood motionless, observing the empty parking lot. His face, older than mine, looked troubled, as if he were carrying a heavy burden.

"Maybe asking Jax to change to benefit my own needs was the wrong approach," I pondered quietly. "Maybe if I..."

My thoughts were interrupted once more, as Jax found my eyes with his.

"Elara, I am truly sorry if I've caused you any distress. It was never my intention to do so. I can only imagine how challenging it must be to accept the request to return to Aroonyx. I understand that I'm not the easiest person to relate to on an emotional level. I cannot guarantee that I will be the person you want in your life, but I will do everything in my power to be the person you need."

In that moment, Jax spoke with more feeling then I had ever heard. His voice was quiet but slightly unsteady. It was this rare instant of vulnerability that made him seem more real to me than ever before. I remained focus on his eyes, feeling as though I were seeing him for the first time.

"Thank you," I nodded, feeling comforted.

There was a quiet moment between the two of us in the vast, empty parking lot. An acceptance of our roles on this mission together seemed to unfold, as a we stared at one another.

The remainder of the afternoon had a certain quality to it that was different from any of the other previous visits with Jax. We walked side-by-side, picking up exactly where we left off about whether Cyrus enjoyed English class. There was a calmness between us that was so strong it suddenly felt tangible.

My feet effortlessly directed me to the local pizza restaurant located a stone's throw from the high school. We ate together quietly, speaking only when necessary. Time passed as I sat smiling, watching Jax enjoy his meal.

As soon as I accepted him for who he was, I began to see him in an entirely different perspective. Yes, he was detached and distant, but he was also kind and gentle. Though he wasn't my perfect idea of a companion, he was perfect in every other way. It was on that day that I decided to accept Jax for who he was; a troubled man trying to make the best out of the cards he had been dealt.

Jax wiped his mouth with the paper napkin, then placed it gently on the wooden table.

"You feel anything?" he asked.

"Full. I shouldn't have eaten three whole pieces," I groaned.

A large grin crossed his face before speaking.

"It's almost sundown," he noted, nodding toward the large double doors of the restaurant.

My head turned, noticing the light beginning to fade from the late afternoon sky.

"Are you ready to continue your training?" he asked, raising an eyebrow.

I felt my body begin to feel revived as it did every night. My mind felt clear and refreshed, as though I had just awakened from a restful sleep. I stretched my arms overhead, feeling the soreness of the day's earlier training begin to diminish.

"Ready as I'll ever be," I answered, smiling at Jax.

CHAPTER 26

I winced as I made my way slowly down the stairs.

"I don't remember them being so steep," I complained, my muscles flinching with every small step.

Jax was right about "feeling my training" the next morning. The past week had been more physically demanding than I could have ever imagined. Every morning, Jax met me on the trail, teaching me basic theory of combat and every evening as soon as the sun set we would begin what he like to call "hands-on training."

In this short amount of time, I had successfully achieved how to throw a punch without injuring my hand, escape a surprise attack from behind, block a strike coming from the side, and my least favorite, how to successfully escape the dreaded two-handed choke.

On top of the brutal hands on training, Jax had me perform several strength-training exercises that would have otherwise killed me, had I not the benefit of my nightly power of endurance. Repeatedly, I groaned over sit-ups, lunges, squats and pull ups, until our time was finally up. Every evening I returned home, bruised and bloodied, but felt alive and energized. Every morning I awoke with an agonizing, unsubtle reminder of the previous night's events.

The morning after our first training was so intense that I remained in bed for an hour, crying quietly to myself, literally afraid that I would be unable to stand. Jax instructed me to inform my parents that I had signed up for a self-defense class at one of the local martial-arts schools. I lied, telling them that I had entered a drawing and won six free weeks of intensive training sessions that lasted from 6:00 p.m. to 10:00 p.m. every night of the week. For some odd reason, they believed me.

I sighed with relief as my feet found the bottom of the stairs.

"Elara! Is that you?" my mother called from the living room.

It was Friday morning and my mother sat drinking coffee on the sofa, watching Good Morning America.

"Who else would it be?" I asked, rolling my eyes.

"Quick, come look!" she gasped, pointing to the television screen. "There's this cutest little dog that can walk on his hands!" she said, cheerfully.

"Dogs don't have hands!" I yelled from the hallway, not wanting to walk any farther than necessary.

"Well now you missed it," she scoffed, irritated by my lack of enthusiasm. "He was so cute. They trained him to walk on his hands over to Robin…"

"I'm leaving," I interrupted.

"Not so fast young lady! Come over here," she demanded.

I groaned as I limped into the living room.

"Look at you," she barked. "You look like you've been hit by a bus!"

"I feel like I've been hit by a bus. Wait, no, a semi-truck," I corrected.

"This self-defense class seems a little too intense don't you think?" she asked, making a distasteful face, noticing the large bruise on my neck.

"Mom," I sighed. "I told you it was an intensive session," I reminded.

"Well, I don't like it!" she snapped. "You look like you're training to be a boxer or something."

I burst into laughter, thinking how much easier that idea sounded than what I was really preparing for.

"Look at it this way," I began. "I can get a few bruises now, but be prepared if someone attacks me, or I can quit and in a few months when I move out and am living all alone, just hope that I never find myself in a precarious situation," I said, playing into her fearful thoughts.

"That's not funny, Elara!"

"I'm not laughing, I'm just simply reminding you of the world we live in."

"And I'm reminding you that dinner is at 7:00 tonight."

"I don't get out of training until 10:00," I countered.

"Well tonight you better figure out a way, because you haven't had a meal at home all week," she said, lowering her eyes at me.

"Fine," I said, tossing up my sore arms, and immediately regretting it, "I'll see you at 7:00."

She smiled, satisfied with her win before settling back into her spot on the couch, remote in hand.

I limped to the front door, slipping my feet into the old pair of boots, wishing they would lace themselves. There I stood, debating whether they even needed to be tied, then finally surrendered, groaning as I bent forward to secure the brown laces. I inhaled deeply as I stood outside the front door, mentally preparing myself for day ahead.

The air was chilly but felt warmer as the sun finally showed its face in the cloudless sky. My mood brightened once I was out of the house and back outdoors. I had spent more time outside during the past week than in the last month alone and suddenly found myself preferring the change.

I walked gingerly toward the trail, listening to the birds chirping, sounding pleased with the bright day. I found myself turning my head frequently, checking behind to see if Jax was lurking, waiting to pounce. His surprise attacks were not to be taken lightly and each time I never saw him coming.

The sound of a car coming up from behind caused me to flinch as my arms instinctively moved to the guard position. The man driving the car did a double take, looking at me as though I were mental. I waved awkwardly trying to act as though my defensive move was just that, a casual wave. I could have sworn he sped off quicker than he had approached. I laughed to myself, knowing even Jax would have found the situation humorous.

I noticed the entrance to the trail not far ahead, feeling my stomach churn with excitement. Accepting Jax for who he was and simply letting go of any desire to change him transformed our relationship altogether. It was only through this acceptance that I had the ability to notice him in a different light. Once I stopped focusing on what I found to be his faults, I began to see him in a lighter way. I observed him smiling and laughing more than ever. His once-distant, quiet, and closed-off demeanor I now saw as moments of contemplation and reflection. I didn't ask about his past, knowing that his time here on Earth was most likely an escape from whatever troubles he dealt with back on Aroonyx. We had found a rhythm that we were both comfortable with and finally felt content, if not pleased, to be around one another.

I peered carefully into the shaded trail, straining to hear the slightest crunch of mulch under Jax's boots, but was surprised to see him standing in plain view. His head looked away slightly as he waved, acknowledging my presence. Painfully I hobbled over to where he stood, smiling, but then quickly frowning.

"Jax!" I exclaimed. "What happened?" I gasped, pointing to the three-inch gash that ran horizontally across the side of his unshaven face.

"Ran into an old acquaintance," he said, shrugging his shoulders.

Seeing Jax injured was unsettling. I had always assumed he was impermeable to harm. He was fast, agile, and could always predict which maneuver I was about to throw at him before I even had the chance to make contact. The thought of someone being able to get close enough to harm him was alarming.

"We should get you to a doctor. That looks *really* bad," I cringed, grimacing as I looked closer at the wound.

"I'm fine," he said, brushing me off. "It's not that bad."

"Not that bad? Jax, it looks like someone tried to slice your face off!"

"I believe that was his intention," he said, pushing up the sleeves of his shirt.

I shivered, imagining what sort of person was foolish enough to challenge Jax.

"Why didn't you just jump and get out of there?" I asked, bewildered.

"Two reasons, Elara. Firstly, I am unable to jump if someone is restraining me in a forceful way. Secondly, as I informed you before, it's not possible for me to jump for selfish reasons."

"Selfish reasons?" I questioned. "Jax, how is it selfish wanting to escape from a life-threatening situation?"

"It's selfish when that life-threatening situation is your own," he finished, as if I should have already known this bit of information.

"Well, that gash looks deep. It looks like you need stitches," I persisted, scrunching up my face as I spoke.

"Elara," he said, resting a hand on my shoulder. "I appreciate your concern, but we have a much more pressing situation to address today," he announced, ignoring my request.

My eyes glanced to his arm, noticing dried blood on the sleeve of his shirt.

"And what could be more important than seeking medical attention?" I asked.

Jax removed his hand from my shoulder, before crossing his arms.

"Cyrus is home," he said.

My jaw fell open, as my stomach filled with butterflies. The last week had been focused solely on my training. Every day I kept reminding myself that I needed to figure out a way to tell Cyrus, but every day I convinced myself that it could wait until the next.

"But I thought he wasn't coming back until Saturday!" I cried, feeling short of breath.

"He wasn't, but I sense something is wrong and that's why he and his family came home early. I can't get close enough to see exactly what the situation entails, but I could hear a lot of arguing going on inside their home."

"What do you think it could be?" I asked, becoming more frantic by the minute.

"I don't know, but I feel that it has something to do with what you told him the last time the two of you spoke," he said reluctantly, as if withholding information.

I suddenly felt protective of Cyrus, wanting to help any way I could.

"I need to get over there right away," I said looking at Jax.

"I think that's a very good idea."

"What do I say?" I asked, a nervous lump forming in my throat.

"First, you need to calm down," soothed Jax, noticing my discomfort. "Regardless of what he says, remember that he is your twin brother and the two of you have a deep bond that most will never understand. Be patient with him, Elara, and remember how you felt those first few weeks. I will check in on you to make sure things aren't getting out of hand if that makes you feel better."

"Yes, that would definitely make me feel better. Thank you, Jax," I replied, reaching out a hand.

"That's why I'm here," he said squeezing my hand gently, then vanished instantly, right before my eyes.

I flinched, startled by his disappearing act. My hand, still outstretched, held nothing but empty space. I inhaled, taking in a long deep breath.

"You can do this, Elara," I affirmed to myself, as I began a faster than usual pace down the trail back toward the entrance. I reached into my back pocket, retrieving the small phone, and searched for Cyrus's contact information. My finger paused over his name. I couldn't call him and tell him I was headed over to his house, especially not after what Jax had said. I would have to take my chances and hope he would see me. I had never been to Cyrus's home, but remembered he had told me that he lived not far from the entrance of my community. I searched his address on the maps application, relieved to see that it was only a twenty-two-minute walk away. I hobbled along as quickly as my sore legs would carry me, racking my brain about how to explain to Cyrus that he was from another planet.

I breathed heavily as I approached the tall, wrought-iron gates that stood at the entrance of his community. A gray-haired, over-weight security guard sat in the opulently decorated guard shack at the front of the well-manicured entrance.

Walking slowly up to the tiny window, I waved, making my presence known.

"Hi," I huffed, still short of breath. "I'm here to visit Cyrus Lofton," I stated, moving the strands of hair that had escaped my pony tail out of my face.

"Is Mr. Lofton expecting you?" he asked, irritated by my presence.

"Uh, yeah, they just got back from their trip and he had borrowed my ...uh..." I stuttered, trying to come up with a reason to my visit.

The security guard tapped his fat thumb rhythmically on the window ledge, clearly not buying my story.

"Let me just call the Loftons and verify that they are expecting you," he began, reaching for the tan cordless phone.

"NO!" I yelled, louder than intended.

Annoyed with my outburst, he held the phone in hand while dangling his thumb over the numbers in a taunting like motion.

"You see, his mom and I don't really get along so I was just hoping to knock and grab my shirt from him," I continued, not realizing what I had said.

"You let Mr. Lofton borrow your shirt?" he asked, looking unamused while crossing his plump arms.

"What?" I asked, quickly reviewing our dialogue exchange.

His thick, gray eyebrows raised, implying that he needed an explanation.

"You see, it's this old concert T-shirt that we sometimes swap back and forth so...."

"I don't want the details of what you young kids are doing these days," he said, reaching over his desk.

"He's going to turn me away," I thought, feeling frustrated and wondering if I could scale the large electric gate.

A loud clicking noise startled me, as I watched the tall iron gates slowly open, granting me access.

"Thank you," I rejoiced, smiling at the guard.

"Kids these days," he murmured, shaking his head.

Relieved, I rushed through the gates, pushing past the pain that radiated throughout my legs. Fortunately, Cyrus's street was only blocks from the main entrance. Giant brick and stucco homes surrounded a pristine, emerald-green golf course.

I gawked as not two-car, but four-car garages were standard with every home site.

Cyrus obviously came from a family with more money than most, but he never mentioned anything about the privileged life he lived. He was always humble and kind, seemingly unaffected by worldly goods.

Double-checking the address on my phone, I stopped, starring up at the enormous stone and brick home which sat at the end of a large cul-de-sac. It reminded me of a miniature castle. The only thing missing was a draw bridge and moat. A large brick, semi-circular drive way took up most the front yard. Not four, but six garages lined the far end of the house. My eyes scanned the three opened ones in hopes of finding Cyrus's black Camaro. I exhaled, feeling both relief and anxiety wash over me once I saw his car parked in the far-right garage. Rolling my shoulders back and standing tall, I mustered every ounce of courage I could find, taking a small step onto the brick driveway.

I walked slowly up the steep stairs that led to the front door, which was easily twelve feet tall. My hand rested inches from the door, wishing Jax were here to convince me I had permission to knock. I shook my head, trying to shoo away any doubt about what I was about to do and knocked loudly three times. Within seconds, a small, dark-haired woman, wearing a uniform, opened the massive wooden door.

"Yes?" she asked in a soft voice.

"Uh... I'm here to see...."

"Who is it, Gloria?" called a woman's voice from somewhere inside the mansion.

"A girl," the small woman replied, motioning to where I was standing.

The sound of clicking heels echoed loudly through the halls, stopping behind the towering door.

The tiny woman lowered her head and quickly walked away as a tall, blonde woman came into view. She could have easily passed as Cyrus's biological mother. Her tan skin glowed in contrast to the stark white sleeves of her pressed blouse and her sleek blonde hair rested neatly on her shoulders. She sniffled loudly, wiping beneath her eye. Black mascara ran down the sides of her cheeks, streaking her flawless complexion.

"Cyrus is not having visitors right now," she managed, her voice slightly shaking.

I felt panicked, unsure if I should push past her yelling for Cyrus or run as fast as I could back to the trail.

"Who is it?" yelled a deep voice, from inside the home.

She looked at me, shaking her head before responding.

"I don't know honey, some … solicitor," she said, motioning for me to leave as she began shutting the door.

Shocked by her response, I yelled through the closing door. "Cyrus, it's Elara!"

She jumped, startled by my behavior. Her eyes, resembling daggers, glared as though I had declared a personal vendetta against her.

Footsteps thundered down the stairs, echoing through the large home. I felt the familiar warming sensation take hold, as a large, tan hand moved between the closing door and the door frame.

"Cyrus, you're not leaving this house today!" the woman spoke, her voice on the verge of tears. "We still have to sit down and discuss everything that happened," she pleaded.

"Move away from the door, mother."

"Don't do this Cyrus! You're upset and your father thinks it's best…."

"My father?" he bellowed. "I could care less what that man thinks is best!"

"Cyrus, please," she begged.

"Step away from the door, mother!" he yelled, causing me to jump backward.

My hands shook uncontrollably with heat as I thought back to Jax's warning of the dangers of Solins during the day if they felt cornered.

"Please move away from the door," I quietly beseeched his mother.

Relieved, I watched as she side-stepped, just seconds before Cyrus threw the door open with a loud BANG! Covering her face with her delicate hands, she ran off, sobbing uncontrollably. Cyrus blew past me while storming down the steep front steps and heading toward the garages.

"Cyrus!" I called, wondering if he had even noticed me standing there.

"Get in the car, Elara!" he shouted, continuing his fast pace.

"Why? Where are we going?" I asked, heading down the steps.

"Just get in the car!" he roared.

"Okay, just stop yelling!" I demanded, running to catch up.

"I'm not yelling... yet," he snapped, opening the driver's side door.

CHAPTER 27

I gulped, questioning whether it was safe to get inside the car. Jax's expression of "I told you so" entered my mind, as I rested my hand on the passenger door handle, unsure what to do next. I felt the heavy door push open from the inside of the car, as Cyrus started the engine. He motioned quickly for me enter the vehicle. Without thinking, I slid onto the cool, black leather seat, slamming the door behind me.

Cyrus shifted into reverse, flying out of the garage, then switched into first gear, sending my body shooting forward. Frantically, I reached for my seatbelt. Once I secured it, I grabbed the handle above the window with my right hand keeping my left outstretched to brace myself from his erratic driving.

"Cyrus! Slow down! You're going to kill us," I said, flinching as he rounded a corner, ignoring a stop sign.

He down shifted, slowing the car as my head once again jerked forward.

"Where are we going?" I asked, noticing Cyrus's appearance for the first time that day.

His usual, calm, collective self was completely disheveled. His short white-blond hair, always gelled to perfection, lay flat and lifeless on his head while his worn hoodie somehow managed to get tucked in the back of his loose shorts but not the front. He was missing his belt and the strangest part of all was that he wore flip-flops in the near freezing weather. I had never seen Cyrus so undone. His face was red and his eyes darted back and forth, reminding me of a suspect on the run.

"Cyrus," I began cautiously. "Where are we going?"

My voice was calm, as if I were trying to talk someone down from the ledge of a tall building.

"I don't know yet. I just need to drive."

We blew through the entrance of the community, only pausing to allow the gates to open just enough to squeeze through. I watched as the security guard almost fell off his chair watching us drive away.

Cyrus headed out of Woodward, merging onto the busy highway, reaching eighty-five miles an hour within seconds. I exhaled loudly, gripping the assist handle tighter. Within seconds the car slowed to the appropriate speed limit.

"Thanks," I said, acknowledging Cyrus's efforts.

I watched anxiously, as his hand gripped the steering wheel, afraid he would rip it off the column once more.

"So how was your trip," I said, instantly regretting my decision to speak.

His laugh, resembling that of a maniacal villain out of movie, caused me to rethink my decision to enter the vehicle.

"Oh, where to begin," he said, speeding up to change lanes. "First we can start with the exciting news that you decided to share with me on Friday before school. Yes, that was interesting. You informed me that not only were we brother and sister but twins," he said, moving his hand off the steering wheel, gesturing to the both of us. "I spend the day completely bewildered, then hurried home to catch an evening flight for our family's yearly ski trip. I sit on the flight observing both of my parents, feeling more and more upset by your words. "These are my parents," I thought, "I've known them my entire life. Why would Elara say such things?" I kept asking myself.

"I may not agree with their plans for my future, but they wouldn't lie to me for eighteen years. I felt better, convinced that you were mistaken, and decided to let go of these foolish thoughts and just enjoy the slopes. The first few days went by smoothly, until my father decided to once again bring up the fact that I had not heard back from Notre Dame."

I hissed in fright, as Cyrus dodged around a slower vehicle, while wailing on the horn, displaying his frustration.

"Now, here's where the vacation got really exciting. I finally decided to come clean and tell my father that I had not heard back from Notre Dame, because I never applied. He became irate, telling me I was irresponsible and didn't appreciate everything he and my mother had done for me over the years. We continued arguing heavily until my mother burst into the hotel room informing us she could hear us all the way from the elevator. She begged my father not to spoil the trip and to drop it until we returned home. He refused, and in the midst of his anger, managed to say to mother just loud enough so I could hear, ". . . doesn't even matter he was never really my son anyway."

My eyes closed tightly, genuinely hurting for Cyrus. He rarely ever spoke about his father but when he did his mood always changed. I had always wondered why, until now. I had never imagined his father to be so cruel.

"What did you say?" I asked.

"Everything you told me on Friday came flooding back into my mind. I stood there in shock and then suddenly this feeling of intense anger came over me. It was more than just an emotional experience, it was physical. It felt like my entire body was vibrating with heat that needed to escape. I looked my mother directly into her eyes and asked if I was adopted. You know what she did? She lied straight to my face and said I was ridiculous to think such things. My father on the other hand, quickly corrected her, saying 'Yeah, we adopted you' as though he were reading the stats from my last football game."

"Oh, Cyrus, I'm so sorry they handled it that way," I said, shaking my head.

"Here's where it gets really interesting," he continued. "My father then decided it was a good idea to get in my face and inform me that maybe they should have chosen a different child, one who would appreciate the opportunities they had given."

"Oh no," I thought.

"Everything after that was sort of a blur. It was like time stopped as I watched my body react to this intense anger that was radiating from within me. I didn't think I even pushed him that hard. I just wanted him out of my face. I'm not a violent person, Elara!"

"I know you're not, Cyrus!"

"He flew clear across the hotel room, into the full-length mirror, shattering it everywhere. My mother looked at me as though I had just committed a murder."

"Was he hurt?" I asked cautiously.

"Not really, it sounded a lot worse than it looked. Fortunately, he only had a small cut on his head, but that didn't stop hotel security from running up to our room. My mother, being the expert liar in the family, told the hotel staff the mirror somehow managed to fall off the wall onto my poor innocent father. Management informed us the cost of the hotel room stay would be on them, then they brought us room service - along with an EMT to check on my father's injury. I didn't stick around long after security left. I packed and headed straight for the airport, catching the next flight back to Houston. My mother and father were not far behind."

"Wow," I sighed, watching us zoom past the cars on the busy highway. "I don't even know what to say, Cyrus. I'm so sorry that happened. When do you get back?"

"Late last night. I haven't spoken to, or even as much as looked at my father since he got home. They flew in early this morning. My mother is a complete mess right now. Her perfect little world is crumbling beneath her," he said, changing lanes once more.

I looked over at Cyrus, feeling truly empathetic to his situation. I thought I had endured a rough couple of weeks. I can't imagine how I would have handled things, if my parents had not been understanding and supportive.

It bothered me seeing Cyrus coming unraveled. He was the strong, calm, practical one, who always knew the right thing to say when I was stressed or anxious. I wanted to be supportive, but I didn't have a clue where to begin. I racked my brain in search of a way to tell Cyrus about our parents, Jax, and the plan of returning to Aroonyx to defeat Zenith. I suddenly felt sick to my stomach and instinctively reached for the button to let down the window. Cyrus glanced over, once he noticed the loud buzz and cool air coming from the passenger side of the car.

"You okay?" he asked, sounding slightly more like himself.

I nodded, not wanting to speak; I was afraid I would vomit all over the leather dash board. As the crisp outside air blew into my warm face, I took small, short breaths, attempting to calm my nervous stomach.

"So, this Jax guy you mentioned. He's the same guy who told you about us being adopted? Who is he?" he asked, diving right in.

My head spun; my heart raced.

"Can I have some of that?" I managed, pointing to the half-full water bottle sitting in the cup holder.

"Uh … it's been in here for like a week," he warned.

Not caring, I grabbed the bottle, twisted off the cap and gulped down the remainder of the water. I exhaled, feeling some relief then screwed the cap back on before placing it back into the cup holder.

"Jax is someone from our past. Funny enough, he knew us when we were born," I began, completely unsure of what I was trying to say.

"Elara, correct me if I'm wrong, but he didn't look that much older than us when I almost hit him with my car," Cyrus interrupted.

"That's because he's not that much older," I laughed aloud, nervously.

"Well, now I'm confused," Cyrus said, shaking his head.

"Cyrus, I was trying to explain all of this to you on Friday but as you know that didn't go over very well, so I'm just going to come clean and lay it all out on the table. You are going to think that I have lost my mind, but I beg of you, please do not allow yourself to get upset. I really need you to stay as calm as humanly possible. Can you do that?" I asked, rotating in my seat to face him.

"You already told me that not only am I adopted, but that we're twins. I'm not sure what else you could say that could top that."

"You'd be surprised," I murmured, under my breath. "Cyrus, the reason Jax doesn't look much older than us is because he isn't that much older. You and I, and Jax, are all from another planet where time moves much slower than here on Earth."

Just hearing myself speak sounded like a joke. How did Jax manage to explain any of this? When he spoke, everything, though crazy sounding, somehow made sense. When I spoke, it sounded like I was trying to explain the plot for the latest science-fiction movie.

"Right," Cyrus mumbled, shifting the car into a higher gear.

"Okay, I understand that probably didn't make any sense. Also, I'm aware of the fact that everything I just told you sounded completely mental, but it's the truth!"

"Elara, let me just stop you right there. Do you even hear yourself right now?"

I smiled, remembering my response to Jax when he informed me that I was from another planet.

"Cyrus, there's no easy or simple way to explain any of this. You can't deny the fact that something within you has changed since your eighteenth birthday."

I watched Cyrus process this bit of information. He inhaled deeply as his eyes remained focused on the road ahead.

"Don't you find it strange, that suddenly after your birthday you're able to display the strength of ten men?" I asked, still twisted uncomfortably in my seat.

"Probably just adrenaline," he remarked, brushing me off.

"Adrenaline? Really? You were the one who told me it wasn't adrenaline that day at practice. Everyone noticed your super-human like strength. Then the incident with your father? You can't think these are just coincidences! Every time I am around you, I feel this strange surge of heat radiate throughout my body. It's like a gentle vibration that ripples through my veins. You were in the car when I ripped this right off," I motioned, pulling down on the repaired assist handle. "And, let's not forget about the steering wheel! You watched at NASA when I barely touched Cliff, but somehow manage to send him flying into Taylor. When I'm around you, Cyrus, it as though..." I stopped, finally assembling the missing puzzle piece. "I share your Solin traits!"

Quickly, I recalled every moment that I had spent with Cyrus, confirming this theory.

"Cyrus," I cried, pointing toward the windshield. "Quick, tell me what that sign way up in the distance reads."

"What?" he asked, confused by my question.

"Just do it," I snapped.

"Uh ... Cracker Barrel," he answered, unamused.

"No! The green road sign, way beyond that, right before the exit for the Beltway," I corrected.

Cyrus leaned forward, glancing over at me as though I had completely lost my mind.

"Greenspoint," he replied flatly.

"Ah ha! I can read it too!" I celebrated.

"Good for you," he said glancing at me suspiciously.

"Cyrus, don't you get it! That sign is like half a mile away from us right now. No human can read a sign that far away and the exciting part is that now I can read it too! Try another one," I said, wiggling anxiously in my seat.

"Elara, you're really starting to freak me out. Let' just …."

Our conversation was cut short by a familiar popping noise, amplified due to the confined space of the vehicle. In an instant, Jax appeared out of thin air, sitting cramped in the back seat of Cyrus's car.

CHAPTER 28

"What the…" profanity escaped Cyrus's mouth, as he swerved into the right lane, barely missing a motorcyclist. He then over-corrected, sending Jax slamming into the left side of the car. The infuriated driver of the motorcycle displayed his anger with a one-fingered gesture as he quickly sped away from Cyrus down the long stretch of highway.

"Fascinating," said Jax, shifting his body back onto the seat behind my own. "I've never jumped inside of a vehicle."

"Really?" I asked smiling, turning my head to acknowledge Jax.

His injured face was covered by a large, beige bandage and his shirt appeared clean, free of dried blood. I felt satisfied, knowing he had taken my advice and sought medical attention.

"Can someone tell me what the hell is going on?!" Cyrus yelled. "Who are you? How did you get into my car?" he continued, eyeing Jax in the rearview mirror.

"Well, this is Jax," I said, pointing to the back seat. "You may want to put that seat belt on pretty tight," I whispered to Jax, motioning to the black belt.

He nodded in approval before speaking,

"Cyrus, I know you have a lot of emotions coming up right now. I also understand that you feel hurt, angry and confused by everything that has happened over the last week, but I need you to focus on driving this car safely. Why don't you head on over to your favorite spot on Crystal Beach where we can talk all of this through. I promise that by the end of the day you will understand everything that Elara has been trying to explain."

I shook my head, amazed at Jax's ability to make the strangest situation sound easier than it appeared. His silky voice and calming tone was hypnotic. Cyrus immediately slowed the car, and relaxed his tight grip on the steering wheel.

"How do you know about Crystal Beach?" Cyrus asked, his tone resigned.

"I have kept a close watch on you for your entire life," Jax said, leaning back against the black leather seat.

Cyrus glanced in my direction, just enough for me to notice.

"I'm aware that you believe this is the first time we have met and I recognize that the circumstance in which we are meeting today is a bit unconventional, but rest assured that even though you do not know me, I do know *you,* very well. I watched from a distance when you won your first football game; scoring three touchdowns. Your father stood on the sidelines, looking prouder than ever."

Cyrus's jaw clenched tightly, as Jax spoke. Nervously, I glanced back and forth between Cyrus and Jax's reflection in the rear-view mirror.

"I watched you comfort your mother at your grandfather's funeral, staying close to her side the entire day. I observed you take the blame when your friend stole that bicycle from the park. I also know that you and your father have never seen eye-to-eye on your future and I know that you drive to the exact same spot on Crystal Beach every time you need to clear your head."

I felt uncomfortable, as though I were eaves-dropping on a private conversation between Jax and Cyrus. I turned my head to look out the passenger window, pretending I was not sitting in the car listening to Cyrus's life review.

"I also watched you come home late last night," Jax continued. "Angry, hurt and confused that your parents lied to you for so long. I am aware of the relationship you have with your father, Cyrus. He has always been tough on you because he thinks that is how a father shows love to his son."

"Yeah, well, he's not my father, is he?" Cyrus added, changing lanes.

Jax sat quietly, rubbing the deep scar on the palm of his hand, lost deep in thought. The only noise that could be heard was the rush of passing vehicles. Minutes ticked away, as I sat unmoving with my head still turned away, afraid to speak.

"I shouldn't be here," I thought. "Jax was wrong. He should have told Cyrus all of this alone, exactly as he did with me. This was too much information for him to process and my presence was not helping the situation."

"Cyrus, why don't you just pull over somewhere and I can call my mom to pick me up?" I asked, hopeful my suggestion would relieve some of the tension.

"No!" Cyrus and Jax replied in unison.

I nodded, sinking back into the seat as if scolded by both parents. Jax moved forward in his seat as he spoke quietly, his head facing toward Cyrus.

"Cyrus, I also know that regardless of how crazy you think all of this is, somewhere deep down inside you know it to be true. Take me appearing out of thin air into your vehicle as an example. Any other person would have immediately pulled over and run from their car if they didn't crash it first, but not you. You and your sister here," Jax said nodding in my direction, "...are not like most people, Cyrus."

Cyrus sighed, letting out a long, deep breath while closing his eyes momentarily.

"Why don't you just drive down to Crystal Beach and listen as I try my best to clarify everything you have just heard," Jax advised, leaning back in his seat once more.

Cyrus nodded in agreement, continuing the drive down the long stretch of highway. Time passed slowly as Jax started from the beginning, explaining to Cyrus the differences between Earth and Aroonyx. He then described Solins and

Lunins, motioning toward my seat when describing the contrasting features between the two inhabitants. Once he heard Jax explain the super strength and incredible eyesight every Solin possesses, Cyrus seemed relieved, almost relaxed.

I wanted to join in on the conversation and inform Jax about my new discovery of being able to display Solin traits, but quickly changed my mind, not wanting to take the focus off Cyrus.

We exited onto a different stretch of highway after passing the tall, glass windows of the buildings that created the downtown Houston skyline. Jax effortlessly informed Cyrus on the history of Aroonyx, beginning with Arun's reign, just as he did during our time together. Cyrus drove quietly, never questioning or commenting on any of the information he heard.

I found it helpful listening to Jax speak about our past for the second time, now fully absorbing small details I had apparently missed. I watched Cyrus's jaw clench and his hand squeeze the steering wheel tighter when Jax spoke about the night of our parents' death. By the time Jax clarified the reason for their death, finally mentioning Zenith's name, it looked as though Cyrus wanted to punch a hole in the glass windshield.

I interjected every now and then, trying to reassure Cyrus that I also had a difficult time believing everything Jax had told me. I spoke of my own intense emotions that had come up when I heard of our parents' death. My attempts were feeble, but I hoped he would find comfort in knowing I was sitting in his position not long ago.

We were in the car for well over two hours before we finally reached our first stopping point. As the car slowed to a crawl, I did a double-take wondering where in the world he was taking us.

"Are we boarding a ferry?" I asked, gawking at the large red-and-white boat that sat idled at the end of an old dock.

"It's the only way to get to Crystal Beach," Cyrus commented quietly.

"I've never been on a ferry boat," I smiled.

It was clear that I was the only one excited about this part of the journey. Jax and Cyrus remained quiet as the car slowly pulled onto the old boat. A man standing aboard the vessel gestured for us to park behind a blue pick-up truck. Cyrus pulled into the open space as directed, shifted the car into neutral while engaging the emergency break and then turned off the ignition. He exhaled, opening the door in one swift motion and climbed out, stretching his arms over his head.

"Elara," Jax whispered from the back seat. "I need some time to speak with Cyrus alone."

"Of course," I replied, feeling relived to be excused from the awkward situation, but found myself curious as to Jax's sudden desire to exclude me from the conversation.

I unfolded out of the low riding car, releasing the handle of the seat so that Jax could exit the vehicle. He smiled at me briefly, then motioned with a subtle nod for Cyrus to follow him. Complying, Cyrus trailed closely behind Jax, keeping his hands tucked into his pockets. Jax stopped to lean over the side of the ship with his hands outstretched on either side of him while Cyrus stood close by, looking uncomfortable.

I decided to head to the upper deck of the boat, leaving the two of them alone. The steep metal stairs led to a spacious indoor cabin. Looking out through the large window, I noticed only a handful of people had chosen to leave their vehicles. Most sat inside the comfort of their cars, checking their phones or chatting to one another.

The sun shone brightly in the clear blue sky while the seagulls above flew in organized chaos, searching for food. An obnoxiously loud horn blew, signaling our departure. I gazed out the tall window as the ferry chugged slowly along the calm, murky seas. Tall palm trees lined the distant shore, their long leaves twisting and bending in the coastal breeze.

Walking toward one of the many empty seats, I pulled my cell phone out of my back pocket, noticing I had missed a text from my mother. I quickly replied to her, explaining that I was hanging out at the mall and would be home later. Not wanting any further interruptions, I put the phone on silent before slipping it back into my pocket.

I sat tapping the toe of my boot anxiously on the worn floor, wondering why Jax had to converse with Cyrus privately. Cramped from sitting in the small car for so long, I decided to walk over to another large window that gave me a perfect view of Cyrus and Jax. Cyrus spoke animatedly, which I found surprising, considering the mood he was in when I left. He looked relaxed, as if talking with an old friend. Jax stood with his arms crossed, nodding his head, acknowledging Cyrus as he spoke. Cyrus appeared to laugh as Jax smirked, then shook his head while turning to point to the exact spot where I stood observing their conversation. Embarrassed that my cover had been blown, I dropped to the floor, cringing as my muscles protested the unplanned move. Quickly, I crawled on hands and knees toward the front of the cabin, feeling my face flush. This crawling maneuver reminded me of the first night I had seen Jax through my bedroom window.

"I wonder if he found that humorous as well?" I thought, annoyed.

An older man, eyeing my predicament around the edge of his newspaper, watched until I eventually made it to the opposite end of the cabin. I stood, slowly peeking over the sill of another massive window, leaving only my forehead and eyes exposed. To my disappointment, Cyrus and Jax were no longer in sight.

The horn of the ferry blew loudly once more, startling me. Out of the front window I could see another dock. Heading down the steep, rusting stairs, I turned the corner to find both Jax and Cyrus, sitting in the car continuing their conversation. Unsure of where to go next, I began heading to the opposite side of the vessel. I stopped when I noticed Cyrus's arm waving out of the driver's-side window, motioning for me to rejoin the group. I walked quickly back to the car and opened the door softly, not wanting to interrupt, and slid back onto the cool leather seat.

"It's just a quick drive once we get onto the dock," said Cyrus, as if reading my mind.

"Cool," I replied unable to think of any other response. "So…" I started, unsure of how to ask Cyrus and Jax about how their private chat went.

"Everything is going to be fine Elara," Jax assured, answering my unspoken question.

"Cool," I repeated, feeling more and more child-like with every word I spoke.

Cyrus laughed and for the first time that day, he sounded like the Cyrus I knew so well. I joined in; looking over at him, relieved to have my friend back. Jax sat quietly in the back seat, allowing us this time to ourselves.

We pulled off the ferry boat onto a rickety dock and then slowly maneuvered onto a small paved road. We sat, now comfortably in silence, while Cyrus drove to a stretch of beach that looked as though it had been deserted long ago. He pulled the Camaro up next to a grassy sand dune and turned off the ignition. My eyes scanned the long stretch of beach, searching for anyone else crazy enough to be outside in the freezing temperature. A pack of stray dogs ran together, chasing each other through the surf, then headed over the sand dunes disappearing from sight.

"Is it usually this empty?" I asked, reaching for the door handle.

"The summer can get a little busier but typically, tourists prefer Galveston," replied Cyrus.

"Well, then I guess we have the whole place to ourselves," I said, climbing out of the car.

"That's why I come here," he said, stepping out of the vehicle.

Jax climbed out of the car, unaffected that he had been confined to a space half the size of his body twice today. He smiled casually in my direction, his blue eyes locking onto mine.

Cyrus motioned for us to follow, and the three of us made our way over the small grassy sand dunes.

"His choice of shoes makes perfect sense now," I thought, watching Cyrus's flip flops glide easily over the dunes.

I struggled with every step as my boots sank into the soft beige sand while Jax walked smoothly next to me, his boots managing to maneuver effortlessly. Cyrus continued his quick pace until he reached the shore line.

The greenish-blue waves lapped gently onto the wet sand, bringing sea weed and other debris onto the shore. The wind, much stronger on the coast line, sent strands of my hair flying in every direction. Large cargo ships, which I could see in great detail thanks to Cyrus's proximity, chugged along smoothly over the vast gulf.

"I'm going to take a walk," said Jax, turning away from me and Cyrus.

It was clear the two of us were not invited.

"Okay. We'll be ... here," I said, pointing to our feet in the sand.

Jax nodded, walking away from where Cyrus and I stood, never looking back.

"Is it just me, or is he a little odd?" Cyrus asked, watching Jax walk slowly down the empty beach.

I laughed at his observation, turning to face him.

"He grows on you over time," I said.

Cyrus smiled his large, pearly-white grin, then plopped down onto the cool sand. I followed suit, grimacing with the pain radiating from my sore muscles.

"You, okay, sis?" he asked, smirking.

"Ah ... that sounded weird!" I exclaimed, making a face at his sister reference.

"It's like Star Wars!" Cyrus proclaimed. "You know, when Luke had a crush on Leia, but then found out they were twins!"

"Oh geez ... stop it, Cyrus!" I exclaimed, punching his shoulder, sending him toppling over on his side.

"Ouch," he complained, rubbing his arm. "When did you learn how to throw a punch?"

"I've had some intense training as of lately," I said, pulling up my sleeves, proudly showing off my bruises.

"Man, Jax wasn't lying about this hands-on training we have to do, huh?" he asked, taking a closer look the black-and-blue marks on my arms.

"So, he told you about how we needed to prepare?" I asked, curiously.

"He mentioned it briefly. Said something about training me in the day and then you at night."

"Cyrus," I started in a more serious tone.

"I'm sorry, Elara," he interrupted.

I looked at him, confused by his response.

"I'm sorry I didn't believe you when you first told me everything."

"Cyrus, please!" I reassured. "You don't have to apologize for anything. It took me weeks to wrap my head around all of this . . . and honestly, I still wake up every morning wondering if it's all a dream."

"Jax did mention that you were pretty hard to convince."

"Oh, did he?" I asked, thinking back to their private conversation on the ferry boat.

"Maybe a little bit," he added, trying to recover.

"I've missed hanging out with you Cyrus."

"Me too," he said, gently nudging my shoulder with his.

We sat there quietly together, watching the waves crash onto the shore. Cyrus kicked off his black flip-flops, burying his feet in the cool sand and then laid onto his back, resting both hands under his head.

"Let me get this straight. We're supposed to train and prepare as if going to war, then return to Aranyx with Jax as our guide?"

"Aroonyx," I corrected.

"Right, Aroonyx and then attempt to defeat some megalomaniac and his group of murderous followers?" he asked, staring up at the clear sky while he spoke.

"That's the plan," I said, lying down next to Cyrus.

I paused before asking the next question, afraid of his response.

"So, you are considering going back?"

Cyrus sighed, closing his eyes.

"Elara, my entire life has been precisely planned out. Did you know I don't even love football?"

"What? I asked, utterly shocked.

"Yeah, I mean I'm good at it and enjoy the game, but I don't love it. That's why I never applied to Notre Dame. I knew I would get in, thanks to my father's connections, but I don't want to play football in college. I never wanted to. That was my father's plan, not mine. I wanted to go to a local college and take four long years to figure out what the hell I was going to do with my life."

I laughed aloud at his honesty, feeling relieved about my own uncertainties.

"Then you and Jax come along and turn my world as I know it upside down. I don't know if it was when he mentioned our parents' death, or when he spoke of how cruel Zenith has been, but something inside of me changed. If I have an opportunity to make a positive difference by helping the people of Aroonyx rid themselves of Zenith, and it is my *own* choice to do so, then damn right I'm going back Elara."

I gave him a huge grin, exhaling loudly.

"How about you?" he asked, turning his head over on the sand to meet my gaze. "Do you want to go back?"

"Yeah," I answered, my voice trailing off.

"That doesn't sound like a confident yes," he said, rolling over on his side, still facing me.

"I mean I'd be lying to you if I said that I wasn't scared, or terrified for that matter, but I can't imagine not going back. It's like I have two separate lives now. One here on Earth, that in some strange way feels finished and another one back on Aroonyx that is completely unfinished."

"I understand, Elara. I feel the exact same way. It's like everything Jax has told us can't be unheard you know?"

"Exactly!" I exclaimed. "How would we ever go back to our old lives now that we know all of this information?"

"We can't! That's why we have to go back," he finished.

"I wish you knew how relieved it makes me feel to hear you say that, Cyrus. This whole time I thought you would put up a fight about going back."

"No, I'm saving that fight for when we get there."

"I'm so glad we are on the same page now. Even if Jax could take me back to Aroonyx alone, I would not want to go without you by my side," I said smiling, looking over at Cyrus.

"I'm happy you feel that way and honestly, I don't know if I would be comfortable with you going back alone with him, anyway."

"What do you mean by that?"

"Do you really trust him?" Cyrus asked, his amber eyes more focused than I had seen all day.

"Who? Jax?" I asked, sitting up on the cool sand.

"No, the ferry-boat captain. Of course, I mean Jax," he continued.

I ran my fingers through my long hair, shaking off tiny sand particles.

"Jax is a tough one to figure out. I think he has led a very challenging life that I have learned to not ask questions about. When I first met him, I wasn't sure about anything, but as time passed, everything he said about our powers and our past kept making more and more sense. It's like a part of me didn't want to believe him, but for some reason every time he spoke, his words made it impossible not to believe him."

"I know what you mean," said Cyrus, rolling over on his back.

"But to answer your question, yes, for some reason I do trust him. Somehow, I feel connected to him. Jax is our only window to this life we've never known. I mean he knew our parents, which is just…."

"Weird," Cyrus interjected.

"Yeah, it still seems surreal when I think about it," I said, watching a large cargo ship pass slowly along the horizon.

"I would have like to have met them," Cyrus said, in a more somber tone.

"Me too. I will have to show you the picture of them that Jax gave me that night we met on the trail. At first it was a little unsettling to see, but it did give me some closure. Our father looked exactly like you do now, just older."

"I would appreciate that," he said, sitting up.

We both turned our heads, noticing Jax now standing only a few feet away from where we sat comfortably in the sand.

"Man, he can really sneak up on you," Cyrus murmured under his breath while standing.

"You have no idea," I replied, reaching for Cyrus's outstretched hand as he helped me to my feet.

Jax walked the remaining few steps, forming a circle among the three of us. The cool, strong ocean breeze whipped around us as Jax crossed his arms. His eyes shifted back and forth between Cyrus and me, as if weighing his options before quietly speaking in his calm, silky voice.

"There's something I want to try."

CHAPTER 29

Cyrus and I exchanged curious glances, unsure of Jax's request.

"What do you want us to do?" I asked, dusting more sand off the back of my pants.

"Elara, you get to sit this one out. I want to try something alone with Cyrus."

"Finally, I just get to watch," I said excitedly, taking a seat on the cool sand once more.

Glaring at me, Cyrus began, "Okay, so what do you want try?"

"I want to test your strength while there is still daylight," answered Jax, pointing to the afternoon sun.

"All right," smirked Cyrus, pushing up the thick sleeves of his hoody.

Jax stood unmoving, observing Cyrus like a lion stalking its prey. I laughed quietly, eager to see a Solin's strength against Jax's advanced skills. I wiggled anxiously, hugging my knees tightly, as if I were ringside at a prize fight.

"Okay Cyrus, imagine you're at football practice doing some drills and I'm a teammate. I want you to try blocking my attack with any force necessary."

My eyes widened at Jax's instruction.

"This is going to be interesting to watch," I thought.

"All right," agreed Cyrus, rolling his neck and shoulders while crouching in a low defensive stance. "Go for it," he taunted Jax.

In an instant, Jax rushed Cyrus, moving quicker than he had ever done when he trained with me. The sickening thud of the two of them colliding was instantaneous as Cyrus successfully blocked Jax, shooting his hands forward precisely at the right moment. Jax flew, easily ten feet, in the opposite direction, landing hard on the cold sand.

My jaw, had it not been attached to my head would have hit the ground. Cyrus stood with his hands outstretched, looking equally as stunned. He glanced at me, unsure if he should smile or frown. I clapped loudly, giving him the approval he was seeking, then jumped up, running to Jax. He was quick to recover from the hard fall, dusting himself off while shaking sand from his black hair.

"You mentioned Solins were strong, but I never imagined...." I began excitedly.

"During our training, you gave me the impression that you believe I am impermeable to harm. I wanted you to see first-hand the powerful strength of a Solin," Jax said firmly.

He then motioned for me to take a seat once more as he walked back to where Cyrus stood, still staring at his two hands.

"The feeling you are experiencing," Jax began, still removing sand from the back of his shirt. "That tingling sensation you get right before and after you use your power – that's normal with every Solin. When you feel anxious, angered or protective, you may notice that feeling begin to radiate throughout your entire body and then concentrate in your hands."

I thought back to the incident at NASA, feeling relieved by Jax's explanation about what I felt that day. Cyrus turned his hands over, looking relieved as well.

"It will begin to dissipate as soon as the situation has been resolved," Jax finished.

"Yeah, I felt that way at the hotel room with my dad. I hardly touched him and he went flying as far as you just did."

"It isn't about the amount of force you use, Cyrus. The energy coming out of your hands is so powerful that it barely needs to make contact to have the effect you just witnessed."

"Wow," said Cyrus, glancing in my direction.

"Now that you are aware of the magnitude of your strength, I'm going to test you at a more advanced level," Jax said, pushing up his sleeves while reaching into his back pocket.

In the blink of an eye, Jax had the grey knife with its sharp blade exposed, ready at his side.

"Whoa there," Cyrus gasped, holding his hands up in an "I surrender" stance. "I wasn't aware that we used knives in any football drills," he said, looking nervously in my direction.

I shrugged, completely bewildered at Jax's antics.

"Prepare yourself, because this time I'm coming at you full force," spoke Jax, in a steady voice.

"What? I don't even have a…"

Cyrus didn't get to finish his sentence, as Jax ran faster than I had ever seen him run. Cyrus, looking completely confused, stood motionless, unsure of how to block someone with a knife. Jax approached him within seconds, then quickly side-stepped Cyrus's feeble blocking attempt. Before I could blink, Jax was behind Cyrus, immobilizing him in the grueling locking hold position. The only difference was that instead of using his hand around Cyrus's mouth, he held the sharp knife blade to Cyrus's throat. I jumped to my feet, seeing the fear in Cyrus's eyes.

"Jax!" I yelled, running over to the two of them.

"Okay, I get it. I need a lot of training," Cyrus whispered, barely able to speak. "Dude, put the knife down," he pleaded.

"Jax stop!" I shouted. "That's enough. He gets it."

"Elara, I want you to notice how if properly restrained, a Solin's strength becomes inadequate. The harder he struggles, the deeper my knife pushes into his neck. He knows that if he uses his strength to try to push me off, he risks the chance of this knife hitting the main artery in his neck."

Jax spoke eerily, calmly, as if explaining the placid weather conditions.

A small line of dark red blood, quickly began to trickle down Cyrus's neck. My heart thumped loudly in my chest, unsure of what to do next.

"Stop it Jax! You're hurting him!" I yelled, pointing to the curved line of blood that dripped down onto his hoodie.

Jax's eyes remained focused, unmoving. I had never seen him act this way before. Yes, his training tactics were unconventional, but he had never before looked unstable. A darker side appeared to take over him, completely unaffected by the pain he was causing Cyrus.

"Drop the knife, Jax!" I shouted, taking a step forward.

Jax remained silent, while Cyrus's eyes looked at me as if begging for help.

The warming sensation I had grown accustomed to while being around Cyrus, began moving through my body faster than I had ever experienced it before. The cool weather outside was unnoticeable, as the fire inside surged through my veins.

"I'm going to ask you one more time, Jax. Drop the knife!" I demanded, taking another step closer. With each step, the intensity of heat grew as if it wanted to escape out of my hands.

Jax stood his ground, unmoving.

I watched as my body rushed Jax, moving effortlessly, one foot in front of the other. Instantly, my hand slid into the tight space between Jax's arm and Cyrus's throat. Twisting Jax's arm and knife away from Cyrus's injured neck, I then shoved Jax, feeling the heat leave my hands, sending him flying fifteen feet into the frigid surf.

I stood there motionless, unsure as to the feat I had just performed. Cyrus, gasping at my side, grabbed his neck, wiping the blood away. My head snapped toward the surf where Jax stood soaking wet, laughing while clapping his hands.

"This is it," I thought to myself. "Jax, has finally lost his mind. Keeping all of those trapped emotions in for so long has finally taken its toll on him."

I watched Jax display a huge grin as he shook the water from his hair and jogged back to where Cyrus and I stood.

"What the hell were you thinking?" Cyrus barked, still holding his neck.

My hands began radiating heat, as I felt Cyrus's anger grow. I grabbed his arm, squeezing it tightly in hopes of calming him.

"I apologize for the unorthodox training back there," Jax began, approaching us with caution, but still smiling.

His arms were up as he spoke, showing us he was unarmed, the knife secure in his back pocket.

"Forgive me, Cyrus, but I needed to tap into Elara's protective side to see if it would trigger her to defend you," he said, watching Cyrus holding his neck.

Jax turned, looking at me in apology.

"I am sorry if I frightened you, Elara, but I knew you would have just stood there and watched had I not pushed you to your limit. I had to test you both to see if there was any possibility that the two of you could share each other's traits."

"Well, I could have told you that!" I snapped at Jax.

"What?" asked Jax, his eyes narrowing.

I stuttered, feeling as though I were about to be in serious trouble.

"I ... wasn't certain until today. We were in the car and I noticed I could see equally as far as Cyrus."

"You mean to tell me you have known this the whole time?" Jax argued, sounding genuinely angry.

"Does anybody care that my neck probably needs stitches?" Cyrus asked, still holding a hand over his dripping wound.

"You don't need stitches," Jax assured, sounding annoyed.

"Well it won't stop bleeding," replied Cyrus, removing his hand from the wound allowing blood to rush out of the deep cut.

"Just use your shirt and tie it around your neck. The pressure will stop the bleeding," Jax instructed as if it were common knowledge.

"Why didn't I think of that," Cyrus said, rolling his eyes while moving his arms out of the long sleeves.

I turned my head back to face Jax.

"I wasn't sure until today Jax! I wanted to wait…."

"Wait until I sliced your brother's neck?" he said, wiping water from his face.

"How was I supposed to know you were going to literally threaten him?" I said, crossing my arms.

I glanced over, noticing the now shirtless Cyrus, attempting to tie his hoodie around his bleeding neck.

Turning away from Jax, I walked to where Cyrus stood, motioning for him to let me to help.

"You're doing it wrong," I snickered, untying the now blood-stained shirt.

"Well, I don't know how to do this," he said, tossing me the thick hoody.

Had I not known Cyrus were my brother, I most likely would have blushed while helping him with his make-shift bandage. He was much more muscular than I had remembered. His tan skin was covered in goose bumps but glowed in the afternoon sun while his perfectly chiseled abdomen looked like something out of a fitness magazine.

"There," I said, finishing my attempt.

I turned around, facing Jax once more. He stood unmoved, but clearly freezing from his dive in the cold surf.

"I'm sorry Jax. I wanted to tell you about these weird things that kept happening to Cyrus and me when we were around each other, but I wasn't sure what was happening or how you would take it. I was going to tell you when you jumped into the car today, but that didn't seem like an appropriate time, either. I didn't want to take any attention away from Cyrus," I said, looking at the white sand, feeling as though I had let Jax down.

Jax sighed, pushing his wet hair out of his face, looking at me and then at Cyrus.

"I'm going to go make a fire," he suddenly spoke, turning away from us both.

"How is he going to make a fire?" Cyrus asked, still looking a bit comical, as though he were wearing a super-hero cape.

"Oh, you'll see," I said, motioning for Cyrus to follow Jax.

CHAPTER 30

Cyrus watched Jax conjure a fire from only palm-tree shedding's, looking equally as impressed as I had the night under the bridge. The sun rested lower the late afternoon sky, casting a warm, orange glow over the barren beach. The temperature began to drop at a rapid rate, so I was grateful for the warm fire.

I crossed my legs, running my fingers through my long, black hair, continuing to rid myself of sand. Cyrus sat next to me, adjusting the makeshift bandage, checking to see if his wound had closed enough to remove the hoodie from his neck. I watched Jax kick off his worn, gray boots, turning them upside down to drain the murky water. My face flushed when he removed the wet, tight-fitting shirt from his body. Casually, he draped it over a stick that he had placed firmly into the sand near the fire. My eyes widened, taking note of his perfect physique. He could not have looked more different than Cyrus, but equally as strong. Cyrus's muscles were large, well defined; Jax's body was muscular and lean. Not an ounce of fat could be seen on his imperfect skin, making every muscle on his torso even more apparent. Several deep, pale scars lined his toned abdomen and back. I felt a sharp nudge on my shoulder, pulling me out my trance-like stare. I turned to see Cyrus raise his eyebrows, pointing to Jax teasingly.

"You're drooling," he whispered, so only I could hear.

"Stop it," I mouthed, embarrassed that I had been called out by Cyrus. I rested my head into my hands, feeling my face redden even more. Inhaling, then exhaling deeply, I attempted to regain my composure by forcing my eyes to stay focused on only the burning fire.

Jax removed the wet, beige bandage from his face, before tossing it onto the glowing flames. He then carefully checked his freshly stitched wound for blood. I noticed Cyrus's eyes take note of Jax's injury. Immediately he removed the hoodie from around his neck. I laughed quietly, whispering to Cyrus.

"About time you manned up," I teased.

He glared, rolling his eyes then tossed the blood-stained hoodie into the fire.

"I'll be back," he said, quickly standing. "I'm going to grab a shirt from my car."

Jax and I watched Cyrus walk back over the sand dunes toward his parked car. I sat uncomfortably across from Jax, trying to keep my eyes off his perfect figure that now glowed in the bright flames.

"I didn't mean to frighten you back there," he said, attempting to make eye contact.

I compelled my eyes to meet his, hoping they would stay put and not wander.

"I wished you would have just asked me about our powers before trying something that crazy," I stated.

"I wish you would've just told me so I didn't have to," he countered.

Jax leaned over the fire, rotating his shirt on the stick as if roasting a chicken. He ran his fingers through his dark, wet hair, slicking it back out of his handsome face.

"Elara, we can't keep secrets from each other. I need full disclosure from you and your brother if this is going to work."

"I know," I replied, shifting my weight in the cool sand. "I'm not keeping anything else from you."

"Good," he said smiling, his deep blue eyes never leaving mine.

"I see you took my advice and saw a doctor," I boasted, nodding to his wound.

"I saw a friend," Jax corrected.

The thought of Jax having friends seemed strange considering he had previously spoke of living a solitary life.

"Your friend knows how to administer stitches?" I asked curiously.

"Yes, she does," Jax answered.

When I heard that his "friend" was a girl, an uncomfortable feeling of jealousy took hold.

"Well good for her," I replied, looking back at the fire.

I didn't have to look at Jax to know he was smirking at my sarcastic comment. Thankfully, Cyrus returned and interrupted us.

"So now what?" he asked, taking a seat, now wearing a clean Woodward football shirt.

"You are equally as impatient as your sister," Jax commented, clasping his hands together.

Cyrus shrugged, looking over at me smiling.

"I want to test and see if you share Elara's traits as she does yours, but we need to wait until the sun has set," Jax said, motioning to the position of the sun, which was falling closer to the horizon.

"This test better not involve knives," Cyrus quickly stated, looking firmly at Jax.

Jax laughed, shaking his head.

"No more knife lessons … yet," he teased. "All I'm going to do is check to see if your night vision is equal to that of Elara's and then have you do some sprints to see if you experience the same cardiovascular stamina that Lunins display."

Cyrus nodded in agreement, looking over his shoulder at the setting sun.

"I thought we should take some time before it gets dark to discuss our plans of returning to Aroonyx," said Jax, looking back and forth between the two of us.

"I think that's a great idea," I replied, eager to set a game plan in motion.

"Before I discuss the logistics of your return, I first need to ask you a question," he stated decisively, looking only at Cyrus.

"Shoot," he replied, staring at Jax.

"I need you to be completely honest with me right now. Is your intention of returning to Aroonyx based on vengeance?" Jax asked.

"What? No!" Cyrus exclaimed. "I mean, don't get me wrong. When I think about the reason for our parents' death, I feel like punching a wall, but I don't want to return to seek revenge. Like I said to Elara earlier, the things you've told us Jax, they can't be erased from our minds. Our lives are completely disrupted now. There is no way I could go back to my old life. Also, I'll be glad to get away from my adoptive parents," he finished, his voice fading.

"Cyrus, don't be like that," I pleaded.

"Why? They lied to me for eighteen years, Elara!" he snapped.

"As did mine! I'm not saying the way your parents handled the situation was appropriate by any means, but at least try to see the situation with compassion."

"Compassion? Why, because of all the compassion they have showed me?"

"They showed you compassion the day they decided to take you home," I began, turning to face him. "You could've ended up stuck in the system, constantly in and out of foster homes, but you got lucky, Cyrus. You and your father's issues aside, they gave you a privileged life.

"You know, I felt the same way about my parents until I walked down stairs one day feeling angry, hurt and betrayed. But then something suddenly changed inside of me when I saw them drinking their coffee together. It was only through compassion that I was able to see the situation differently; see it for what it truly was. They were just two people doing the best they could with the circumstances they were given. They were never trying to hurt me by keeping this deep secret for eighteen years. My parents kept this massive secret out of love for me! Once I stopped being selfish and acknowledged the burden they had been carrying for my entire life, I saw them with loving eyes, instead of eyes filled with anger."

Jax nodded in approval as I spoke, looking at Cyrus.

"I don't know, Elara. I'm not like you," Cyrus began.

"Yes, you are Cyrus! You are always helping people out, taking them under your wing, showing kindness when others choose not to and standing up for what you believe in. I know you're hurt and angry right now, which is understandable, but don't leave for Aroonyx still mad at your parents. Talk to your mom, Cyrus. She loves you and your love for her hasn't changed just because you know she isn't your biological mother."

Cyrus nodded, looking down at the sand absorbing my words carefully.

"I can't make any promises," he said, lifting his head.

"I'm not asking you to," I replied.

Jax cleared his throat, moving our focus back to the conversation.

"Cyrus, I'm relieved to hear that your reasons for wanting to return are selfless."

"So, what are the logistics?" asked Cyrus, clearly wanting the focus off him and his parents' relationship.

"I'll get right to it then. From this point on we will be racing against the clock. I feel that the best time for the three of us to return to Aroonyx will be at the end of the summer."

My heart skipped a beat, hearing a specific time frame. The thought of returning had always seemed unreal until now.

"How did you figure that time line?" questioned Cyrus, tossing sand back and forth between his tan hands.

"I figured the two of you would want to graduate from high school and this will give us ample time to train and prepare your parents for your new endeavor."

"Yeah . . . about that," I interrupted. "What exactly are we telling our parents?"

Jax sighed, sitting up straighter.

"You're going to tell them that you have decided to join the military," he said.

I laughed hard, almost falling back into the sand had it not been for Cyrus's quick arm.

"Right," I laughed still. "Because my parents will definitely believe that plan."

Cyrus remained quiet, deep in thought as Jax spoke once more.

"I know right now it sounds far-fetched, Elara, but look at it from this perspective. You have already informed your parents that you are taking self-defense classes, you do not have any college plans and with Galveston being so close to Houston, the Coast Guard would be the obvious choice, would it not?" he asked. "Cyrus, now at odds with his father and no college plans for himself, has decided to join the Navy," Jax continued.

"Yeah, but," I began protesting.

"It just may work," Cyrus interjected, dropping the sand from his hands. "My parents would buy it and the idea would piss off my dad," he said grinning.

Jax nodded at Cyrus, pleased by his enthusiasm.

"Okay, so what if I am able to convince my parents that their only daughter, who has never swum a lap in her life, now suddenly wants to join the Coast Guard? They will still want to hear from us. What are we going to do? Call them collect from Aroonyx?" I asked, shaking my head at the absurdity of Jax's request.

"Coast Guard boot camp is eight weeks, followed by another twelve weeks of "A" School. The Navy's boot camp is eight weeks long. Cyrus will then inform his parents that he has been accepted into the Navy Seals BUDS training, which buys us another twenty-one weeks. Only letters will be delivered to your parents during this time. I figure after training is over we can stall them with more letters explaining that your hectic military schedules are the reason you have been unable to visit. I would imagine that we could continue this charade for a year tops, before they would begin to speculate."

I sat completely stunned, listening to Jax. As usual, he was ten steps ahead of us.

"So, we get our folks to believe we are joining the military and then at the end of summer we return to Aroonyx? How are these letters even going to get back to our parents? Are you just going to jump back and forth, acting as a mail carrier?" Cyrus asked, eyeing me cautiously.

I shook my head, anxiously wanting to hear Jax's answer.

"That's a good question. You will need to pre-write every letter to your parents. To be on the safe side, I would write one a week for the time during boot camp then one a month for the advanced training, continuing with that pace until the year is up. You will need to find someone you trust that can mail these letters weekly and then monthly for you both."

"Well, I don't have anyone that can do that," I said, frustrated.

"Coach Burnell will do it for us if I ask him. He has been more of a father figure to me then my own father ever has," Cyrus said, looking back and forth between Jax and me.

"Good, then it's settled," Jax continued.

Mentally, I began doing the math, adding up the number of weeks Jax predicted us to be away from Earth.

"Jax? How did you come up with these numbers?" I asked.

"What numbers?"

"Your saying we'll be gone from Earth for a year. That's only six months on Aroonyx right?" I questioned.

"Yes. If we have not defeated Zenith within six months, then...." his voice trailed off.

"Then what?" Cyrus and I asked in unison.

"Then I am unsure if we will ever be able to," he finished, looking away as he spoke.

"You're giving us only six months to overthrow Zenith?" asked Cyrus, bewildered.

Jax nodded.

"And if we're not successful then you just take us back to Earth?" Cyrus continued, looking between me and Jax.

Jax rubbed his face with both hands, looking uneasy for the first time that day. He sat quietly with his eyes closed. I looked around, noticing my night vision in full effect as the sun had disappeared beneath the horizon.

"What is it, Jax?" I asked, sensing something terribly wrong.

He remained silent as if collecting his thoughts, then slowly opened his eyes before speaking.

"The reason I am giving us this short amount of time to defeat Zenith is simple. The odds of the three of us surviving longer than six months on Aroonyx will be slim to none, once our intention to remove him from his position is known."

My stomach churned, looking over at Cyrus. His facial expression was equal to that of my own.

"But if we fail, you can just jump and take us back," Cyrus stated, almost pleading.

Jax paused, finding Cyrus's eyes then mine before continuing.

"I don't know if I'll be able to bring you back to Earth," Jax admitted, closing his eyes once more.

"What?!" I gasped, standing up.

My head spun, making me dizzy. Cyrus was quickly at my side, his hand steadying me.

"You're only telling us this now!" I barked, breathing hard.

"That is kind of an important fact to leave out, Jax," Cyrus snapped, still holding my arm.

My adoptive parents' faces flashed before my eyes, followed quickly by the thought of never seeing them again. Warm tears formed in my eyes as I shook my head back and forth.

"Jax, you said jumping had to do with intention. How would it be selfish to bring us back if we were in harm's way?" I asked, as Cyrus helped me sit back down on the cool sand.

"I just have a feeling."

"Not another feeling," I groaned.

Jax pulled his hands from his face, avoiding the freshly stitched gash while making eye contact with us once more.

"I intuit that you will be able to return to Earth once Zenith is defeated and the people of Aroonyx are free from his destructive ways. When you were first born, I could jump to Earth because my reasons were purely selfless. I was told by your parents to keep you safe. Never once did I think of myself. I am still able to return to Earth because I continue to make sure that the two of you are safe and prepared for this journey: another selfless reason.

"Once we are all back on Aroonyx, I will no longer will have a selfless reason to return to Earth. My intention is to bring you back and defeat Zenith, regardless of what challenges or dangers may arise. That intention will not change, even if we find ourselves in precarious situations. I could be wrong, but you both need to know the gravity of the situation."

"I think we understand the gravity of the situation perfectly, Jax!" Cyrus barked. "You're telling us that if we are unsuccessful in defeating Zenith within six months, then we will be stuck on Aroonyx and most likely be killed. It's a suicide mission!" he continued.

The fire crackled loudly as white smoke rose like a snake from the burning brush. Jax stood, commanding our attention.

"I see that when you look at it from that perspective, the outcome appears bleak, but you must understand that we now have the upper hand over Zenith. It is rare for twins to be born on Aroonyx and never have twins looked different from one another or had the ability to share each other's traits. This will come as a huge blow to Zenith. He is a very troubled man who reacts strictly on emotion. Once he receives word of this…."

Jax shook his head, smiling.

"He will come undone. There has never been a threat to him, until now." Jax continued, motioning to both of us. "He's a weak man, Cyrus and weak men are no match for true power."

I exhaled, looking over at Cyrus.

"Well, then, I guess there is some light at the end of the tunnel," he said glancing over at me, then looking at Jax.

"I have one more question," I said. "Say we are unsuccessful at defeating Zenith and unable to return to Earth. The letters to our parents will eventually stop and then what? They never hear from us again, only to find out that our entire military life was just a ruse? That would crush them!"

Jax reached for his damp shirt, slipping it over his head and then pulling it over his chiseled abdomen. He walked around the fire, standing close to both of us.

"I understand your concerns, Elara. It will be the ultimate sacrifice, to leave loved ones behind, unsure if you will ever see them again. This is a sacrifice you both must be willing to accept. I cannot make this decision for you, for the choice to return is yours alone." Jax added, looking firmly at me and Cyrus. "I want you both to take this weekend and reflect on everything we have discussed today. If you choose to return, we will move forward with the plan. Do not concern yourselves with the details. They will unfold as we move along," Jax said, intuiting my uneasiness. "However, if you choose to stay here on Earth, I will return to Aroonyx and you will never have to worry about me interfering in your lives again."

"I'm in! I don't need the weekend to think things over," Cyrus stated firmly, crossing his muscular arms.

"I appreciate your enthusiasm, but I don't want an answer until Monday," Jax reaffirmed. "Cyrus, look behind you out to sea and tell me the color of that passing ship," Jax began, surprising us both with his change of subject.

Obeying, Cyrus turned his head toward the vast ocean.

"Uh...blue and grey," he answered nonchalantly.

"Very good," nodded Jax, a wide grin crossing his face. "It is getting late and the ferry will be leaving soon. I don't want the two of you stuck on the island."

"I thought you were going to test to see if I share Elara's powers?" Cyrus asked curiously.

"I just did," Jax replied, still smiling.

"I'm confused again," said Cyrus, looking back and forth between Jax and me.

I laughed, catching on to Jax's little trick.

"What?" Cyrus asked.

"Cyrus! It's completely dark outside. There's no way you could have seen the colors of that ship had you not the ability to share my powers!" I said, excitedly.

Cyrus looked around the beach, wildly turning in a fast circle around where he stood.

"It's not dark?" he asked, flabbergasted.

Jax and I shook our heads, laughing loudly together.

"Pretty cool, huh?" I said, nudging Cyrus's arm.

He nodded in agreement, marveling at his well-lit surroundings.

"Don't you want to test my endurance?" he asked, looking at Jax.

"You both have had a long day and I feel confident that you have the ability to share all of her Lunin traits. Also, I need to be getting back to Aroonyx. There are a few things that require my attention."

"Okay," Cyrus and I replied.

"I will see you both on Monday. Cyrus...." Jax said, reaching out his hand.

The two of them shook hands firmly, the way men do after a successful business meeting. Jax then offered his hand to mine, squeezing it gently, before vanishing right in front of us.

"Do you think we will ever get used to him disappearing like that?" Cyrus asked, looking over at me, shocked by what he had just witnessed.

"Probably not," I laughed, shaking my head.

"We should get going if we want to catch the last ferry," Cyrus noted, rubbing his cold arms.

I pulled the small phone from my back pocket, gasping when I saw the clock read 7:14 p.m. I had three missed calls from my mother and even more text messages.

"Ugh," I groaned.

"What?" Cyrus asked, beginning the walk toward the car.

"I'm in so much trouble," I said, dreading the inevitable talk my mother would have planned by the time I got home.

"Well, only a few more months and that concern will be no more," Cyrus said cheerfully.

My heart sank with his words. I stopped in my tracks, feeling the weight of the decision I had to make. Sensing my discomfort, Cyrus threw a strong arm over my shoulder, encouraging me to keep moving.

"Come on, sis," he said playfully.

We walked side-by-side the rest of the way to the car, at peace with each other's company.

"You know," he said, opening the passenger side door. "I think this next year will be the most interesting year of our lives."

I slid onto the black leather seat for the final time that day, looking up at Cyrus before speaking.

"I couldn't agree more," I nodded, forcing a smile.

CHAPTER 31

It was hot and I was sweating. The Texas summer was in full effect and sitting next to Cyrus in U.S. History was not helping the intense heat that radiated throughout my body. Cyrus turned his head, sensing my discomfort, then nodded toward the clock hanging on the back wall of the classroom, which read 2:44 p.m. I sighed loudly as my foot bobbed up and down nervously. It was the last day of our senior year and I hadn't listened to one word of Mrs. Sampson's speech on what to expect during the first year of college. My mind was preoccupied with only one thought. Why had Jax not returned to Earth?

It had been five months since Cyrus and I had made our decision to return to Aroonyx. When not attending class, we had spent our time training daily with Jax. He would train with Cyrus in the mornings before school then with both Cyrus and me in the afternoons and finally, with me alone during the late evenings. I had mastered the art of sneaking out of my house to meet him on the trail. The plan, as Jax had predicted, unfolded much smoother than I could have ever imagined. Cyrus's parents loved the idea of him joining the Navy. He finally forgave his mother, but unfortunately, the relationship between him and his father had not improved.

My parents laughed when I informed them of my plans.

"Coast Guard? Sweetie, you can hardly swim," my mother had teased.

It took a month of convincing, but eventually they agreed when my father spoke frankly to her one day.

"Emily, she's eighteen. Elara is an adult and I think she will excel at anything she puts her mind to."

I teared up while listening to my father's kind words, regretting the fact that I had lied to them.

"Stop," Cyrus complained, kicking my foot under the desk.

"Sorry," I exhaled loudly, once more.

I noticed Kayle glaring angrily at Cyrus from several rows over. When Cyrus and I returned to school after winter break, rumors flew that we had started dating. Cyrus, finding the humor in it all, encouraged these rumors by throwing his arm over my shoulder any time we walked past Hillary or Kayle.

The final bell of the day rang, sounding loudly through the school hallways. Seniors jumped out of their chairs, cheering. Hands were slapped, hugs were given and used notebooks were tossed into the over-flowing trash can as students left the classroom for the last time.

I jumped to my feet, eager to head to the trail, hoping Jax would be back. Cyrus slowly rose from his seat then stretched his arms overhead. Our training had a tangible effect on both of our bodies. Cyrus's muscles, now larger and more defined, made his shirts look even smaller. My gains, though less noticeable were still apparent. The hint of a six-pack was visible on my pale stomach and my arms and legs, though still slender, were more defined. When fellow classmates questioned our fitness routine we lied, informing them that our newly found passion was CrossFit.

"Elara, you have got to calm down," Cyrus said, turning to face me.

"I can't calm down. It's been over a week! Jax has never been gone this long. I have a feeling that something is terribly wrong," I pressed.

"Your boyfriend's going to be just fine," he taunted, heading toward the door of the classroom.

I blushed, irritated that Cyrus thought it an appropriate time to tease.

The relationship between Jax and me had grown, as he typically spent more time with me than Cyrus during our training sessions. We would spend the late evenings together training, then sit together for hours afterwards talking about life on Aroonyx. I would be lying if I said I hadn't developed feelings for him, but I knew better than to let my adolescent crush distract us from the task at hand. The quiet moments we shared made me wonder if Jax felt the same way as I did, but that idea always quickly dissolved when I would look over and find him distracted, lost deep in thought.

"Why don't we do something fun tonight? Get your mind off Jax for a while," Cyrus asked, walking down the busy hallway.

I side-stepped an excited freshman, careful not to make physical contact with him, being in such close proximity to Cyrus.

"I won't be able to relax until I know he's okay."

"Come on, Elara! It's the last day of our senior year! We've been training almost every day for the past five months. We deserve a break, you know … a little celebration," he beamed, looking in my direction.

"Maybe," I said, eyeing him cautiously.

The early summer air, thick with humidity, met us like a hammer as we exited the large double doors of the school.

"I don't know, Cyrus," I said back-tracking. "I won't be any fun tonight. All I'm going to do is sit there pretending to relax, when all I'm really doing is worrying about…."

"Jax!" said Cyrus.

"Exactly," I murmured.

"No, Elara! Jax! He's here!"

"What?" I gasped, my eyes frantically scanning the school grounds.

"Over there! He's standing right next to my car!" he continued, pointing to the crowded parking lot.

A wave of relief washed over me when I saw Jax, looking unharmed, right where Cyrus said he was.

"Come on," I said, racing down the steep concrete stairs.

I darted around reversing cars, never letting my eyes leave Jax, fearful he would disappear once more.

"I told you he was okay!" bragged Cyrus, as we approached the vehicle.

Jax leaned against Cyrus's car, looking rustically handsome, as usual. The only difference was that he looked as though he hadn't shaved in days and his hair hung even further into his eyes, giving his appearance an extra mysterious appeal. I watched as fellow female classmates slowed their fast pace to admire his presence, whispering to one another quietly.

"Quick, get into the car," Jax said, motioning for us to hurry. His urgency was nothing short of alarming.

I glared at Cyrus, giving him the "I told you so" face while shaking my head.

Cyrus unlocked the vehicle then got into the driver's seat. Jax climbed into the cramped back seat as I took my place on the front passenger side.

I twisted my body around on the hot leather seat, looking at Jax.

"Where have you been!" I scolded, hearing my mother's voice echoing in my tone. "We've been worried sick!"

"Elara has been worried. I figured you were okay," corrected Cyrus.

Ignoring Cyrus, I continued.

"We didn't know what to think! I started to expect the worst, thinking the Collectors had taken you or that Zenith…."

"No," Jax interrupted, shaking his head as if my thoughts were irrational.

"Then, where were you?" I demanded.

"I didn't mean to worry you," he said, looking only at me while he spoke. "I was unable to jump back."

"What, like you were busy or something?" Cyrus asked, starting the engine of the car to allow the warm A/C to blow into our even warmer faces.

Jax laughed nervously.

"No, I was physically unable to get back to Earth."

"What?" we asked in unison.

"How is that possible?" I asked, rotating further in my seat.

Jax sat quietly, watching students pile into their cars, then speed out of the emptying parking lot.

"I don't know for sure, but something has definitely changed. I'm afraid we are running out of time to prepare for your return."

"What are you saying?" asked Cyrus, crossing his arms.

Jax exhaled deeply, looking back and forth between the two of us.

"We need to leave for Aroonyx sooner than planned."

"Okay, so how much longer do we have? Mid-summer?" I asked.

"We need to leave by Monday."

"What?" I gasped, looking at Cyrus as though Jax had lost his mind.

"Dude, that's like four months earlier than we had planned!" Cyrus exclaimed, shaking his head. "We haven't even finished our training and what would we tell our parents?" he asked.

I was grateful for Cyrus's ability to ask questions, because in that moment I found myself utterly speechless.

"We'll continue your training once we're back on Aroonyx. The weapons training can wait. You are now both well versed in hand-to-hand combat. I feel confident you will be able to defend yourselves if necessary," Jax said calmly.

I felt my head begin to spin, as I reached for the air vent, placing my face only inches from the cooling air.

"As far as your parents are concerned, I will take care of it."

This strange statement snapped me out of the daze I found myself stuck in.

"What are you going to do?" I asked, not moving my face from the vent.

"I will call both of your parents, pretending to be your recruiters and inform them that your enlisted date was moved up to early summer and that you will need to leave for boot camp on Monday morning."

"That's only three days away!" I wheezed, feeling myself beginning to panic.

"Relax, Elara," Jax soothed. "I promise you, it will all be okay."

"It's too soon," argued Cyrus. "We're not ready."

Jax's tone suddenly changed dramatically to one more direct.

"If we choose to wait until the end of summer, there is a possibility that I may never be able to return to Earth again. If that happens, all our efforts will have been for nothing. I am not willing to take that chance."

The weight of the situation took hold, as I rested my head against the warm passenger window. The three of us sat quietly, while staring out of the front windshield, observing the happy faces of smiling students. They appeared worry-free, piling into each other's vehicles, laughing while enjoying their music. There was a stark contrast between our tone and that of the scene outside.

"Okay," Cyrus stated, clapping his strong hands together. "Then we go," he nodded, looking at me.

I slowly shook my head in agreement, but was unable to speak.

"Cyrus, would you please dial your mother's number?" Jax asked, motioning to the phone resting in the empty cup holder.

"You want to do this now?" Cyrus asked, picking up his phone.

"Now is the only time we have," Jax said, holding his hand out for the phone.

I sat there listening to Jax first impersonate a Navy officer to Cyrus's mother and then a Coast Guard officer to my own. His silky voice flowed through the receiver as though he had made the call a hundred times.

Finished, Jax rested the silver phone back in the cup holder.

"I want the two of you to prepare those letters for your parents and take the weekend to spend with your loved ones. I will do everything in my power to meet you on the trail come Monday morning. Let's just hope I can get back."

Cyrus and I nodded, feeling the weight of our decision.

Within an instant Jax had vanished, leaving Cyrus and me alone in the car. My eyes filled with tears and I let them flow down my cheeks, not caring if anyone noticed. Without speaking, Cyrus reached over and took my hand into his, holding it tightly.

The weekend passed quicker than I had hoped. Graduation day was emotional, not because I had finished high school, but because I had finished a life I had grown attached to and must finally let go.

I secretly handed my letters to Cyrus, asking him to tell Coach Burnell thank you from the bottom of my heart. Cyrus and I stayed apart that weekend, spending time with our families, as Jax had requested. I absorbed every moment with my parents, studying and observing them as though trying to make more memories than the physical world allowed. Time was against me as I watched the minutes of my old life tick away at a rapid rate.

Monday morning arrived all too quickly. The alarm on the bedside table beeped loudly as I rolled over, gently pressing the off button. My eyes felt heavy, for I had not slept a wink the night before, knowing that this day may be the last I would ever see my parents. As Jax had instructed, I dressed comfortably in canvas shorts, a sleeveless shirt and a pair of closed-toed shoes. He told Cyrus and me that the intensity of heat on Aroonyx would come as a surprise to us both.

I stood in front of the large bathroom mirror, reflecting on the person who stared back. I was not the same person who first noticed her appearance in this very same mirror only a year ago. Physically, I was stronger and tougher, but mentally, I was exhausted. I trusted that the decision I had made to return to Aroonyx was selfless, but the selfish part of me wanted to stay living the comfortable, safe life, I knew so well.

I wrapped my hair into a high bun, slipping an extra hair tie over my wrist. I walked out of the bathroom, taking one final moment to observe the peaceful bedroom. I reached down to grab my old back pack and checked the contents one final time. It contained only a few articles of clothing, toiletries, and an old pair of boots. Jax was unsure if we would be able to jump back to Aroonyx with any items at all, but said to pack something light, just in case.

My hand hesitated on the bedroom doorknob, remembering the old portrait Jax had given me that night on the trail. I quickly walked to the bedside table and lifted the lamp to remove the picture before slipping into my back pocket.

Somberly, I made my way down the wooden stairs of the quiet home, feeling like a condemned prisoner about to face their demise. My eyes welled up as soon as I heard my parents' footsteps. My mother and father greeted me with open arms, smiling. I ran to both of them, hugging each one tighter than I ever had, not wanting to let go.

"Are you sure we can't take you to the bus stop?" my mother asked, tears streaming down her face.

"No," I managed in a small voice. "I think I need to walk and take a minute to collect myself," I answered, telling only half the truth.

"Honey, we are so proud of you," my father beamed, wiping a single tear from his cheek.

The emotions that arose were too intense to handle. I kissed them both gently on the cheek before running to the front door, unable to look back. I couldn't say goodbye, not like this. Not knowing that I had lied to the two people who cared for me the most.

"We love you!" was the last thing I heard before shutting the wooden door. I ran to the trail without stopping, hoping my cramping muscles would somehow mask the intense pain that hovered over my heart. The sun shone brightly in the warm summer sky as the subtle wind blew gently, cooling my clammy skin.

My heart raced as I stepped onto the path. I paused, unsure if I could command my body to take the final, few steps. I exhaled loudly as my hands trembled at my side. Slowly I entered the shaded trail, relieved to see Cyrus and Jax waiting for me. They stood side-by-side, silently watching me walk the remaining distance to where they stood. I nodded, acknowledging their presence, then closed the gap by forming a circle among the three of us.

Cyrus stood, looking focused, a small back pack hung over his broad shoulders. He smiled quickly in my direction, nodding his approval of our decision.

Jax exhaled deeply, closing his eyes only momentarily. The time for casual conversation had passed. Jax looked back and forth between the two of us, his face more determined than ever.

"Are you ready?" he asked.

My heart thumped, feeling my fight-or-flight instincts take over. I shifted my weight uncomfortably, my eyes darting nervously between Cyrus and Jax.

Cyrus nodded, rolling and popping his neck loudly as though preparing for battle. Jax reached out both of his hands, motioning for each of us to each take one. Cyrus grabbed Jax's hand without hesitation as I stood immobile, as if incapable of taking that final step.

Jax inhaled slowly as if attempting to steady my own breathing, then gently took my hand in his. I watched Cyrus close his dark, amber eyes while letting out a slow, deep breath. A sudden calming sensation radiated throughout my entire body as Jax squeezed my hand firmly, looking over at me. His expression, though calm and composed, had a certain quality of uncertainty. He nodded, then smiled, reassuring me. Jax's deep blue eyes locked onto mine for the last time as everything faded into the oblivion.

Epilogue

The man sat at a large wooden table enjoying his warm meal alone. He never ate with the others because the incessant chatter drove him mad, and he found their constant effort to stay in his good favor irritating.

It was mid-day but the vast room was dark; the rectangular windows that bordered the perimeter were closed and tightly locked. Taking a sip from a silver mug, he paused before swallowing as a rhythmic knock sounded loudly on the tall, black wooden door.

"What have I told you about interrupting me?" he bellowed.

The large door slowly opened, exposing a tall Solin who cautiously poked his head inside the room.

"I'm sorry sir," he stuttered. "I don't mean to interrupt your meal, but there's a man here with information that you'll want to hear."

The man sighed, tossing his fork onto his plate.

"And what information is that?" he asked in a patronizing tone while drumming his fingers against the top of the aged table.

Sensing his irritation, the Solin quickly added, "He says he saw a man disappear from the side of the cliff this morning."

The man's fingers paused upon, hearing these words. "Bring him to me."

Only seconds passed before the tall Solin entered the room with an elderly man at his side. The old man's tan, aged face was full of wrinkles and filled with trepidation as he took in the appearance of the man at the table. He took a hesitant step forward, glancing momentarily at the man's uniquely colored eyes: one blue and one orange, staring down at him fiercely.

"You will bow before Zenith!" demanded the Solin as he shoved the man onto the wooden floor.

The older man fell hard, barely able to catch himself with both hands. He slowly climbed to one knee while hanging his head low.

Zenith leaned back against the tall chair, exhaling loudly as he gestured for the man to speak.

"Sir," the man stammered. "I was at the far end of the cliff just now when I noticed a young man vanish right before my eyes."

Zenith's eyes narrowed at the elderly man as he sat up straighter in his seat.

"Was he Solin or Lunin?" he asked sternly.

"Lunin, sir. Probably early twenty's or so," the man answered.

Zenith clenched his tan hand into a tight fist, his nostrils flaring.

The kneeling man shifted uncomfortably as he proceeded to look down, away from Zenith's gaze.

"You will tell us the exact spot where you saw the young man jump," Zenith demanded, standing alongside the long table.

"I will, sir, but there's more," he added nervously.

Zenith walked over to the man then signaled for him to stand. He hobbled up to both feet but continued to look away, afraid to make direct eye contact with Zenith.

"Speak!" Zenith shouted.

The man flinched at his harsh tone, then quickly continued.

"I've never seen a Seeker with my own eyes, and I was curious, so I stayed in the same spot, hoping to see him return," he said with a slightly shaky voice.

"And?" Zenith pressed, never taking his eyes off the man.

"At first, I couldn't believe my eyes, but sure enough, he appeared in the exact same spot he had left, and not only did he return, but he returned with two others. A young man and young woman."

Zenith's jaw clenched together as he processed the man's words. He closed his eyes briefly, then inhaled slowly. Anger surged through his body as he took a step closer to the frightened man.

"The young man and woman, were they Solin or Lunin?" he asked.

"The young man was Solin and the young woman was Lunin. They appeared close in age," he added.

Zenith paused, attempting to collect himself before speaking once more.

"Elio, have this man tell you exactly where on the cliff he saw Jax and the twins appear. Then I want you to send four Solins to scout the area. If they bring any reports of their whereabouts, dispatch the Inner Circle immediately. I want the three of them brought to me without delay. You have your orders, now go!" he yelled, waving them both away.

Elio nodded at Zenith before walking up to the elder Solin. He grabbed him tightly by the arm, then turned, exiting quietly through the tall wooden door.

Zenith stood motionless, but his hands shook violently with rage. He whipped his body around and stormed off back toward the large table. Unable to finish his meal, he sneered at the half-eaten plate of food, and in one violent movement, flipped the heavy wooden table over on its side. Everything flew off the table and crashed loudly against the floor as he yelled out in anger. He exhaled deeply, observing the room quietly.

He had waited nine, long years for this opportunity. He had always wondered if Jax was foolish enough to bring the twins back to Aroonyx. It was only a matter of time before his Collectors would capture Jax and the twins. He exulted, thinking of how they would soon cower before him in the dimly lit room where he stood. The fear he had kept hidden for so many years would no longer be a concern once *they* were gone.

Zenith pulled a large, black folded knife from his back pocket before taking a seat on the elaborate wooden chair once more. In one smooth motion, he exposed the sharp blade and slowly turned the knife over in his hand. Hurling the knife across the room toward the tall door, he watched as it spun, handle over blade. It then precisely hit the targeted door, slicing through the aged wood. The knife swayed gently back and forth from the forceful throw. A wicked grin crept slowly across Zenith's face. He had tried to end their lives on that fateful night, but was unsuccessful. Next time he would not fail by leaving it to chance.

Acknowledgements

Firstly, I must thank God. This book would have not been possible without the Grace of God holding my hand through every step of the way.

To the work of Dr. David R. Hawkins, I am eternally grateful.

To my dear husband, your love and support has not only lifted me, but carried me through this entire journey. Without you, I would have never had the courage to take the first step. You are the love of my life, my partner and soul mate. Thank you for inspiring the best parts of C & J.

Emerson, you are my biggest blessing! Thank you for being the world's most patient child and for truly loving my characters more than anyone I know.

Sunny, thank you for your love, guidance and selfless service to mankind.

Tom Bird, thank you for giving me the confidence to believe that I am an author and for validating the work.

John Hodgkinson and Sabrina Fritts, thank you for steering me in the right direction.

Family and friends, you know who you are, and I appreciate your love and support.

My sweet mother, thank you for being my biggest cheerleader, for everything you do and for your generosity.

To my mother-in-law, thank you for rising to the call when needed.

Ashley Rafiner, you are my soul sister! Thank you for your unwavering friendship and for always believing in me.

A very special thanks to Dan Smith of Bastille and Ryan O'Neal of Sleeping at Last, and to the other talented members that help create the music I love so much. Your music has held my hand through this entire journey. Your lyrics have shaped these characters and scenes more than you'll ever know. Thank you from the bottom of my heart for your gift of storytelling through music.

To the readers of this book. Thank you for joining me on this exciting adventure. I hope after reading this book you find yourself looking at others with more compassion and forgiveness than you ever did before.

About the Author

J.M. Buckler resides in Austin, TX with her husband and their four-year-old son. Every day she thanks God for the gift of writing. The intention of this book is to show readers that even when faced with a challenge, they always have the ability to see things differently.